ST. NICHOLAS
SALVAGE & WRECKING

DANA HAYNES

ST. NICHOLAS
SALVAGE & WRECKING

**BLACK
STONE**
PUBLISHING

Printed in the United States of America
Originally published in hardcover by Blackstone Publishing in 2019

First paperback edition: 2020
ISBN 978-1-09-409106-8
Fiction / Thrillers / Suspense

1 3 5 7 9 10 8 6 4 2

CIP data for this book is available
from the Library of Congress

Blackstone Publishing
31 Mistletoe Rd.
Ashland, OR 97520

www.BlackstonePublishing.com

To Tim King and Andy Priebe: two friends who helped research stories and who listened to my endless pitches. Tim traveled with me to many of the locations in this book. Andy helped me with my flights of imagination. Deepest gratitude for the stories we've created together.

To Katy: "We that are true lovers run into strange capers."

PROLOGUE

SEVASTOPOL, CRIMEA
Three Years Ago

If you look up "bedlam" on any crime-fighting website, they will link you to Sevastopol and the Ukrainian drug runner, Pantomime.

Anything that couldn't go bad *did*. Anything that *could* go bad caught fire.

American law enforcement, European intelligence agencies, Russian military—all coming together with the intent of stopping one criminal, the number one drug-running kingpin in the entire Black Sea region. Each with their own agenda, each with their own chain of command, each with their own political oversight.

Bedlam.

From the beginning, sparks flashed between one of the Americans, a feisty, wiry investigator from the US Marshal's Service, and one of the Spanish intelligence officers, a tall, angular woman who tended to stand in the back of the room during briefings, arms crossed, looking dark and sullen. His name was Michael Patrick Finnigan, and he wanted a completely proper, by-the-book,

American-style arrest, leading to an indictment, leading to a trial, leading to prison time.

Her name (and it took Finnigan three days before anyone would tell him this) was Katalin Fiero Dahar. She seemed perpetually angry. She also seemed to have bad clock, constantly checking her watch and sighing irritably.

They were calling the Ukrainian drug runner Pantomime. During one of the heated, shouted, pointless "Tower of Babel" meetings, Finnigan demanded a proper arrest of Pantomime. Fiero said it would be faster to shoot the fat bastard.

"That's not our job!" the American snapped back.

She swiped long, straight hair away from her eyes. "Don't be naive."

Finnigan fumed. "This has to be done right. We need to put him away."

"Yes, this has to be done right," the Spaniard countered. "We need to put him down."

"We're law enforcement!"

She stormed out of the room. "*You're* law enforcement."

A day passed. Embassies sent contradictory messages to the participating agencies. Wires got crossed. Pecking orders got pecked to death. Finnigan took the time to look into the intense, angry Spaniard. She was nominally a soldier, but without rank, insignia, or unit affiliation. She held herself apart from the other Spanish officials. He learned she was part Algerian. The others in her party treated her like sweaty dynamite, ready to explode at any time.

Fiero also asked about the annoying American. He'd been a cop in New York City, she found, then joined the Marshal's Service. His countrymen called him "the Boy Scout" and "Honest John," behind his back and shook their heads.

The less Finnigan learned about Fiero, the harder he dug. He poked and prodded.

A prosecutor from Cordoba finally spoke to him off the record. "Fiero? Leave that one alone."

"Why?"

The man looked around to make sure they were alone. His voice dropped. "That one is the *Oscura Sicaria.*"

Finnigan looked it up.

The Dark Assassin.

It all came to a head on the night they'd planned for Pantomime's arrest. The various agents, including Finnigan, were spread throughout a sprawling maritime warehouse and train yard outside Sevastopol. Communications were spotty; cooperation more so. Was this a military or law-enforcement operation? Would Pantomime be taken inside the warehouse or outside? Which agency was in charge? The Americans wanted to go all in; the Russians threatened to pull out.

Shortly after midnight, Finnigan heard the distinct crack of gunfire. His earpiece squawked. *"Pantomime down! Pantomime down!"*

Finnigan was outside, near the train tracks. He spun, eyes looking everywhere, hand lingering near his holstered Glock. Down? The drug runner wasn't even supposed to arrive for another hour! Confusion and tumult assaulted him through his earpiece. *"Who fired? ... Target's dead, Jesus ... All units, fall back to the rally point ... Find the shooter! ... Belay that!"*

Finnigan turned and caught the faintest glimpse of someone leaping off the roof of the warehouse, ink black against a jet-black sky; no more than the suggestion of movement. The form—if it was a form, and not a figment of his imagination amidst the confusion—dropped straight down onto the roof of an unmoving

Russian freight train. Finnigan was maybe two hundred yards back. He yelled into his mic, "Got the shooter! In pursuit!"

The radios went nuts. *Who responded? Who is that? ... Hold position! Do not engage ... All units, help Finnigan! ... All units, stop the American!"*

Finnigan ignored it all, sprinted in the direction of the shadow.

He ripped the earpiece away, felt it bounce against his shoulder blade as he hauled ass into the train yard, running parallel to the train.

He heard a *ka-thunk*, and then again and again, all up and down the line, the repeated sound echoing off the faded warehouse fronts. The engine safeties had disengaged, the mile-long freight train gearing up to leave the grimy, rat-infested station.

Finnigan didn't know any details yet. The target, Pantomime, was down? He'd been shot? That meant a crime. That was all Finnigan needed to know. Like a dumb dog chasing a ball, he didn't need to know why he was chasing it, he just needed to catch it.

He picked up his speed.

Finnigan ran parallel to the train. He heard the faintest tap of rubber soles on metal, and felt sure that the hitter was running the length of the train, too. But up top, leaping from car to car.

Fiero. The Spaniard/Algerian/whatever. She'd been the only person on the joint task force who appeared athletic enough to do that.

"Stop!" he bellowed as she continued to flee in a sprint. "Hey! Police! Stop!"

She ran along the top of the train in the direction of the engine cars, which were a half-mile ahead of Finnigan's location.

Now the train started to move. It began with a palsy lurch, a giant dragon stirring from a century's sleep. It would travel a foot per minute; then a yard per minute. Then the train would be racing into the night, toward Dzhankoy and the narrow crossing

of the Sea of Azov. Get that far, and the train and the suspect—
Fiero?—would be gone forever.

"Stop, goddamn it!"

Finnigan kept sprinting, inhaling deep, the air of the old train
yard a stew of lead and asbestos and every carcinogen known to
man. He heard English and Spanish and Russian and French,
tinny and incoherent, bubbling from the earpiece that swung behind him on its pigtail wire. The task force hadn't even been able to
agree on a common tongue, let alone a common definition of *win*.

Finnigan wasn't a big man. At five-eight, he was light and fast.
He liked to say, "I'm faster than any bastard who's tougher'n me,
but I'm tougher than any bastard who's faster'n me."

That'd been his father's mantra when the old man was a
New York City cop. The same for Finnigan's uncles and grandfather. Nobody ever picked the Finnigan boys to win a basketball
game—just the fight after the game.

He ran faster than the iron behemoth and caught up to the
connector between two of the cars. There he saw a flash of leg,
way up high, leaping from one car to the other.

Katalin Fiero Dahar. The *Oscura Sicaria*. He had no doubts
about that now.

The train was still much slower than Finnigan, but it was
picking up speed. Fiero had selected her thousand-ton magic carpet well.

Finnigan picked it up, boots pounding into the loose gravel,
sprinting now, arms pumping, pulling ahead of this car. He
reached the next space between cars; kept running.

"I will goddamn shoot you!" he bellowed. "Stop running!"

He thought he caught a glimpse of her jumping in his peripheral vision. She was now a second behind him. He sprinted on.

The train chugged, gaining a little momentum.

Finnigan got to the end of the next car, then ten paces beyond, and stopped, dropping to one knee, gravel digging into his skin, his right knee up, bracing his right elbow. He drew his Glock auto, clutched his right wrist with his left hand. He aimed.

He had no hope of hitting the crazy Spaniard while she jumped between cars. She was just too damn fast.

So, he fired before she jumped. He aimed for the vertical wall that made up the rear of the next car, aiming above the door. He was going for a bank shot. His bullets, he hoped, would hit the iron and ricochet back into her path. Maybe get her to stop or to stumble. Maybe.

He fired twice, one shot after the other, sparks flying off the iron wall of the boxy car, both bullets caroming backward and upward into the night.

He heard a muffled grunt. Then nothing.

He knelt, listening. The train threw up a terrible racket despite—or perhaps because of—its glacially slow start.

No chance I actually hit her! he thought. It had been an in-the-dark Hail Mary. The equivalent of casting a fishing line into a lake and bonking the fish on the top of the head with the lead weight.

But Finnigan heard the distinctive crunch of boots landing on gravel on the far side of the slow-rolling train.

She'd hopped down.

He holstered his weapon and dodged between two of the cars. He climbed up on the ironwork, tossed his leg over the coupling device, and hopped down on the far side.

The Spaniard tackled him.

Finnigan saw her coming and twisted, hip-checking her away. He slammed back into the moving car and bounced off it, going to one knee.

She was up and running, perpendicular to the tracks now, toward a cavernous abandoned warehouse thirty paces on.

She limped, favoring one leg.

Finnigan preened a little, thinking he'd hit her with the bank shot. That would be one to brag about at the bars until … well, forever. He rose to follow, already shaping the anecdotes in his head, when his vision warped. The planet's gravity shifted. He stumbled and put a hand to his midriff.

Felt a knife handle.

His first thought: *Why is there a knife handle in my shirt?*

Then: *Oh.*

He yanked the knife out, let it clatter to the stones. He realized something had deflected the blow—his ballistic vest; his belt perhaps. Rather than a four-inch-deep incision, the blade had sliced him laterally—long, but not deep. The bolster of the knife had caught in the cloth of his shirt, which now bloomed with a dark stain of blood.

He raced after her, one hand on the stomach wound.

Fiero disappeared into the warehouse.

The place was abandoned, falling apart, asymmetrical. The north end had collapsed under some winter's snow, maybe, or fallen victim to termites. The south end stood, black and foreboding, a hole in the dark sky, a silhouette of structure.

He ran inside.

Twenty paces in, his left leg forgot how to lift properly and he tripped on an old flue brick, sprawling. It was too dark to see much. His hand felt sticky with blood. He sensed, more than saw, a solid substance a few feet to his left and crab walked toward it, left hand on the ground, supporting himself. He reached the old, creosote-soaked wooden beam and collapsed against it. He sat, drew his Glock, and tried to breathe normally.

The pain pulsed in his gut.

He heard the distinctive ratchet of a handgun slide in the dark, somewhere to his left.

She spoke English. "You're the American? Finnigan?"

He remembered now that her voice was low and husky; a smoker's voice, though she sure as hell didn't run like a smoker.

He said, "Fiero, right?"

She began to swear; at least, he assumed from the venom sound that it was swearing. It was a Gatling gun goulash of Spanish and Arabic. She drifted to English at the end.

"You shot me! Son of a whore!"

"You stabbed me."

He waited, trying to triangulate her position.

She said, "Yes, well ... You shot me first."

Seconds ticked by.

And Finnigan snorted a laugh.

He had no earthly idea why. It was the simple petulance of her comment.

A second later, and she laughed, too.

"You're psychotic," he said.

"Yes. Try to keep that in mind."

"Where did I shoot you?"

She said, "Hip."

"Hurt?"

"Just a graze."

Finnigan settled back against the pillar. "You have the right to remain silent."

"You haven't met many Spanish women."

They both laughed. Which, for Finnigan, hurt like hell. Bats flitted overhead, sonar bouncing. The train outside chugged and hissed, and finally passed on by.

He said, "We wanted the asshole alive. To face charges."

She said, "We wanted the asshole dead. He'd faced charges before. So, what? He was let off."

"So, you just executed him?"

"Last time the Americans arrested him, they put him in

Witness Protection. From there, he ran his rackets across the globe. And you knew it!"

She wasn't wrong. The Ukrainian had flipped, providing evidence for almost a dozen major arrests. And yes, he'd continued to profit from his own evils throughout.

Finnigan felt the wound, right above his beltline. It hurt but it wasn't fatal. It likely had begun clotting while he sat there. He wiped sweat off his forehead. They sat in silence.

After a while, Finnigan lowered the hammer on his gun, sure that she could hear it. He holstered the weapon and then stood, grunting, one hand tacky with creosote, the other tacky with blood. Depending on where she was, he might have been backlit by the barn door. He started back the way he'd come—toward the entrance and the tracks and the night.

Halfway there, he stopped. "You can't just assassinate people."

"You can't pretend to stop people like that with arrest warrants. My ends may not justify my means, but neither do yours."

"Your way isn't justice."

"Yes, but yours isn't either."

Finnigan reached the exit and looked back over his shoulder, into the pitch black. The darkness stared back at him. Far away, sirens blared and men in boots ran on gravel. Behind his back, his earpiece chirped nonsensically, like a grown-up in a *Peanuts* special.

"Look, my way doesn't always work," Finnigan said, "but there are rules, lady. We follow the rules, or we're just as bad as the bad guys."

The darkness said, "My way doesn't always work, either. I know this. But when your precious rules don't work, then what? Do nothing? That way is just as bad as your *bad guys*."

"So where does that leave us?"

He stood, clutching his gut, waiting.

The darkness said, "I don't know. Do you?"

Finnigan listened to the muted cacophony of his earpiece, listened to the fading sound of the freight train heading toward Russia. Thought about how little he cared that Pantomime was dead.

He turned toward the darkness and said, "I've got an idea."

C01

Six months after Michael Patrick Finnigan and Katalin Fiero Dahar met—and wounded—each other in Ukraine, they were in business together.

Both had had their fill of bureaucracy. Both wanted to see their work *mean* something.

But Finnigan had set one inviolate restriction: "We'll break rules. We'll break laws. But we aren't assassins."

Fiero agreed. Reluctantly.

Finnigan was a cop, through and through. He was a slow, methodical, and imaginative investigator. Fiero was a spy. She could get into places and be whomever she needed to be to get to the truth.

Fiero had a contact in the International Criminal Court, an anonymous go-between who threw a few thousand dollars their way, under the table, to connect "actionable evidence" to a wily Portuguese smuggler. The smuggler had evaded capture for a decade. It took Finnigan and Fiero three days. The evidence was rock solid, the conviction a slam dunk.

(Fiero hadn't understood the colloquialism *slam dunk*. Finnigan explained it to her.)

Their source at the court—an Englishman, it turned out—sent more cases their way. Harder cases. With more money on the line.

What they were doing wasn't legal, in the strictest sense. Okay, it wasn't legal in *any* sense. Shan Greyson—they eventually learned his name—their back-channel liaison to the court, knew a banker who could help hide the profits.

And Fiero knew mercenaries for the times when violence ensued.

They made a hundred thousand euros by the end of the year and five hundred thousand by the end of the next. All of it tax-free.

They had a list of enemies by the middle of their first month together. That happens when you arrest people and sneak them across borders to The Hague.

As their profits and their profile grew, the partners created a false front. Honestly, they needed two—one to hide their profits and another to hide from their families.

A Cyprus-based firm handled the legal and insurance paperwork for maritime salvage operations. Cypriot banking is byzantine enough that the new company would never have to show clients or a profit. The money that poured in was expertly cloaked.

For the world at large, Fiero and Finnigan used their contacts to create false identifications for themselves as independent researchers for some far-flung subsidiary agency of the European Union. Finnigan hired a burnout bureaucrat from Manchester who'd retired to the Cypriot city of Gazimağusa, and he churned out two or three breathtakingly dull reports under their names per year. Should anyone look—and nobody had—a paper trail of pristine dullness lay scattered about them like hedge trimmings.

They also signed a nonaggression pact with the Central

Intelligence Service of the Cyprus Police. In one of their very first cases, they had stumbled upon a con man who'd stolen nearly a half-million euros from the police retirement fund. The partners got the money and returned it, no questions asked, no finder fee expected. An Inspector Rafael Triadis, Nicosia Division, had called upon them shortly thereafter to figure out what their game was. Put simply, they were going after criminals, but without the traditional protection of being in law enforcement or connected to any government. They needed a safe haven. In return for which, they would offer their services to Inspector Triadis on occasion.

Triadis had served as a soldier in Sarajevo during the years-long siege in the 1990s. He held a fierce loathing for war criminals. They reached an agreement and Triadis had even thrown in an introduction to his cousin, who owned an empty office over a Turkish restaurant in Kyrenia.

Now all that was needed was a name for the company.

One night over way too much vodka, they came upon St. Nicholas Salvage & Wrecking.

The origin of the name was the partners' secret.

CO2

The club wasn't easy to find. It featured no signage out front. It was up a narrow flight of stairs, tucked above the office of a legal advocate, and nobody would think to enter through the door unless they were seeking an attorney—not a drink. The illuminati of Belgium's international diplomatic corps had used the place for years as a clandestine spot for those times when one wanted complete anonymity. Many affairs of state, and affairs of the heart, began in this nameless place.

Katalin Fiero Dahar looked the part. Michael Finnigan didn't.

She wore a slim black suit with stilettos. He wore blue chinos and a blue, unstructured jacket—and thought the blues matched. He was the only one who thought so. They walked up the narrow steps, Fiero in the lead, toward the hush of the bar and away from the murmur of the street. She looked back over her shoulder, shaking laser-straight hair out of her eyes. "We need to see about getting you a suit."

Finnigan said, "This is a suit."

She blinked at him and smiled.

Thomas Shannon Greyson waited for them at the bar. English, matchstick lean, aristocratic, and charming, he knew the waitstaff by name, knew what football clubs they fancied—although he didn't visit the nameless club but a few times per year. He turned as the duo entered, beaming at them.

He presented a Champagne cocktail in a tall crystal flute to Fiero. Bubbles glistened from the top. "The Champagne is from a vineyard outside of Troyes," he said, his voice pure Eton. "The brandy is a little Armagnac *hors d'âge* that I've grown fond of. The bitters I discovered in a deplorable cathouse in Trinidad."

Fiero took the glass.

He handed Finnigan a larger glass. "Pabst."

"Sweet."

Shan, as he was known to friends, led the way deeper into the gloom of the distinguished club, to an oxblood-red wooden booth with heavy, drawn curtains of green baize. They sidled in, Shan on one side, the partners on the other. The Englishman already had a whiskey and soda waiting. He favored them with his satyr's grin, lifted his glass an inch.

"To St. Nicholas Salvage & Wrecking."

They sipped.

"Been meaning to ask you for ages: Where did you come up with that name for your company?" he asked, turning to Fiero. "Michael is Irish Catholic but you're Muslim, so I assume it has nothing to do with Kris Kringle."

"My *mother's* Muslim," she corrected. "What can we do for you?"

By *you*, she meant Madame Hélene Betancourt of Switzerland, the ranking judge of the International Criminal Court.

Their company, St. Nicholas Salvage & Wrecking, had now done work for Judge Betancourt on five other occasions, but they never met with her. Nor would her name come up in this day's conversation. Although the company was well paid for its work, no agency on earth would ever be able to link the money back to the venerable judge.

Bounty hunting, by and large, is both illegal and vulgar.

Hence Thomas Shannon Greyson, in his bespoke suits and besotted by his own self-image, was the perfect go-between.

The Englishman turned his gaze on the American. Finnigan looked as disheveled as usual, with his mop of wavy black hair and a half-day's growth of beard. Michael Finnigan was one of those men who develop a five o'clock shadow at ten in the morning.

"It is good to see you, Michael. How've you been?"

"Drunk. You?"

"Sometimes; not as often as you'd think."

Fiero had never been good at small talk. She asked again, "What's this about?"

Shan reached down onto the bench beside his coat and produced an iPad, with a flash drive sticking out of the side like an arrowhead. He swiped it open and turned it to face the partners. "There's this fellow lives in Serbia. Lazar Aleksić. He's an extremely bad person, and Our Mutual Friend would like very much to see him appear before the International Court."

Fiero studied the image: he was a youth, midtwenties, blond and handsome. Shan reached over and used a fingertip to bring up more images: The blond kid skiing. The blond kid at a bar with a looker in a strapless gown. The blond kid amid the crowd at a bullfight, smoking a cigarette and laughing hysterically.

She looked up at Shan. "Why?"

"Which part?"

"Why arrest this man, and why us? Start with the first part."

"He's pimping underage refugees to pedophiles throughout Europe."

Fiero said, simply, "Ah."

"If I'm right, this tumor of a human is running girls and boys throughout half of the eurozone. Dozens, maybe scores of kids. Syrians, Afghans, Egyptians. Anyone fleeing to Europe for a new life. And our young Master Aleksić is on absolutely nobody's radar. Not the local police. Not Interpol. Nobody."

Finnigan reached over and made the images disappear. He expected a PDF and found it: a file on Lazar Aleksić. He started scanning the details.

Fiero said, "That explains *why him*. Now: *why us*."

"Three reasons," the Englishman said. "The first is this: As our Michael is about to tell you, we have a great deal of smoke, but no fire. We need an independent agency that will link Lazar Aleksić to his victims. Second, he never leaves Belgrade, Serbia. Where, I assure you, he is surrounded by an army of underlings with firearms. He's also bought protection from the Serbian Police."

Finnigan was scanning the PDF on the tablet computer. He drained his beer. "This all you've got?"

"Unfortunately, yes."

Fiero leaned in toward the American and placed an arm on his shoulder, resting her chin on the back of her hand. She peered at the screen as Finnigan scrolled through the document. Shan Greyson waited, watching.

They were an unusual pair, he thought. Lovers? One suspected so, at first. But they acted more like siblings. Or at least very good friends. Shan fancied himself an avid reader of others' body language, and he had trouble figuring out what the principal owners of St. Nicholas Salvage & Wrecking were to each other.

Finnigan said, "Guy's mobbed up in Belgrade?"

"He is indeed."

Fiero brushed long hair away from her face. "You said there was a third reason why the judge … sorry, why *you* wanted to hire us?"

Shan finished his drink and checked his watch. "There is. Come. I'd like to show you something."

Four blocks away, an association of international attorneys was just finishing the dinner portion of their annual conference. Shan Greyson led the way into the auditorium, handed several folded bills to a waiter, and took the partners to the back of the room, where the coatracks stood sentinel.

The speaker for the evening was the director of the Levant Crisis Group at the United Nations High Commission for Refugees. The director had a patrician's frame, an actor's profile, and a resonant baritone. He was a man born to make speeches. He had silver hair and a conservative suit and a sky-blue enamel lapel pin shaped like a dove in flight.

Almost 160 guests of the international conference on international law had attended the dinner to hear his keynote address. The attendees sat around white-clothed tables and ate prime rib. There were no vacant seats. Liveried waitstaff provided wine and coffee as the guest of honor took the podium without the aid of notes—and spoke for forty-five minutes straight.

Finnigan, Fiero, and Shan Greyson stood in the back and, the way the lights hit the stage, it was unlikely the speaker could spot them. Attorneys at the rearmost tables could see them; several kept turning to eye the tall, dark woman in the slim suit and stiletto heels. Fiero didn't appear to notice. Finnigan did, and smiled.

The UN official spoke with passion about the tsunami of immigrants pouring into Europe from Syria, Afghanistan, Sudan, South Sudan, Iraq, Libya, and Egypt. He spoke about the Christian mission of Europeans to help the downtrodden, but also about the enormous burden this had placed on the economy of each member nation. He set the historic landscape, comparing this to the great, forced immigrations of World Wars I and II. He talked with granular detail about the Schengen Agreement, which allowed for free and unfettered border crossings for both people and freight between European nations. He praised the history and ethos of Islam, but warned of the dark stain of Islamist forces.

He was an electrifying speaker, even in English, which wasn't his native tongue. When he wrapped it up, the room rose as one in a spontaneous burst of applause. Photojournalists bathed the lectern in strobes.

The speaker moved to the head table and kissed a plump little woman in a cashmere sweater and pearls. She beamed benevolently at him; clearly the doting wife.

As the applause continued, Fiero leaned toward the Englishman. "We know where the UN stands on the refugee crisis. What's this got to do with your Serbian bastard?"

Finnigan leaned in. "Also, you said there were *three* reasons you wanted us involved."

Shan said, "Right you are. My enfant terrible is Lazar Aleksić. And our fine speaker for the day, the director of the Levant Crisis Group at the United Nations High Commission for Refugees, is Miloš Aleksić. Lazar's loving dad."

He pointed toward the wife at the head table. "Marija Aleksić, Lazar's mum."

Finnigan scratched his stubbly cheek. "Holy shit."

Shan said, "Indeed!"

A waiter walked by with a tray of Champagne flutes held shoulder-high. Fiero snagged one, en passant, and drained it in a go.

"We're in."

C03

Rare was the Friday night that didn't find Jane Koury and Lanni Connors meeting for drinks at Callahan's in Bayswater. The pub was a favorite of young journalists and journalism students, providing cheap beer, half-decent wine, and a relatively good chance of not getting groped at the bar. Jane and Lanni seldom missed a weekend together of chardonnay and moping.

Both had been out of school for two years. Both were underemployed; Jane working for peanuts at three news websites, Lanni waiting tables and writing for free on entertainment sites for the exposure. They'd known all the way through school that things would be tough once they got out. But the actual reality of it hit them like a lorry.

Which was why Jane's wicked grin caught her best mate by surprise that Friday.

"Good lord!" Lanni set down the drinks and huddled in for a good chat. "You've met someone!"

"Have I? I have hell!" Jane laughed. Like a lot of second-generation

Syrians, she dressed in typical London fashion—tonight it was jeans, a sweater, and suede boots. Her grandmother might not have approved, but nobody Jane's age wore anything resembling traditional Arabic clothing. At least, not in her circles. She was young—only twenty-two—but thanks to a round face and petite build, she was constantly mistaken for a teenager. It was a source of great humor—and possibly a bit of resentment—from the taller and curvier Lanni, whose ancestors had sacked the Scottish coast in longboats.

"I'm not seeing anyone," Jane said. "I've got the most brilliant idea ever. 'Bout my career."

Lanni rolled her eyes. "I'd like a brilliant idea about my career. Remind me again: What's my career?"

Jane reached over and squeezed her hand. "You're going to be writing for the London *Times* before you're thirty and running it by forty. Fact."

"Not at the pace I'm—"

Jane held up a hand and said, "Fact! It's science, and you can't argue science. Reporter by thirty. Managing editor by forty. Shut up and drink."

Lanni did as she was told. Her best friend had more faith in her trajectory than Lanni did herself. Which was why she hadn't revealed to Jane that she'd been gathering brochures for doctoral programs in English literature. If she were going to be a Poor Underemployed Londoner, she might as well be Dr. Poor Underemployed Londoner.

"So, what's your daft plan?" Lanni asked.

Jane unfolded a page from the *Guardian*. The newsprint was folded precisely, which was Jane's way with everything. It showed a map of the Middle East and Southern Europe, with the Mediterranean as a big blue blob on the left.

"Hundreds of thousands of refugees are making the trip, by foot, from Syria to Turkey, to Europe. Hundreds! Of thousands!"

"I know!" she said, shaking her head. "Breaks your heart."

"I don't want to break hearts, I want to break stories. Lanni … I'm going."

Lanni sipped her white wine. "Where?"

"Syria."

Lanni then, promptly, spat white wine across the *Guardian*.

"You're not! That's rubbish! There's no tourism in Syria these days! Nobody's going there but the Red Cross and soldiers!"

"And journalists."

"No!" Lanni said adamantly. "Reporters aren't! Do you not know how many journalists have died in the last couple of years in Syria? Gobs!" She said *gobs* as if it were a finite and measurable number, divisible by itself and one.

"My uncle lives in Hama. He's an editor. I've already written to him, told him my plan."

"Which is what?" Lanni's voice ratcheted up in disbelief. This didn't seem like Jane's usual but brief foray into a new career opportunity, but instead something she'd thought out.

"I'm flying to Beirut. One of his photographers is meeting me there and driving me across the border. I want to focus on refugees. I'll join one of the routes moving north. I plan to interview children; just children."

"You're not!" Lanni protested. "Love, that's bonkers! You'll be at risk!"

Jane shrugged. She reached over to her tote, which shared the third chair with Lanni's bag, and produced an airplane boarding ticket.

Lanni shrieked, and suddenly all eyes in the pub were on her.

"Shhh! God, everyone's looking!"

"Jane," she replied in a muted tone, "this is barking mad! You can't! It's dangerous!"

"Less so since ISIS, or Daesh, or whatever, was kicked out," she said. "Only Damascus and the cities around it are still at war. The rest is just … well, refugees."

"But—"

"And I'm in good shape. I've hiked through Ireland and Wales," Jane said. "I've run half marathons! I'm in great shape. And I look like this,"—she pointed with both index fingers at her youthful, round face—"so kids always open up to me."

"You don't speak Arabic!"

"Hello! *Koury?* I speak Arabic with a Syrian accent. Look …"

She produced her driver's license. Lanni peered at it.

It wasn't made out to Jane Koury. It was made out to Jinan Koury.

"That's my real name. Nobody calls me that, but it's my name."

Lanni realized that tears were forming in her blue eyes. "Is this for real then? You're doing this?"

Jinan Koury of London grinned at her best mate, cupped both of Lanni's hands in her own. "I am! I really am!"

C04

St. Nicholas Salvage & Wrecking owned a seaplane, currently revving up in the waters of Amsterdam. Finnigan decided he'd rendezvous there with Lachlan Sumner, their pilot, and bring it down to their headquarters in Cyprus. Sumner, a rangy New Zealander, had flown for oil companies, putting down planes everywhere from Alaska to Qatar. There was pretty much no place he couldn't fly to.

Fiero hopped a flight to Berlin to see an old friend from her intelligence-service days.

The articles of incorporation for St. Nicholas Salvage & Wrecking were a bit arcane and not easy to track down. The company was headquartered in Kyrenia, Cyprus, which meant, technically, that it was a Cypriot company. But since 1974, the island had been split lengthwise—two-thirds Greek, and one-third Turkish. To the government of Cyprus, and to all but one of the 193 members of the United Nations, the island had one government and a Turkish occupying force. To the Turks, the island featured two independent nations, much like Haiti and the Dominican Republic.

Kyrenia is on the north, on the Turkish side, and from its shore one can see Turkey on a clear day. It's a small, provincial tourist town with a lovely old marina that houses a few dozen luxury sailboats, a semicircle of restaurants, hotels, and Russian casinos, plus a small commercial core, all hemmed in by the Mediterranean to the north and the craggy Pentadactyl mountain range to the south. A mammoth fortress overlooks the commercial bay and an identical, mostly unused bay to the east of the town—from the air, the two bays and the fortress look like a capital *W*, with the looming stone fort between the inlets. The bay to the west has a functioning seawall to protect the sailboats. The bay to the east does not, and is used mainly by local companies.

Companies such as St. Nicholas Salvage & Wrecking, which had purchased the rights to tie down a de Havilland DHC-6-300 Twin Otter seaplane in the lesser-used bay.

Thanks to the bifurcated nature of life on Cyprus since the 1974 civil war, tracking down information on a company based out of Kyrenia is difficult at best.

Plus, the island is known for its obtuse and opaque banking regulations. It had become a favorite haven for Russian mobsters hoping to hide money from their country's crooked government.

Sauce for the goose … The murkiness of the Cypriot banking and business world worked just as well for Michael Finnigan and Katalin Fiero Dahar.

After visiting her friend in Berlin, Fiero flew commercial to Larnaca, Cyprus, the country's only large commercial airport. Cyprus is a small country—the best method of getting from one city to the next is taxi, and the price rarely rises above thirty euros.

St. Nicholas Salvage & Wrecking kept a Land Rover in a garage close to Larnaca, just past the salt marsh lakes with their massive flocks of flamingos. Fiero threw her overnight bag in the back and checked the lockbox to make sure she had euros for the Greek side of the island and Turkish lira for the north. She drove straight through, circling the capital of Nicosia, crossing at the UN checkpoint, and got to Kyrenia inside of two hours.

Bridget Sumner—wife of their pilot, Lachlan Sumner—ran the shop when the principals were away. Fiero got back to find everything tidy and a note from Bridget informing them that she was at home but could run back if needed.

St. Nicholas Salvage & Wrecking kept a suite of offices on three levels, perched precariously above a restaurant that overlooked the commercial marina. A flood of tourists—mostly Turkish and British—strolled the promenade below the oatmeal-colored abode. The office was set back enough to provide privacy from the people below.

Fiero showered and changed into raggedy cutoff jeans and a vintage Ramones T-shirt. She poured herself a vodka and sat out on their tight little balcony. She'd rescued two floatable cushions from a friend's boat and used them as a seat on the balcony and a support behind her back. The Turkish restaurant below did the most amazing seafood, and the aromas of saffron and ginger floating up to their loft never ceased to amaze. The town gleamed, especially at night, with its combination of late nineteenth-century and prewar Romanticism. The great, rocky fortress loomed to the east, reminding the town of its Venetian and Ottoman history. The French House of Lusignan had ruled its slice of the Mediterranean from this island, back when its kingdom included Jerusalem and Armenia. Aphrodite had come from this oblong rock in the sea, if one believed that sort of thing. (Fiero sometimes did.) Pygmalion's statue had come to life on this island. Othello had served here before his encounter with Iago. Or, so the story goes.

Fiero studied the files on the encrypted flash drive that Shan Greyson had given them. She sipped her vodka until the sun set, then went inside to pull on a ratty, stretched-out sweater, grabbed another bottle of vodka from the icebox in the staff kitchen, and padded back out to the balcony to sit on her cushions, reading now beneath the light pouring out of the office window.

She and Finnigan kept living quarters on the top level of the three-floor suite.

Her mother texted her from Madrid. Khadija Dahar's birthday was coming up. There would be no good way to avoid seeing the family. No matter how much she tried.

She called it a night around one. She awoke at ten, threw on gym shorts and a jog top and shoes, and ran eight miles, east toward the town of Bellapais, doing the hill work that she preferred three days per week. Thanks to the elevation gain, her long, deeply tanned body was sheathed in sweat by the time she returned downtown. The village was coming alive, the air smelling of fresh shellfish and ground coffee. The midday Muslim call to prayer—the *Zuhr*—reverberated from minarets up and down the valley. The sound always reminded her of her mother, and of growing up in the Muslim quarter of Cádiz.

She showered and got a plate of olives, feta, and fresh bread from the restaurant downstairs, along with a beaten copper plate with a cup of good Turkish coffee and a sealed, plastic container of water; the way it's always served on Cyprus. She recognized a happy sound and stepped out on the balcony to watch as the company's de Havilland Otter descended from the skies, its twin Pratt & Whitneys purring. The Otter was outfitted with pontoons that summer, although she often was rigged in STOL—Short Takeoff and Landing—formation with a fixed tricycle gear. Fiero watched as the Kiwi, Lachlan Sumner, brought the plane in, as light as a love song.

Fiero retrieved her mobile phone from the desk in her suite and hit the number one speed dial.

Finnigan spoke up over the roar of the twin engines. She could tell by the audio quality that he'd taken the call over the Otter's headsets. "Yo."

She shielded her eyes and watched as their plane cruised beyond the great Venetian fortress, toward the lesser bay and out of sight.

"Smoke," she said, watching. "Little fire. We need to get started on this."

Finnigan said, "Agreed. Hey. It's your mom's birthday on Thursday."

Fiero said, "Shut up," and disconnected.

C05

It worked like a charm. Jane Koury—*Jinan*, she reminded herself—flew from Gatwick to Ankara, then took a smaller plane to
Beirut. Tamer Awad, a thirty-year-old photojournalist from the
newspaper in Hama, met her at the airport. She'd purchased a
hijab from a shop near Gatwick, and had gone to YouTube to
remind herself how to drape it around her head and shoulders.
She hadn't worn one in ages.

"You look fine," Tamer said. "How's your Arabic?"

Jane laughed. "I'm Syrian, Tamer. I speak fluent Arabic."

The journalist's smile faltered. "What's that accent?"

Jane blushed. "It's Syrian."

The guy laughed. He pointed to his Nissan Sentra, parked
just outside the airport gates. "If you say so ..."

C06

Over a lunch of grilled lamb and salads with Turkish olive oil and lemon, the partners shared what they'd learned about Lazar Aleksić.

"What is this kid, nineteen?" he asked.

"He's twenty-five."

Finnigan just shook his head. "They get younger every year."

"It's not *his* youth that bothers me. His victims are underage. According to Shan, maybe as young as twelve or thirteen."

Finnigan looked momentarily ill. "Selling them to pimps and whorehouses. But also private buyers. That's just ..." He rubbed his eyes with the heels of his hands.

"Evil. I know."

They ordered white wine.

Fiero nibbled on her lamb. She wore black, as always—a simple tank and matchstick jeans with suede ankle boots. She'd pulled her hair back in the Spanish style: parted in the middle and in a low chignon at the base of her neck. Finnigan also wore a standard outfit: 501s and a button-down shirt, untucked. His tousled haircut was a few weeks past its sell-by date. He hadn't shaved since Bruges, but it all looked good on him.

Fiero pointed toward the laptop between them. "Aleksić grew up very rich. There are stories of his getting into trouble with the law in Serbia, in France, in Belgium, and his father bailing him out."

"His father, who is director of a UN Middle Eastern refugee program."

"Which means serious clout," she added.

"What's Junior been doing since he came of age?"

"According to Shan, he's connected with Serbian mobsters. Whether Miloš Aleksić knows or not …" She gave a very Iberian shrug, conveying tons.

"Mobsters?"

"Formerly Serbian military. The same military that committed atrocities in the 1990s, during the Yugoslavian civil war. When the war ended, they turned to organized crime."

The owner of the restaurant swung by the table with their wine. He didn't mind Fiero Dahar—a half-Muslim woman— sharing liquor with Finnigan. Cyprus is a most secular country, even by Turkish standards.

"Who're the victims?"

She took a moment to bring up a map of Europe and the Mediterranean. "Since the wars in Syria and Afghanistan, the refugee trail into Europe has looked like this …" She pointed to the screen. "From the Middle East, north into Turkey. From there, refugees take three routes. The middle route is Turkey to Greece, Greece to Macedonia and Kosovo, then on to Serbia and parts farther north, such as Hungary. Or, they head from Macedonia through Bosnia and Croatia, and on to Austria."

Finnigan nodded.

"The northern route goes Turkey to Bulgaria to Romania to Hungary. The western route goes Turkey by boat from the southern coast to Greece, then across the Adriatic by boat to Italy."

"So. The middle route." He licked lemon juice off his fingers. "You need someone in Serbia to exploit the refugees."

"Serbia or Kosovo, yes. Closer to Greece and you find too many observers. From the UN, from the media, from the Red Cross and Red Crescent."

Finnigan thought about it a while. "In the Marshal's Service, we liked to keep our eyes on the borders. Borders create bottlenecks. That's where coyotes exploit victims."

"Coyotes?"

"Colloquialism. Traffickers."

"Ah. Anyway, I see your point. Does Aleksić make contact with his victims in Belgrade? Or where they come across the border, in Kosovo?"

"We need to connect Aleksić to his victims. We need to know where he gathers them." He leaned back, sipped his wine, mulled over the problem. "Jeez, I'd love to put this *vantz* in prison."

"Is *vantz* like *coyote*?"

"No, it means bedbug. But in this case, yeah."

"To prey on little children, and on refugees …" Fiero's eyes had taken on a stormy, slate-gray sheen. Her partner knew the warning signs when he saw them.

"We don't get paid if Aleksić's dead."

She leveled that gray gaze on him for a while, and Finnigan held it, returned serve.

She finally gave him a warning smile. "I don't kill everyone I meet."

Finnigan signaled for the check. "Not for lack of trying."

After lunch, he returned to their office over the town of Kyrenia, checked his watch, and did his calculations for the time back in the States. He called a few friends from the Marshal's Service, from the DEA, and the FBI. He thought about it a while, then looked up a number for a guy who worked for the New York State Police, and who'd worked a number of cases involving the Little Odessa gangs in the US from the post-Soviet era. They hadn't spoken in a while.

The state cop called him back inside of five minutes. "Finnigan himself calls me. I think wonders just ceased."

Finnigan threw open the double doors to the narrow balcony overlooking the sailboats of the Kyrenian marina. The sky was crystalline, and Turkey shimmered near the horizon. "How's it going? How's Caroline?"

"She's good. You still bumming around Europe, writing love ballads and reading Yeats?"

"It's Keats this year, you soulless bastard. Hey, you know anyone who knows anyone connected to the scene in Belgrade, Serbia?"

The statie laughed. "You *consulting* on this thing, Mickey?"

"I'm asking." He didn't elaborate.

The guy said, "This a Saint Nicholas thing? I'm not as stupid as I look."

"Don't see how you could be." Finnigan hadn't realized that his old friends knew he was bounty hunting. But then again, this particular state cop collected knowledge the way some people collect stamps. There didn't seem much point in denying it. "Yeah, it's that. My partner and me are looking at a guy runs underage vics for whorehouses and private collectors. Guy targets Middle Eastern refugees."

"Ah, jeez …"

"Yeah."

Finnigan listened to the pause over the phone. Below their

office, British expats laughed and strolled the curved boardwalk, on their way to one of the many casinos in town.

"You know who would know for sure, right?"

Finnigan said, "Let's not get into that, OK?"

"How's Paddy doin'?"

"Don't know. Guy we're looking into, he may be using ex-Serb military. Death squad guys from the civil war in the nineties. What I need is someone elsewhere in Europe who can point me to the receiving side of the network. I want to work it from that end, heading *toward* Belgrade."

"Makes sense. Not a lot of Micks badging their way around Belgrade, I figure. Okay, I'll ask around."

"Thanks. This is a bad guy. Buys and sells children. Breaks up refugee families. We'd really like to put him away."

"You maybe don't know this, buddy, but St. Nicholas is gaining a reputation. A good one. I'll ask around."

"Thanks, man."

He was about to hang up as his friend cut back in. "No problem. But call your old man. 'Kay?"

Finnigan got some laundry going and changed the sheets on both beds—Fiero treasured her privacy, but having a partner who did laundry? For that, she was willing to cut him some slack.

He took a look at whatever important papers Bridget Sumner had put on his desk. They involved Cypriot banking, and he understood absolutely nothing about them. Bridget left a Post-it telling him to sign them, so he did.

He checked his watch and realized he could get to the capital, Nicosia, for the ten-thirty English Mass at Holy Cross Church. The drive itself took less than a half hour on the small island. Finnigan liked to tell his friends and coworkers that he went to Mass so he wouldn't have to lie to his mom about it later. But really, he went because it was a lifetime's habit. And he enjoyed it.

He slept fitfully that night. The next morning, he again hustled around, cleaned his suite of rooms. He took out the trash. He scanned Facebook and Twitter. He contemplated cleaning out the fridge. He stared into it for a while and threw away some cheese. He said, "Oh, for God's sake ..." and broke down and called his dad.

It was a Saturday, and his father would be camped out in his lounger, beer at hand, watching college sports. Always college sports, regardless of the season. Captain Patrick Finnigan—Paddy to his old friends—couldn't abide pro ball.

"Mickey! How the hell are you?"

Finnigan went to stand before the balcony again. A classic, wood-sided thirty-footer was making a spinnaker run toward the breakwater, the sun glistening off its deck, a long-legged girl in a huge floppy hat lying on a beach towel. "I'm doing good, Dad. What's on the tube?"

"Baseball. Arizona, UC San Diego. Where are you?"

"Cyprus, Dad."

"Sand, sun, and babes."

Patrick Finnigan assumed that Cyprus, Coney Island, and Miami were interchangeable. Not that he could visit any of them. Not with the electronic tether in his ankle bracelet.

They talked about family. They talked about baseball and about politics. Patrick Finnigan couldn't believe how much the politicians were screwing the country; screwing the working man. As always. Michael didn't think his old man had ever voted, but he'd served enough corrupt politicians over the years that he had a right to an opinion.

"Hey, Nicole is up for a promotion. How's *Sergeant* Nicole Finnigan sound?"

His old man sounded so full of pride. His only daughter,

wearing the blue. Finnigan said, "Well, she's the smartest member of the family, so …" and left it at that.

When he'd left the NYPD, his two-years-younger sister had been just about to finish at the academy. Another Finnigan, walking in Paddy's footprints. The day he handed in his badge, Michael had warned his sister about what she was getting into. It was the last time they'd spoken seriously.

"How 'bout you?" Patrick said. "You think much about getting a real job?"

"This job's pretty real, Dad."

The former captain laughed. "Jesus, you work in a goddamn cubicle, Mickey. Guys are out doing shit and you're writing reports."

Finnigan stared at the Eastern Med. "Something like that. It's a job."

He'd never had any intention of saying to his father, *I'm a bounty hunter.* Bounty hunting is illegal. And back in the States, as a New York cop and later as a deputy US Marshal, Michael Finnigan had had zero tolerance for the illegal activities that got his father booted off the force; that got him eighteen months in a federal lockup. Patrick Finnigan's criminal nature is what drove Michael to leave the NYPD in the first place, and he hadn't been shy letting his old man know that.

Michael had been angry and unforgiving. How then, now, to say his own path wasn't exactly on the up-and-up?

"No, look. I'm sorry, kiddo. A job's a job. Lotta guys are on the dole, you know? Being a bean counter in a cube ain't the same as taking welfare. Hey, how's you and Kathy?"

"Katalin."

"You an item, you two?"

"We work in the same office. You doing okay? Staying out of trouble?"

He heard the subtle change of tone in his dad's voice; heard him glug from the beer can. "Just watching some ball, kiddo. Just watching some ball."

"Sure," Michael said. "You're as clean as mom's floor."

He listened to nothing. The thirty-footer came around, aligned for the entry to the marina.

"Your mother's floor wasn't all that clean."

Michael blushed, sorry he'd pushed that particular button.

He knew that his old man had had great contacts in New York's immigrant crime communities, including the Slavs. In his day, Patrick Finnigan had known a little something about everything. He thought about bringing up Belgrade.

Patrick said, "You talked to your mother lately?"

"Last week. She sounds good."

Patrick said. "Good. Good."

The silence reigned. In the background, the crack of an aluminum bat, the soft susurrus of a happy crowd. Somewhere, in Arizona or California, people were buying dogs with spicy mustard, watching hyperathletic cheerleaders, and second-guessing managers. Somewhere, it was America. Somewhere. Just not in Cyprus.

"Hey, Dad, I gotta go."

"You bet," Patrick Finnigan said. "Oh, hey. You remember a jackoff name of Burkovsky at the DA's office?"

Finnigan squeezed his eyes shut and rubbed the lids with the pads of his finger and thumb. "Berkowski."

"Fuckin' guy," Patrick Finnigan said. And then nothing.

"What's going on, Dad?"

"Hmm? Nothing. Burkovsky, Berkowski, the guy's a dickless twerp with nothing better to do."

"Nothing better than what? You into something, Dad?"

"I'm into a fucking baseball game on TV, Mickey. I'm about halfway into a can of Coors. What do you think? I got this bracelet on my ankle, you think maybe I'm taking belly dancing lessons at the junior college?"

Berkowski, with the New York District Attorney's Office, specialized in high-profile corruption cases. Current cases; not old cases. "What's he want with you?"

"Ah, who knows with these Jews?"

Finnigan and Berkowski had gone to the same high school; the Berkowskis were Polish Catholic. "What'd you do?"

Patrick said, "I didn't do anything, Mickey. Okay? Guy's got a hard-on for me. Understand?"

Finnigan rested his forehead against the sill, the breeze of the Mediterranean blowing his hair. He closed his eyes.

"Mickey?"

"Yeah. Hey, I gotta go. Long distance ..."

"Sure. Not made of money."

"Okay," he said. "I'll call next week. Love you. Bye."

It'd been a hell of a childhood.

Paddy Finnigan taught his son to be a tough little bastard. He paid for boxing lessons. He also taught him all the things the other kids could only dream of: How to throw a punch. How to pick a lock. How to count cards.

Paddy taught his daughter, Nicole, much of the same stuff. Partly because she wanted to be a cop like her dad. Partly so she could take care of herself around boys.

"The Finnigans are cops because the world needs rules, and we need someone to make sure everyone plays by the rules," his old man had told both kids, sitting on a stoop and watching the sunset. Mickey was fourteen; Nicole was twelve. "But that don't mean *we* have to follow all of those rules."

Nicole said, "How come?"

"You ever watch basketball?"

"All the time," Mickey said.

"Ever see anyone call a foul on the ref?"

Both kids laughed. But in truth, they'd never thought about it before. "No."

"Course not. The refs keep the peace. But the refs don't have to follow the same rules. They can't. That's not how the world works." Paddy had handed over the bag and bottle. "You remember that."

A decade later, Michael Patrick Finnigan turned out to be an exemplary cadet at the same police academy that had accepted his grandfather and his uncles and his dad. New York's Finest had known two generations of Finnigan Boys, and was happy to accept the third.

Michael had partnered well as a rookie, got placed in a major-crimes unit that most cops would have given their eyeteeth for.

For the first year, a voice in the back of his head warned him that something was wrong. It wasn't just that his old man was popular. It wasn't just that his family had a legacy of law enforcement. No, there was something else.

By the second year, he understood.

The Finnigan Boys were connected. Majorly connected. And Michael would be, too, once he'd earned his bones.

Young Officer Finnigan finally got drunk enough to ask Captain Patrick Finnigan about it, one night in an Irish bar in the Lower East Side.

"This is the way the world works, kiddo," his father had said. "You can be inside. Or you can be outside. And Mickey, inside's a shitload better. In all ways."

Michael Patrick Finnigan resigned from the NYPD a week and a half later. (And Nicole Finnigan's admission to the police academy was accepted the following day.)

Michael had been with the US Marshal's Office for a full two years before the district attorney brought charges of corruption against Captain Patrick Finnigan.

The case took fifteen months to work its way to a guilty verdict.

Deputy US Marshal Michael Patrick Finnigan never returned to New York during that time. He accepted calls from his father, and from his mother, but he knew that the lines were tapped. He begged off from conversation within a minute or two, every time.

He and Nicole stopped talking.

He read about his dad's conviction in *USA Today*, while sitting outside a tavern in Laredo, watching a Texas Ranger sell 10-gauge Benellis out of the back of his pickup to fifteen-year-old Ciudad warlords.

A year later, he'd been assigned to a task force in Crimea, charged with bringing home a Ukrainian drug lord codenamed Pantomime. The Spanish CNI served as a partner agency in the task force, along with their *Oscura Sicaria*, Katalin Fiero Dahar.

With Shan Greyson's flash drive as a starting point, the partners spent the next two days in Kyrenia, doing online research, reaching out to sources, and learning what they could without straying too close to the target. Bridget Sumner brought up articles of incorporation for Lazar Aleksić's company, Ragusa Logistics. Fiero explained that, in European parlance, *logistics* meant *trucking*.

She asked about Patrick over kebabs and ouzo. "Did you ask your father about Serbian organized crime?"

Finnigan nodded and *hmm'd* and focused on his food.

The next day, the investigator from the New York State Police called and said he'd heard of a guy in Italy who maybe could help.

"Guy's a walking shit-show, Mickey. So no need to play nice."

"Thanks, man. Where can we find this guy?"

"Milan. And Finnigan?"

"Yeah?"

"These child traffickers, brother …" the investigator said. "Go get 'em."

C07

Jane Koury underwent two days of orientation, alongside the photojournalist she'd met in Damascus, Tamer Awad. Tamer, she discovered, had won awards—first for his work in Egypt, then during the Syrian civil war. He would be making the trip, too, with the understanding that Jane and Tamer were working first for her uncle's newspaper, and then for whichever European newspaper they could freelance their work out to.

Jane and Tamer went hiking around the city both nights, along both banks of the Orontes River, and it soon became clear that the Londoner, at five-foot-two, could out-march the tall, lanky photographer. Jane got to see the famous *norias*, or water-wheels, of Hama. She began writing stories, both in Arabic for her uncle and in English for Lanni Connors, who was both her best mate and a wicked-good copy editor.

On a Wednesday, Jane and Tamer took off to meet a caravan of cars driving north with refugees, fleeing Homs in the south. It was like some sort of surreal street rally—a thousand older-model cars, all facing north, all filled with children and grandparents, furniture and luggage, dogs, and even goats.

The caravan stopped for dinner near the ancient city of Ebla. Jane walked around the campground with Tamer in tow—he left his cameras in the Nissan. She peeled away from him from time to time to find youths to interview. She looked like a teenager and Tamer, thirty, well, he looked like a guy in his thirties. It quickly became obvious that she had better results approaching kids by herself than in tandem.

The stories were so similar, and so depressing. Jane used the journalist's trick of distancing herself, observing the story from afar, to keep from tearing up.

She spoke to the Bakour family of four, huddled around a campfire and sharing lentil soup. The mother and father immediately wanted to know where she was from—her accent was fooling no one. They consented to a Western journalist talking to their children, mostly because Jane wore the hijab and looked innocuous enough.

Mohamed, fifteen, and Amira, thirteen, told her about the bombings in Homs, and about losing their house and their school. Mohamed looked like an angry grasshopper—all arms and legs, elbows and knees, and a scowl that could melt tin. Amira showed almost no emotion; a side effect of a childhood lived in a war zone.

Jane never touched a notebook for the first hour. During the second, she asked the parents if Tamer could join them. He dropped into the grass and set down his aging canvas camera bag with its well duct-taped shoulder strap. He cleaned lenses and fiddled with filters, listening to the stories. By the time his shutter flipped for the first time, they kids were completely used to his presence.

Jane and Tamer spent the next two and a half hours getting the stories of Mohamed and Amira and their parents.

Jane fought with her internal angels: She was shocked and

saddened by the youths' tale, but also profoundly fulfilled. This—
this!—was journalism! This was important. This was her dream.

Two days later, she got an Instagram that showed Lanni's
toothy grin and an email from the *Irish Times*, which had accepted
her first proposed story on the child refugees of Homs.

C08

Finnigan and Fiero arranged to meet Brad Mason, former agent of the US Drug Enforcement Administration, at a seedy bar in an industrial district outside Milan, close to Malpensa Airport. They'd been told that Mason was a tough guy, a ladies' man, and well bent. He'd come under fire from his old agency for playing both sides against the middle and pocketing the profit.

They had left the de Havilland tied up at Santa Margherita Ligure, on the northern Italian coast, and drove a rental straight north to the rendezvous. Finnigan had cooked up a story about looking for a European source for Mexican cocaine, and felt that Mason might just be the guy to help him out. For a price.

Rather than go directly to the bar for the meeting, they staked out Mason's place in Central Milan first. Bridget Sumner had found the address for them via the magic lantern of her desktop computer back in Kyrenia. They'd hired her for her bookkeeping skills, but she'd proven to be an adept online digger as well.

Finnigan had used every source he knew in Italian law

enforcement, so they had the guy's background and a surveillance photo of him. Forty minutes before the meeting, they saw him stroll out of his apartment, adjusting his fly, and saunter off toward a splashy Stingray convertible.

As soon as he was out of sight, the partners stepped out of their Renault and headed toward his place. Finnigan looked around and said, "Good cop or bad cop?"

Fiero used an open palm to swipe hair away from her face. "I'm not any kind of cop."

Brad Mason arrived at the airport bar ten minutes early and staked out a place where he could watch the door. He had snorted a line in the 'Ray, cruising out to the meeting, and was feeling good, loose and ready. Profits definitely could be up this year, no question about it, and any new contact was worth making. Still, he packed the Smith & Wesson because, hell, why not?

The potential buyer was late. Mason downed his first beer and was halfway through his second when this leggy, languid vision began walking toward the bar. She had to be five-ten, he guessed, with a mane of black hair hanging to the middle of her back, wearing a badass biker jacket and painted-on jeans. Mason hardly noticed the loser with her; some guy for sure, but he was like a planet orbiting too close to the sun; there, but you had to squint to see him.

This, Mason thought, should be good.

Finnigan and Fiero were late on purpose, letting him stew a bit. They entered and moved to his table, Fiero sitting to his left, Finnigan to his right, pinning him in. Finnigan was on his cell phone, saying, "Thanks, Pietro. Appreciate it."

He hung up and smiled. "Mason? How you doing?"

Mason studied Finnigan, noting the couple-days' beard growth, a messy mop of wavy hair, and world-weary slouch. He turned to Fiero, who sat with her fists jammed into the side-slit pockets of the biker jacket. She'd worn sunglasses outside and didn't bother taking them off.

Mason addressed her. "This is a fine day. A fine day. Buy you a drink?"

Finnigan said, "I'm Ken. This is Barbie. Barbie, this is Brad Mason."

Fiero said, "Hallo, Brad Mason."

Mason turned Finnigan. "Something I can help you with, *Ken?*"

"I think, maybe, yeah. We're looking into human trafficking. Middle Eastern refugees moving through Serbia."

Mason glared at him. He had probably forty pounds on Finnigan, plus he was armed. "The fuck do I care?"

"Word is, you know a lot about moving product on the other side of the Adriatic. The former Yugoslavia. We're told you're the man."

"That what you're told?" Rather than wait for a response, he turned back to Fiero, who might have fallen asleep behind the shades. "Ask your boyfriend if he'll go out, find me a pack of cigarettes, will you? I don't mind talking to you, but—"

"Sex workers," Finnigan said. "Underage. Probably Middle Eastern kids, on the refugee trail, coming up through Greece. This ringing any bells?"

Mason turned back. "No, but if you're looking for an underage boy to play with, I might be able to hook you up. Guy like you, you should do really good in some neighborhoods around here."

"Yeah?" Finnigan took no umbrage. "Know anything about organized crime in Serbia?"

"Where?"

Fiero sighed. A Spanish sigh, like a Spanish shrug, can speak whole paragraphs. She stood, hands still in her pockets, leveraging herself upright by the strength and balance of her long legs. "D'you have any money?"

Finnigan: "How much?"

"Hang on." She walked to the bar.

Watching her walk from behind was one of the finest moments of Mason's year to date. He downed his beer. He said, "Sorry I can't help you, *Ken*."

"You're sure you don't know about Serbian gangs?"

"Sorry."

Fiero returned, sunglasses hiding her eyes. "Three hundred."

Finnigan said, "Really? That seem high to you?"

She shrugged.

"Okay." He pulled out his wallet, handed her a wad of euros. She walked back to the bartender, handed him the bills.

Mason watched her ass. "That is some Prime Grade A talent there. What're you, her brother? Her driver?"

"I drive sometimes, yeah."

Mason kept his eyes on her, as she talked to the bartender. It seemed like a serious discussion.

"What the hell is she buying for three hundred? Champagne?"

"We live in a service economy, Mason. Not a product economy. She's buying a service. Less and less people are making shit and selling it." Finnigan paused, thinking. "Maybe it's *fewer and fewer*."

Mason said, "It's time for you to fuck off."

"Know the name Lazar Aleksić?"

"Nope."

"Anyone in Serbia you can recommend we start with?"

"Wish I could help, *Ken*."

Fiero was walking back now, the bartender still watching her, and also watching the two strangers in the booth. Mason said,

"I don't know who steered you my way. I don't know anything about anything."

She drew her hands out of her side pockets, planted her boots shoulder-width apart, grabbed a handful of Mason's hair at the back of his head, and drove him face-first into the table.

Cartilage crackled. The glass of beer went flying.

Mason found himself blinded by blood in his eyes and a searing laser of pain that ricocheted through his brain as if the interior of his skull had become a concave disco ball.

Finnigan said, "Three hundred? For a broken nose?"

"His bar, his prices." Fiero yanked Mason's head back, straining his neck.

"God! Jesus!" He tried spitting out blood, realizing it was draining from his nose, through his nasal passage, into his gullet.

"Serbia," she said, her voice revealing no hint of emotion, shades hiding her eyes. "Whored-out refugee children."

Mason spat up a bloody gob. "I don't know the fuck you're—"

She slammed her left fist into his gut and, when he hunched in, she again drove his face into the table. He felt as much as heard more cracking from his nose.

She pulled him back up and Mason puked down the front of his blood-sodden shirt.

"Serbia. Whored-out refugee children."

Mason drooled blood and beer and breakfast down his front. He gasped for air. "Jesus ... you bitch ..." He tried to struggle but had no leverage. He pawed for the Smith he kept in a kidney holster. The holster was empty.

Finnigan had taken it; set it on the table.

Fiero said, "How much do we have left?"

"Lessee ..." Finnigan took Mason's wallet, started rifling through his money. "Mason's got, ah, twelve hundred in euros. Figure, if a broken nose goes for three ..."

Mason raised both hands, palms forward, fingers splayed, and blinked blood out of his eyes. "Okay! All right! All right!" He spat to clear his mouth. The pain was like a drizzle of Tabasco oozing through his skull.

"Basha! Driton Basha! He runs"—Mason spat again—"runs all the kids coming outta Serbia!"

Fiero said, "Who is he?"

"I don't know! I sell to pimps, time to time! Okay? They say Driton Basha! I don't ask questions."

He blinked tears out of his eyes.

Finnigan thumbed through his wallet and took out his Italian driver's license, pink laminate with *Patente Di Guida* and *Repubblica Italiana* in the upper corners.

He said, "Thanks, man. The name Driton Basha doesn't pan out, we come back. If it does, and we find out you've talked to him, or to anyone mobbed up in Serbia, then we give him this and tell 'em we chatted. Yeah?"

"Fucking …" He tried wiping his face, and the searing pain from his nose made him weep.

Finnigan reached into his jacket pocket and produced a human figure, six inches high, with a base. It was painted lead; a cowboy twirling a lariat over his head. It looked just like the figurine that stood on the table at the entrance to Mason's apartment, where he kept his keys.

Finnigan said, "Here's the other news. We stopped at your place before coming here. We found a shitload of coke behind your fridge, dude. Like, enough to distribute to friends and family. I'll be honest with you: I'm a cop. Once I saw all that blow, I felt obligated to contact Pietro Calpano at the Carabinieri. He runs the drugs and vice squad in Milan. You know him? Good guy. Terrible tennis player. Pietro appreciated the tip, said they'd hit your apartment about, ah …" Finnigan checked his watch.

Mason groaned. "You son of a—"

"I was you, I'd lay low for a while. They might have the tags for that kick-ass Stingray; I don't know. But I wouldn't bet my freedom on it. I'd get out of Italy fast as I could. You got friends elsewhere? I'd go hang out in Elsewhere."

Mason tried to breathe through his mouth.

Fiero reached for Mason's gun and took out the bullets, dumping them in his pocket. He stood and nodded to Fiero. "We good?"

Fiero deadpanned him through her shades. "Barbie?"

"I thought it was funny."

"Ken has no genitalia."

They moved toward the door. Finnigan left all of Mason's money in front of the bartender, turned back to his partner. "Was hoping you wouldn't go there."

C09

The refugee caravan wisely avoided Aleppo, the site of major fighting for well over two years. Jane had seen the international wire stories, with photos of bomb-devastated neighborhoods, of total destruction that brought to mind the Allied bombing of Berlin or Dresden. She repressed her emotions when conducting interviews; shared them via Skype with her girlfriend back home.

Azaz, they were assured, would be the preferred stopping point before making the transition into Turkey.

By now the refugee caravan had joined many, many others. Jane Koury estimated that three thousand people were camped out in the perimeter of the fallow farmland outside the town. But Tamer Awad had been checking stories on the net and knew that the refugee population of Azaz was closer to twenty thousand. "There are other camps, dotted all over," he told her that night. "This is one of the smaller ones."

Jane interviewed Mohamed and Amira Bakour several times. Theirs was not a snapshot story, she understood. They were on a journey, and, if possible, Jane wanted to stay with them until they reached Europe. The parents liked her, and had noticed that Mohamed, fifteen, lost a little of his angry edge as he talked to the young Londoner. Amira, thirteen, had turned the reporter into some kind of idol. The parents laughed when Amira began pronouncing words with a strange, London dialect, mimicking her newfound friend.

The *Irish Times* had picked up four of Jane's stories. And, to her delight and amazement, a wire service had selected two of them, which appeared first in the *Guardian*, then the *Boston Globe*. Tamer's photos were amazing and evocative, and the decision to focus on just the Bakour siblings now seemed brilliant. It's impossible for an audience to identify with twenty thousand traumatized people camping outside Azaz. But easy to identify with an angry big brother and his shell-shocked little sister.

That night, Tamer Awad paid another family for two cans of Fresca from an ice chest and the journalists popped them by moonlight, toasting the cans together. "I'm selling photos to Getty Images," Tamer said with a wicked grin. "Don't tell your uncle, but when we get to Ankara, I'm putting out my résumé to every paper in Europe."

"You're not going back to Hama?" Jane asked, nudging his shoulder.

"Your uncle is a great and scholarly man—may the Prophet bless his household—but he pays crap."

"Don't settle for just any paper." Jane sipped her soda, felt the carbonation tickle her nose. "You're going to be a staff photographer for the London *Times*. Or the *New York Times*. You'll see."

Tamer grinned in the night. "You're the big gun here, Jinan. Don't think I don't know it. I'm just hitching a ride on your comet."

Jane beamed with pride. She huddled her squall coat around her narrow shoulders. "Turkey?"

"Tomorrow. There's a Red Cross / Red Crescent camp just on the other side of the border, due north on the D.850." Tamer pointed toward the glow of the highway, which connects Northwestern Syria with Turkey. "It's going to take the family the better part of a day, maybe two, to get through the checkpoint. I recommend we hustle and get through first, and wait for them in the camp."

"Sounds good. Ready for a hike in Turkey?"

"Thankfully, the Koran specifically says that penitent women must always carry the camera bag. I looked it up. Just be grateful I didn't bring tripods."

"It says that, does it?" She nestled in next to her friend. "We'll see."

CIO

Lachlan Sumner flew the de Havilland back to the firm's operating base in Kyrenia, where the partners took care of such mundane responsibilities as laundry and Lachlan restocked the seaplane. Nobody was happy about breaking off the investigation, but the birthday of Fiero's mother wasn't to be missed. Not without reverberations that would last throughout the year.

Alexandro Fiero, Katalin's father, was a director of the United Nations Educational, Scientific, and Cultural Organization, or UNESCO, the agency dedicated to peace and collaboration between nations, and protecting the world's cultural sites. He was also executive director of a Spanish philanthropy known as the Galician Trust. He co-owned two or three—or possibly four—companies, and sat on the boards of directors for a handful of others. Finnigan honestly couldn't keep up on how the patrician Spaniard defined *my job* from week to week. His diverse interests kept him flying constantly from European capital to capital, and he averaged less than a week per month back home in Madrid.

Her mother, Khadija Dahar, traveled almost as much and almost never to the same destinations. As a liberal, pro-Euro political academic, who wore the traditional hijab with Saint Laurent, she'd become a darling of the Left, appearing on television and in debates as the New European Muslim Woman.

Her daughter often thought that *the New European Muslim Woman* was a bit like Cro-Magnon Man: the skeletal remains of a bygone era. But she didn't say that at home.

Since none of the three family members could be trusted to appear in Madrid on the same week, Finnigan had suggested they meet in Nicosia, the capital of Cyprus. Fiero objected; she wanted to keep her family as far away from St. Nicholas Salvage & Wrecking as possible. But Finnigan argued that the capital would suffice. And her parents did know she was living on the island situated in the Eastern Mediterranean, like the center pivot of a clock that ticked off time, clockwise, between Greece at ten o'clock, Turkey, Syria, Lebanon, Israel, and Egypt at six o'clock.

Nicosia is the last split capital on earth, like Berlin before it. The south is controlled by the Greece-friendly Cypriot government, while the north is occupied by Turkish troops who invaded in 1974. Of course, Turkish Cypriots often said the south was occupied by Greece. Political affairs are, as usual, a matter of perspective.

Drive around Nicosia, and you have to cross United Nations checkpoints. Cut through the middle of the capital, and you cross the Green Line—a Cypriot border station with Cypriot police in one shack, with all signage in Greek, and twenty paces on, a Turkish border station with Turkish soldiers checking passports.

The inner, walled city of Nicosia includes a vibrant pedestrian-only sector stuffed with shops, restaurants, and hotels. On the Greek side, business is vibrant and the foot traffic heavy. The same is true, to a lesser degree, on the Turkish side. But the Turkish side also includes a winding dead zone: gray, half-demolished buildings with missing roofs, mortar holes, and the remnants of tank treads, exactly one block wide and running the entire length of the Green Line. No remnants of the 1974 civil war are evident on the Greek side; they're hard to miss on the Turkish side.

As neutral territory for a Fiero Family reunion, Nicosia couldn't be beat. Alexandro could rhapsodize about the economic potential of the island, and Khadija could admire the secular Muslim culture of the north. And, as Finnigan often said, the coffee on both sides was spectacular. If you didn't like Greek food, there was Turkish fair aplenty, "and if you didn't like either, then you should die with a freezer full of tofu."

Finnigan chose a Lebanese place on the south side, on the pedestrian-only thoroughfare but tucked away enough to be invisible to the mainly Russian, British, and British Commonwealth tourists. Lebanese food is neutral, so Katalin's parents would have a hard time picking a fight over favoritism.

Finnigan wore a relatively nice blazer and black trousers with loafers. He'd even shaved. He thought he looked urbane and sophisticated. Most everyone else thought he looked like a graduate student doing his impression of a grown-up.

Fiero wore a flowing skirt of sky blue and a blush-pink sweater under a jacket, with riding boots. The outfit made Finnigan grin; he was used to her in either bad-girl leathers, or power suits of midnight black. None of that wardrobe ever made an appearance when Fiero and her mom came within shouting distance of each other.

Fiero could switch to a fashionable look in an instant and, with her hair in a low knot and parted in the middle, she immediately looked like she fit in as a stylish young Madrileña. Her tote bag felt uncomfortably light on her shoulder; no weapons.

She wouldn't wear the hijab. She accepted her own lack of faith, and didn't care if her parents had a problem with that.

Finnigan didn't say anything, knowing that Fiero was

subconsciously frustrated that her überliberal parents *didn't* protest her position on faith.

They drove the Land Rover from Kyrenia to the northern sector of Nicosia, parking on the Turkish side near the Roccas Bastion, one of the rounded orillons that made the oval city wall look, from the air, like a giant gear.

"Now look," Finnigan said, "this is important. I can't say it enough. Your parents like me. Don't embarrass me."

She smiled brightly and took his elbow as they approached the Green Line checkpoint. "Go fuck a camel."

Alexandro Fiero had flown in from Berlin and Khadija Dahar had flown in from New York City. They'd taken separate cabs from the island's main airport outside Larnaca and arrived thirty minutes apart.

Finnigan's choice of restaurants was inspired. They started with salads of tabbouleh and fattoush, then switched to spicy batata harra, meatballs in tomato sauce, fried cauliflower and halva, the sweet sesame paste studded with fruit and nuts, for dessert. Alexander ordered Lebanese and Greek wines like the connoisseur he was.

The couple adored Finnigan, as the only man their daughter had ever brought home from her work.

It was the *work* part that worried Fiero.

To the world at large, the partners used the cover of St Nicholas Salvage & Wrecking, a maritime recovery company. Thanks to the opaque and blatantly criminal nature of Cypriot banks and corporate law, they had successfully hidden their real job, and real profits, therein.

But that wouldn't work for their parents. Neither Alexandro and Khadija, nor Finnigan's extended family, where likely to believe that either of them knew the first thing about maritime salvage.

It had been their friend Thomas Shannon Greyson who'd come up with a cover for the families. As far as their kin knew, Finnigan and Fiero lived on Cyprus and worked as analysts for the European Union. They were pencil pushers in an obscure and enormous transnational government entity, gathering statistics on violence, to help set policy in Brussels.

The *job* had three advantages: First, it sounded far too boring for a lot of questions. Second, Fiero had been a soldier; Finnigan had been both a city cop and a US Marshal. Their families might well believe they'd taken desk jobs that still revolved around the data of violence, if not real violence. And third, the EU is so massive, so bloated of personnel, that they ran little risk of their parents knowing someone who could rumble them.

"So important, this work," Khadija Dahar said—speaking to Finnigan and not to her daughter, three inches of bangles jangling on each forearm. "Information is power. Those who gather information are every bit the soldiers as those with guns. More so."

She sipped her wine. She might have been born Muslim, but she brought very few of the cultural taboos with her.

Alexandro Fiero spoke at length about the tech revolution and the information economy, urging his daughter and the fine young American to think about what happens after their time as analysts for the EU. "I am glad, very glad, that you chose civil service," he pronounced to his child. "When you joined the army ... well, a waste of education and brilliance, alas."

"When was that?" Finnigan asked, because it was his job to keep the light conversation moving forward; a skill his partner utterly lacked.

"Right after the bombings, of course," Alexandro said. Katalin stiffened, attention on her halva. "For the US, it was September 2001. But for the Spanish, it was the train bombings in 2004. A week after—the craters still smoldering—and Katalin joined the military. Her mother ..." Alexandro mimed his wife's head exploding.

"No, no," Khadija interjected, reaching across the feast to pour wine into Finnigan's glass. "Service is important. I was honored—proud! Katalin's instincts were the instincts of any good citizen. Of course, I was pleased when she took a civilian position with the European Union. Pleased that someone took notice of Katalin's intelligence and education, and knew instantly that she could best help with a computer. Not crawling in some trench with a rifle. And here we are!"

Finnigan sipped his wine. "And here we are!"

Everyone toasted.

Fiero finished her halva without glancing up from the table.

Michael Finnigan wasn't an idiot. He'd never had any intention of going into business with anyone without doing a thorough background check. Up to, and most definitely including, an illegal background check.

He wasn't ever supposed to know Fiero's backstory; indeed, almost no one did.

Katalin Fiero Dahar had grown up as a complete jock. She'd crewed yachts in the Mediterranean. She'd played soccer (football, he corrected himself). She competed in the biathlon, the competition that involved cross-country skiing and rifle shooting. Indeed, she'd made the Spanish national team before turning nineteen.

But within twenty-four hours of the Madrid bombings of 2004, Fiero joined the Spanish Army with the intention of being a soldier. But within the first weeks of boot camp, the recruiters for the Centro Nacional de Inteligencia realized they had something special in the intelligent, educated, and athletic young woman.

Katalin could shoot. Period.

This skill came to the attention of Hugo Llorente, the éminence grise of Spanish Intelligence. For more than three decades, Llorente had run a quiet little bureau within CNI, with a forgettable budget and a low profile. Hundreds of bureaucrats in Madrid had fallen asleep over the department's turgid quarterly reports.

None of them knew that Llorente's division was, to use the colloquialism of international intelligence, a kill shop.

It was Hugo Llorente who first understood what they had in Katalin Fiero Dahar. Here was a woman who could shoot people.

Could, and did, and slept well enough afterward.

Plus she was a polyglot. And stunning. The combination was too much for Llorente to turn down.

Her transition into his elite intelligence unit had happened as soon as she turned twenty-two. She stayed until she turned twenty-eight. There were no records anywhere of her confirmed kills.

Michael Finnigan knew the right people, though. He pieced together her history as a shooter.

One week after he'd confirmed her bona fides, the Turkish occupying government of northern Cyprus OK'd the articles of incorporation for St. Nicholas Salvage & Wrecking.

CII

Lazar Aleksić rarely left Belgrade, Serbia, but his company wasn't based there. He owned a continent-spanning trucking company, Ragusa Logistics, which had its headquarters in Croatia, closer to the heart of Europe's international trucking lanes.

Ever the cop, Finnigan wanted to find out everything he could about Aleksić's legitimate business before tackling his criminal enterprise.

Finnigan bought a cappuccino for Fiero and an Americano for himself. He'd found them a lovely little café, an open-air affair under a striped awning, right on the great and vibrant central square, *Jelačić plac,* in the heart of Zagreb. A dizzying array of citizens and tourists flooded the square, taking photos or enjoying the sunny day, the townies moving with a mission, the visitors moving in circles. A strangely high percentage of the residents, both male and female, could be categorized as good-looking.

"Zagreb would be a good staging point for us," he said.

She sat hunched low, long legs under the table, dressed in black as always, with classic Ray-Bans. "We're too far from Belgrade. We should be there."

The northern half of the former Yugoslavia gets progressively more European as one moves west, and progressively more Slavic as one moves east, from Slovenia through Croatia, to Bosnia-Herzegovina and finally Serbia. Signage on the west side of the country is in English and German and Italian. In the east side, it's in English and Cyrillic.

"Zagreb is good," he argued. "It gives us access to my police contacts and your military contacts in Europe. It gives us access to Ragusa Logistics."

"Why do we care about his legitimate business?"

Finnigan said, "He allegedly ships underage sex slaves around Europe."

"I know. We should be …" Her voice petered out. "*Ships*."

"Yup."

"Okay," she added begrudgingly. "I get that; find out if he uses his own trucking company to move the victims. That's smart. But Aleksić himself isn't here. Shan's research said he never leaves Belgrade."

"Maybe we can find this Driton Basha here."

She shrugged. "Maybe."

"Besides, nobody's friendlier than Zagrebians …" he said. "Zagrebites … Zagreboids … these people. Friendliest folks in Europe."

She turned her head a couple inches his way, revealing his own reflection in her glasses. "Is there anything about me that leads you to believe that I like friendly people?"

They sat and watched the crowd in the square for a while. Fiero sipped her coffee. They'd spent the better part of the previous two days learning everything they could of Aleksić's Ragusa Logistics. They'd watched the warehouse, made note of the comings and goings of trucks and drivers and warehousemen. The place appeared to be legit and likely was.

Fiero ran a pianist's hand through her long, straight locks. He couldn't tell what she was looking at behind the glasses. She might have been looking at the lovely townies or the grinning tourists. Or at the estimable general astride his marble horse.

"Wanna hear an interesting story? General Josip Jelačić …" Finnigan pointed to the statue of the proud general. The cavalry officer wore the fine plumage of a conqueror and held his sword before him, facing east. "The statue pivots on a single axis, so the general, and his horse, can face whichever nation is suspected of being the biggest threat to Croats at any given time. In the nineteenth century, he faced north, sneering at the Austro-Hungarians. After Tito fell and Yugoslavia disintegrated, they pivoted the statue to face east, in order to intimidate the Serbians."

Fiero slouched. She could fall asleep behind those very dark glasses and he'd be none the wiser. A good minute passed, and a slow smile slid across the lower half of her features, appearing almost timidly beneath the glass frames. And finally a laugh. That most coveted and rare of reactions.

"You made that up."

Finnigan used his contacts to find them an apartment with a kitchen, which would serve as their base camp. He didn't know any cops in Croatia, but he knew cops in a lot of other countries who vouched for him. They made inquiries about organized crime in the former Yugoslavia, but kept the name Lazar Aleksić out of it.

He learned something useful: The heart and soul of the eurozone was the Schengen Agreement. The deal was designed to facilitate international commerce throughout Europe, and it did. Spend twenty minutes on the German Autobahn, and you'd pass trucks from Poland and the Czech Republic, France and Portugal, Luxembourg and Lithuania. None of which are required to stop for inspection at international borders, provided they had the appropriate tags on their bumpers.

And the trucks of Lazar Aleksić's Ragusa Logistics had all the right tags.

When the partners figured they'd learned enough about Ragusa's trucks, warehouses, and offices in Zagreb, they bought a used Nissan for cash. They packed up their go-bags and took a road trip due east to Belgrade, the capital of Serbia.

12

The Club Obsidian was one of the city's most prosperous night-spots, located on Bulevar Nikole Tesle. It had been built in the nineteenth century as a library, with thirty-foot-high ceilings and ornate, Gothic design on every surface. The windows were narrow and a dozen feet high, and colored lights set outside and aiming upward threw beams of blue and red and gold and green through the glass and toward the cathedral ceiling. A second floor had been designed in an atrium format, with iron grid walkways along all four sides, the center part of the building open from floor to ceiling. The floor was sectioned off into a dancing area, a seating area, and a low stage. Seven wet bars lined the four walls.

Finnigan and Fiero arrived separately (he paid to get in; the bouncer let her in for free). After casing the place separately, they reconnected on the second floor. The din was so loud, Finnigan could feel the vibrations in his clavicle.

"Nice joint!" he leaned in and almost shouted into her ear.

Fiero leaned toward him, and he could feel her hair on his

neck. "Face the DJ, and you face Jerusalem," she said. "Face that bartender, and you face Mecca."

He laughed. "You learn the damnedest things in a split-faith childhood!"

Finnigan had selected a black shirt and black jeans. Fiero hadn't changed a thing, which was fine. Her usual goth sensibility fit in well. She hadn't even removed her sunglasses. Both had been hit on several times, making their reconnoiter interesting, if cumbersome.

They stood on the second floor, drinks in hand, near the ornate iron railing that dated to the origins of the building. The second-story iron catwalks had allowed the original library patrons to look down upon row after stately row of long tables with green-shaded, gooseneck desk lamps and severe, high-backed chairs, and at the bibliophiles who held no truck with modern notions like microfiche or paperback tomes, but who preferred the aroma of paper mold.

That was then. Today, Finnigan and Fiero looked down at the writhing, Boschian mass of dancers, swaying to a mix of Alicia Keys and Black Sabbath, bolted together uncomfortably but workably by an Asian girl on the DJ stand. She weighed maybe ninety pounds and had seen maybe nineteen summers, and she wore one side of her earphones in place, the other against her neck, and sweated over the turntables like a thoracic surgeon over a chest wound. Spotlights pivoted and threw shafts of cobalt, magenta, and violet around the open space.

Two drunken college boys sidled up to Fiero and asked her something in Serbian. Neither Finnigan nor Fiero spoke Serbian, but the most polite possible guess about their query was, *want to dance?* Other, less polite options might have been possible, too. She turned her opaque glasses toward them and said, "No."

They apparently understood that word at least.

She turned her head back toward Finnigan's cheek and spoke loudly. "Aleksić?"

"Got him."

"Where?"

"Don't feel bad," he said. "I'm a trained law-enforcement officer. I notice everything. See those couches down there, at ten o'clock? One of them's green? Check out the guy. Blond with frosted highlights. He's got a Champagne flute and, to his left, is a bottle of what appears to be Cristal."

Fiero stared through her shades at the bacchanal beneath them. She turned to Finnigan. "You're a trained observer?"

"I am. Don't be ashamed."

"And that's how you describe Aleksić? Blond with highlights?"

"I should have mentioned that his black shirt appears to be silk and that more of the buttons are undone than is absolutely necessary. See? It's all in the details."

Fiero sipped her vodka. "That's a good description."

"Thank you. It's a skill set you develop over time."

"Or, you could have mentioned that he's getting a blow job."

"Nah," Finnigan said. "See, that doesn't work as a description because, as the evening goes on, our buddy Lazar will still be blond with highlights and will still be wearing a black silk shirt. But the blow job's gotta end at some point." He sipped his whiskey. "Presumably."

Fiero barked a quick little laugh, and Finnigan felt good about that. Very few people ever made her laugh, and he chalked it up as a win.

She leaned toward him and said, "Ten."

"Ten what?" Finnigan squinted as one of the jelled strobes dazzled them. He tried to figure out if Fiero was counting the muscle, clearly seated in proximity to Lazar Aleksić. He'd only spotted four of them.

Then she said, "Seven."

"Seven what?"

She sipped her vodka. "Five …"

"I don't …"

She nodded. "… four … three … two …"

Below them, Lazar Aleksić's face contorted, both eyebrows rising, his mouth a perfect oval. The young woman before him began to stand.

Fiero said, "… one."

Finnigan whistled, high-low. "Now *that* is a skill set."

She patted him on the shoulder and strolled away.

13

They separated and kept a discrete eye on Lazar Aleksić until he left Club Obsidian around three. When the partners spotted the telltale signs of Aleksić getting ready to leave, they departed ahead of him. They sat in the Nissan, a block away.

A man of military bearing drove an Escalade up to the front of the club. Two more muscular men escorted the youngster out of the club, along with a lustrous bit of silicone and peroxide in platform heels. The men glared at the other drivers and pedestrians.

"Soldiers," Fiero said.

Finnigan held binoculars so small they fit into the palm of his hand.

"Any idea who Driton Basha is?"

Finnigan shrugged. "Right now, just a name from a stoner asshole ex-cop. Nobody I know has ever heard of him."

The Escalade started up. Fiero, in the driver's seat, turned over the engine of their Nissan.

They turned down Kneza Miloša, into the heart of the

government district and heading toward the Stari Grad, or Old City. She was able to stay well back because the Escalade was so large and easily visible amid the traffic. All of the truck traffic around them bore logos in Cyrillic. A kilometer on, and Fiero spotted Aleksić's car begin to drift out of the lane. She pulled into an alley so quickly the car behind her honked.

Ahead of them, the SUV ducked into the underground parking of a tall tower.

Finnigan got a quick glimpse of the building before they pulled away: it was maybe twenty stories high, overlooking the Stari Grad and the intersection of the Danube and the Sava Rivers. He spotted another likely soldier standing at the egress to the underground parking as a steel door rumbled upward, clearing the way.

Then their Nissan was into the alley and the view was blocked.

Fiero slow-rolled the car to the end of the alley so they could head back the way they'd come. Her plan was to reconnect to the same street they'd just abandoned, and to do a leisurely drive-by of the tower.

"We were told that Serbian mobsters are ex-military?" Finnigan asked.

"Yes."

"These guys look *ex* to you?"

"No."

They traveled back in the opposite direction a few blocks, then reversed course again.

"The choke point for any contraband—guns, drugs, children—is at the borders. Right?"

Fiero nodded.

"So maybe Aleksić isn't working with retired military, like the Serbian mob. Maybe he's working with current military."

"Serbian," she said. "Or Kosovar?"

"The refugees come through Greece, through Macedonia, through Kosovo, then here."

"And maybe this Driton Basha's not some hood or a bent cop?" she responded.

"Maybe he's active military."

They often finished each other's sentences. But, if asked, both would deny it ever happened.

They cruised past the high-rise. Signs on the ground floor—in English and Serbian—advertised office space available for lease starting that coming autumn, as well as storefront retail space to let. The tower looked to be about four-fifths finished, the primary contractors probably going through their final punch lists. Tenants would start moving in within a month or two. Except for the penthouse level—it was brightly lit, the only floor that was, looking like a lighthouse awaiting wayward sailors on a rocky shoal.

"If Aleksić is supported by a standing army …" Finnigan began.

"… we'll need to see if McTavish is available. And here's another thought …"

"… another thought …" Finnigan chimed in with her. "Say Lazar Aleksić is working with the Kosovar military. That explains what *they* bring to the party. What does *he* bring to the party?"

They both said, "Money."

Finnigan said, "That, and connections."

"Links to the rest of Europe."

"Links to the criminal underground."

"Dark money?"

They looked at each other, and spoke in harmony:

"Ways & Means."

C14

Jane Koury and Tamer Awad made it across to the Red Cross / Red Crescent transit point and into Turkey. Mohamed and Amira Bakour did as well.

Their parents did not.

There was some sort of glitch with their paperwork. Jane couldn't figure out what exactly it was. But Tamer had had an inkling that something like this might happen, and he'd armed the kids' father with a prepaid mobile flip phone and charger, just in case. Tamer and Jane had a matching phone, and they had programmed the reciprocal numbers into each.

Jane and Tamer talked to the parents at length, while Mohamed glowered and Amira cried. There was no way of knowing when the parents would get through. It could take days. Meanwhile, a cousin was waiting far, far to the west, with a boat to take the family across the Aegean to Greece. Not a raft either; a proper freighter with a professional crew.

A boat that wouldn't wait forever.

Jane and Tamer could no more cross south back into Syria than their parents could make the crossing north. It was finally decided—after calls to Jane's uncle—that the journalists would stay with the kids for the transit of Turkey and the crossing of the Aegean. The kids, along with the journalists, would reunite with their parents in Greece. They had a dozen other family members waiting for them there.

Jane and Tamer, and Mohamed and Amira Bakour, boarded a train. While most of the families they'd traveled with were heading northwest, toward Ankara, and across the Bosporus and on to Bulgaria, the journalists and the teenage siblings headed due west.

C15

BELGRADE

Major Driton Basha of the Kosovo Security Force pulled off the main highway at Vrčin, a suburb of Belgrade, and tooled around the main drag toward a series of garages that cater to international trucking. He'd made the trip several times and did so now by rote. A transponder on his dashboard opened a rolling chain link gate. The Quonset hut within offered no signage, the corrugated metal rusty and weather-racked. One truck stood back a bit, invisible from the main street. It was adorned with international transit tags on the bumper and the stenciled logo of Ragusa Logistics on the driver's door.

A sergeant in Basha's KSF unit waited outside the hut, smoking. He wore civilian clothes—the same as Basha.

"Major," he snapped to attention as Basha climbed out of his civilian vehicle.

"How many?"

"Four, sir."

Basha said, "Give me one of those." The sergeant smiled and proffered the pack, plus matches. He waited while the major lighted up.

"They're not what we were expecting, sir."

Basha's eyebrows rose. He rarely showed much emotion in front of his men. "How so?"

"Older, sir. Eighteen, maybe twenty."

Basha took a drag on the cigarette, cursing silently. "Show me."

The sergeant unlocked the door behind him.

The interior of the Quonset hut was gutted, vacant except for a couple of cots and an old cable spool that made for a passable table. It was hot inside, the air danced with visible dust fibers; likely asbestos, Basha assumed, but then again, no soldier is ever guaranteed a long life. Wax paper had been applied to the windows, letting in weak, milky light but maintaining privacy. By the dim light, he studied the four refugees who stood or sat around the spool, staring back at him. Three men and a woman. A surprisingly tall scarecrow of a woman, actually. Their clothes were disheveled. Each had a rucksack, set on the floor but not too far from their feet. They were around eighteen or nineteen years old. They were Iraqi, although Basha only knew that because he'd been told that a wave of Iraqi immigrants had just hit the border between Kosovo and Montenegro the day before.

"Who gathered them?" Basha asked.

"Corporal Llumnica," the sergeant said, shaking his head sadly.

The four Iraqis stared at the soldiers, uncomprehending. One of the men asked a question in Arabic. Neither Basha nor his sergeant spoke the language.

"Llumnica is no genius."

The sergeant smiled. "No, sir."

"So the concept of *pedophilia* ..."

"He's not a bad soldier," the sergeant said. "He's an idiot. But he's not a bad soldier."

A second male refugee seemed to ask them a question. The air was hot and decidedly unhealthy in the hut, so Basha and his sergeant stepped back outside into the sunshine. The sergeant relocked the metal door.

"They're no good for the traffickers," Basha said. "There's a factory outside Bratislava that will take them as workers. Ship them to this man." He paused, pulled an old parking ticket out of his wallet, and dashed a name and address, for a commercial site on the west side of the Italy-Slovenia border, north of Trieste. "He'll keep them until the Slovak warehouse can be contacted. They won't net us what the bordellos do—not a tenth as much. But that's no reason to be wasteful."

"Very good, sir."

Basha walked to his car and climbed in.

"Sergeant? Get them some water," he said. "A dead refugee is worth fuck-all on the open market."

"Right away, sir."

Basha got back onto the highway, but it was barely a twenty-minute drive into Belgrade proper. He turned off onto the street that led to the Parliament building, Kneza Miloša. Just past the grand opulence of the Church of St. Sava, he spotted the almost-finished high-rise office building. A KSF soldier stood guard outside and called in to have the garage door opened. Basha pulled onto the darkened ramp and swept swiftly downward into the underground parking. His car, and his *partner's* fleet, were the only vehicles in the vast, echoing space designed for several hundred cars. Lazar's fleet included an armored Escalade, a glistening silver Jaguar, several high-end American motorbikes that the kid couldn't ride, and a beastly metallic Hummer that dwarfed the others, including the Cadillac.

Basha took the stairs to the lobby and walked up to the unfinished concierge's desk, where another guard stood on detail. "Major."

Basha scanned the lobby. The acoustic tiles had not yet been installed and wires hung in lazy loops from the spaces above, in between the air ducts. Rolls of industrial carpet were stacked in one corner. "Did he get in last night?"

The guard said, "He's in, sir," in a tone that conveyed his annoyance.

"Alone?"

"He's with one of his whores, sir."

Basha stared at the soldier, who stood at attention and took the look without comment.

"Sergeant, no one is supposed to …" Basha's voice trailed away. He ran a calloused hand through his iron-gray hair. "God, it's like babysitting a child. All right. Send me up."

The sergeant used his walkie-talkie to call upstairs to the penthouse suite—the only floor currently functioning in the high-rise owned, via several cutout corporations, by Ragusa Logistics. Once tenants began moving in, the elevators would be functional on every floor. For now, they were controlled from the penthouse only, and one of Basha's Kosovar troops manned the station at all times.

Basha turned and marched toward the elevator bank.

Lazar Aleksić had just done a line of coke as Major Driton Basha stepped out of the elevator. Lazar grinned at the taller man, then nodded toward the mirror and the razor on the coffee table before him.

"No, thank you," Basha said.

Lazar slouched back on the butterscotch-colored leather couch. He wore black dress trousers but was barefoot and shirtless. His straw-blond hair stood up on end, complementing the pillow creases on his otherwise smooth cheek. He had a surfer's lean physique and easy smile.

"You should have seen the ho spinning at the Obsidian last night. She was off the chain!"

Basha nodded, understanding none of it.

"You sure you don't want some?" Lazar nudged the coffee table with the sole of one bare foot. "Plenty."

"No. I heard from my unit at the Macedonian border. We—"

Lazar nodded toward the master suite. "There's a girl in there. Best you ever had. She's asleep, but she won't mind if you wanna throw a quick fuck into her."

Basha stood silently. He wanted to pinch the boy's head off his shoulders, but, then again, he always wanted to do that. If Lazar Aleksić wasn't the key to all their profits, he might have.

"I heard from my unit on the Macedonian border," he said. "We are expecting a shipment."

Lazar yawned and scratched his bare chest. "How many?"

"How many do you have buyers for?"

"I could place six girls. Right now." He snapped his fingers to show how easy it would be. "Boys are tougher. Two … No, I could place four."

Basha nodded. "Six girls, four boys. You have buyers for them lined up?"

Lazar's eyes glazed over. He said, "I want a McMuffin."

"I'll have one of the men go—"

"Actually, I want to go to Berlin. Jay-Z is playing there. I love Jay-Z. I want to go tonight."

"Impossible," the major replied softly.

"Bullshit. I'm rich. I can do whatever I want. Bring

bodyguards. Bring as many as you want. Come yourself. You like Jay-Z?"

Basha shook his head. "You have too many enemies. Your family has too many enemies. I can't protect you outside of Belgrade."

"Well, I'm going, so figure it out."

Basha took a deep breath. "How quickly can you get confirmation from your buyers?"

A petulant cloud formed over the youth's fair features. He started to respond as the door to the master suite opened. A girl padded out. She had very large hair and very large breasts, and she wore one of Lazar's T-shirts but nothing else.

She crossed the living room and leaned over the back of the butterscotch couch. Lazar turned toward her and they kissed passionately. Bent at the waist, the T-shirt slipped up over her ass.

They separated. Lazar squeezed one breast. "Go say hi to Driton. He's my friend."

Giggling, she circled the couch and sidled up to the soldier. "God, you're tall! Driton? What kind of name—"

Basha spun the girl around to face Lazar. He drew a narrow, steel dagger from a shoulder-strapped sheath—it looked more like an ice pick than a combat knife—and drove it into her chest, just under her lowest rib and angled up to pierce her heart. The tough, thin blade met no resistance. Slicing through cheese would have been harder.

He withdrew the slim blade. Blood began to spread on her shirt. She opened her mouth wide, eyes wide, and her muscles went statue-rigid. No sound escaped.

"Jesus!" Lazar tried scrambling over the back of the couch to get distance from the nightmarish sight.

Basha held the girl. The red blossom grew on her abdomen. But not really that much. She made an inhaling sound through her open mouth, and her eyes rolled back up into her skull. He released his hold on her, and she fell straight down.

The stain on her T-shirt grew a little. Basha knew how to make sure the blood from her heart leaked into her chest cavity, for the most part. There are times when one wants blood gushing, to send a message. And times when one wishes to avoid a mess.

"Fuck!" Lazar screeched. He pointed. "What did—"

"I would have preferred she not hear my name or see my face," Basha said. He nudged the girl's rump with the toe of his boot. She rolled at the hip, forward an inch, then rolled right back. Inert. "Six girls, four boys. And I assume your buyers would prefer them to be well under the age of sixteen, if possible?"

"Yes!" Lazar bellowed, his hands shaking. "Jesus fuck! Yes! Yes, I … Yes on the girls! I … maybe four boys, I think …"

"You said four. Four boys."

"I can move them! I can move them!"

Basha nodded. "Good. I'll call my unit."

Lazar sprinted for the kitchen, and, a second later, Basha heard him puke in the sink.

Basha sighed and drew his Nextel phone, activating the walkie-talkie feature. "We have a mess to clean up and a body. Over."

"Copy, Major."

"And contact Lieutenant Krasniqi in Elez Han. Tell him six girls, four boys."

"Sir."

Basha returned his phone to his pocket. He knelt and wiped the long, thin pick on the girl's T-shirt. He checked his own sleeves and hands; no splatter. Still crouched over the body, he spoke up. "We'll have the product ready by the end of the week."

"I understand!" The voice from the kitchen was choked with vomit and emotion.

"Good." Basha rose to his full height, returned the stiletto to its shoulder sheath. "I'll talk to you tonight."

At the elevator, he turned and shouted. "My regards to your family."

He heard Lazar Aleksić puke again.

C16

Gunther Kessler had committed many, many crimes during his time at the Zurich branch of Banque du Monte Rosa. So many, in fact, that the bank faced a dilemma.

Commit one banking crime and you'll get fired.

Commit a handful and you'll go to prison.

But commit scores of them—if not hundreds—all in the name of a centuries-old financial establishment, and they have no option but to take the most dramatic response.

Promote you. And then hide you.

Banque du Monte Rosa of Zurich needed a nice, quiet place to store Gunther Kessler, where no international tribunal would look for him. They opted for the quaint lakeside village of Varenna, on Lago de Como in Northwest Italy, within sight of Swiss mountains. Other than the daily inflow of tourists, via ferry from Como or by train, no businessmen ever ventured to Varenna. It seemed the perfect depot to hide a man whose deplorable acts had netted you millions upon millions in profit.

Gunther Kessler remained on the books as a low-level bank employee. He was free to maintain the various illegal projects he'd created for the bank, and to seek out other clients.

One of those clients was St. Nicholas Salvage & Wrecking.

And, like his other private clientele, the partners of St. Nicholas referred to him simply as Ways & Means.

Michael Finnigan flew back to Milan, commercial, and caught the train from Malpensa directly to Lake Como, coming up on the eastern side of the idyllic mountain lake. He arrived a little past noon. With only a messenger bag, Finnigan hopped off the train first and rolled on downhill, into the narrow, shore-hugging community. He walked with the bandy-legged gait of his father and his uncles, as if walking the beat was in the family DNA. He tried to imagine his sister, Nicole, walking a beat, but failed.

He looked scruffy enough that none of the hucksters offered him maps or kites or tchotchkes.

He'd called ahead and thus found Gunther at his usual table in a small teashop, looking dejected. The banker was small and tubby, bald and badly nearsighted. He wore shabby suits and bought inexpensive eyeglasses online to save money. Finnigan knew from past visits that the man would sit in the shop for hours, reusing the same teabag until it was reduced to little more than a mesh net and pencil shavings. No one passing by would suspect that Ways & Means was a criminal mastermind whose personal net worth was in the tens of millions.

The lake looked placid today and one of three ferries making the rounds—like an aquatic crosstown bus—pulled into the dock, the crew shouting "Vaaah … rennn … aaahhh …" as if it were three words. There was little to do in Varenna, so nobody was in a hurry to get to it. Those tourists not sauntering the Candy

Land–like trail along the curvy shore sat on benches and read, or knelt to line up photographs.

Finnigan entered, the bell over the door tinkling, and sat on the far side of the heart-shaped table, on the uncomfortable metal chair with the heart-shaped back. Ways & Means bobbed an aging teabag in a cup of lightly browned water and peered through his thick lenses at the young man.

Finnigan reached into his messenger bag, looked around to make sure they were undetected, and pulled out a stained paper bag. Inside lay three glazed Krispy Kremes, FedExed from a shop in Secaucus, New Jersey, where his niece worked.

Ways & Means peered into the bag and sighed. "These will probably kill me."

"Probably. How you doing?"

The egg-shaped man shrugged. "It could be worse. I'm not sure how, but ..."

The shop owner came and Finnigan asked for a cappuccino. He looked out the window at the slow-footed tourists, several of whom sat under umbrellas, wine glasses in hand. You could physically see people unwind in a town like this, as if a vise grip was being loosened somewhere on their spines.

"You're doing okay?" Finnigan knew to ask again about the man's health. It was expected of him.

"I am in exile, serving my sentence with nothing but ... this." Ways & Means gestured at the window and the paradise beyond.

"Yeah, that's ... tough."

"Last month, I had a scheme to hide some elected officials' money in a little-known firm in Iceland. A nice little mineral exploratory company. Nothing fancy. I thought they might make three, maybe three-point-two percent interest. Who knows? Could've done better." Ways & Means broke off a bit of doughnut and gobbled it down. It might have tasted like paper, for all his facial features showed. "Do you know what happened? The idiots in Iceland discovered chromium. Chromium! My elected officials made three hundred and forty percent interest in a month. Now they're rich and I have to find another obscure company to launder their new profits. I ask you: Is that fair?"

Finnigan never knew whether the small, fat man was joking. Every time they met, he had another hideous tale of ludicrous good luck. "Sisyphus's got nothing on you, man."

He grunted around another mouthful of doughnut. Sitting, as he did, a couple feet from a display case of the finest pastries in all of the Italian lake region. "Sisyphus tried to roll a stone uphill. I do that while *passing* a stone. But what of St. Nicholas? How is Katalin?"

"She's good."

"I'm in love with her. You know this?"

"Most everyone is."

"What can I do for you?"

Finnigan glanced around the shop to make sure they had some privacy. He leaned forward across the painted pink-and-white table. "How do I go about buying underage sex slaves from Syria, here in Europe?"

"What price range are you thinking?"

Finnigan sat back. "Really?"

The other man blinked through thick glasses.

"That's your question? I ask about underage sex slaves and you ask about my price range?"

The fat man shrugged. "I should have started with gender?"

"You're the most morally hollow human being I've ever met."

Ways & Means shook his head, his jowls quivering. "No, no. You're too kind. There are many less moral men than myself. Some come by it quite naturally. I do what I can, but—"

"There's something very wrong with you."

"I am not a fool, Michael. You and the delightful Katalin are bounty hunters. I'm a banker. I can put two and two together."

Finnigan shook his head. "Okay. We think the mob in Belgrade is moving refugee children on the flesh market. We think the army is involved; maybe the Serbian army, maybe Kosovo's army. Katalin is checking that angle. I want to follow the money."

"Wise," the banker said, and sighed with fatigue. The bag in front of him was empty. "Refugees coming via Greece? Through the Balkans?"

"Yeah."

"And ending up in European bordellos?"

"The worst kinds of bordellos. The kinds willing to barter in the slave market."

Ways & Means sat back.

"There might be a way to find out which criminally minded bankers are moving Serbian dinars and exchanging them with euros. Or Bitcoins. If I knew that, I might be able to identify a location on the broker's end."

Finnigan started to smile. "Yeah. That might work."

"I'll look into it. Do you need any emergency capital?"

"Maybe. If we could figure out who's brokering for the buyers, we could pose as potential customers. We'd have to wave around some green. Yeah, we might."

The other man shrugged. "I can provide you with quite a bit of money. I'm in need of laundering some, so …"

"If we bought several slaves … I don't know, a whole shipment, we might be in a position to demand a meeting with the seller. If we flashed some bucks …" Finnigan said, thinking out loud.

"Whatever you need."

"Thanks, man."

"I have no adventures of my own. And speaking of which, may I ask a question? St. Nicholas. I assume you chose the company name to connote the good feelings of Christmas?"

"Why not?" he said. "Let's go with that theory."

The German let out a long, morose sigh. "Kidnapping refugee children … terrible business."

"I know, right?" He pushed back his chair and stood, reaching for his wallet. Ways & Means never paid for these meetings.

"Their profit margin would be so much higher if they'd just use narcotics on local runaways."

"I can never tell when you're joking."

C17

While Finnigan went to follow the money, Fiero drove back west toward Zagreb. From there, she drove down the Dalmatian Coast to the seaside town of Rijeka, Croatia, and rendezvoused with the laconic Lachlan Sumner and their de Havilland Otter.

They flew to Tel Aviv.

The Fly By was a bar near the airport; the kind of place that looked like either health officials had recently shut it down, or they should have. It was the Israeli equivalent of a biker bar. Only instead of bikers, it catered to mercenary soldiers.

Which meant the Fly By was among Tel Aviv's most profitable watering holes.

Fiero had been there several times and was greeted by silent nods and a few raised glasses. The Fly By might have been a place where everybody knows your name, but the soldier-for-hire business isn't keen on using people's names in public.

She told the Ethiopian girl behind the bar that she was there for *Jones*. She was directed to a private nook behind the room with the pool tables. The nook was large enough for only two booths, and one was empty. The space stank of stale beer and fried food. She entered, waited for her eyes to adjust to the gloom.

Brodie McTavish stood and crushed Fiero with a bear hug, literally lifting her boots off the grimy floor. He stood six-six and was built like a Chevy engine block, with a full beard and a tangled mane of hair.

"Jay-sus, but it's you!" he bellowed. "You look a sight!"

They sat and McTavish poured her a glass of cheap, yellow beer. He smacked her on the shoulder with a hand the size of a tetherball. Fiero half suspected she'd have a bruise come morning.

"It's good to see you, an' that's a fact. How've you been?"

"Good," she said. "Maisie?"

He puffed up his chest at the mention of his daughter. "Accepted into a nursing program in Aberdeen!"

"She's twelve!" Fiero laughed.

"She's eighteen if she's a day. But it's true she sat on your lap in a few bars worse than this hellhole."

They talked about family and about cohorts. They toasted those who'd died—a longer list than either liked to admit. McTavish had served in the Royal Dragoon Guards, an armored cavalry regiment of Her Majesty's Army, and had gone into the gun-for-hire business almost two decades earlier. That made him a rare kind of mercenary—the kind in his fifties. He'd plied his trade throughout Africa, the Middle East, the Far East, and South America. And, for the past three years, Brodie McTavish and his band of criminals had been on retainer with St. Nicholas Salvage & Wrecking.

One night, over pitchers of rum drinks in a Jamaican dive in Paris, Judge Betancourt's aide-de-camp, Shan Greyson, had asked about the wisdom of employing a feckless gunhand whose loyalty could be bought on the open market. A very drunk Michael Finnigan had explained it like this: "They say that if the only tool in your toolbox is a hammer, then every problem looks like a nail. I'm a cop. I'm a really good investigator. Katalin's a spook. She has a gift for getting into anywhere and getting anyone to say anything. But sometimes, we're gonna need big guys with an absence of morals and lots of guns. Or, put it another way: we're gonna need hammers. Because not every problem is a nail, but sure as shit, some are."

Now, in the Fly By bar outside Tel Aviv, Fiero made sure they had the alcove to themselves, then leaned in close to the big Scotsman with the Viking beard and crazy hair.

"Any luck tracking down that name?"

He drained his glass and refilled it from the pitcher. "Driton Basha. Aye. Don't know him, but I found some men who do."

"And …?"

"Kosovo." McTavish pronounced it as three distinct words with three very long vowels, like he was practicing an alien tongue. Klingon, maybe. "Flyspeck nation in the auld country of Yugo-fuck-yourself. Has its own military these days. Kosovo Security Force. Replaced the Blue Helmets of KFOR."

Fiero knew the reference. International troops under the banner of the United Nations—the so-called Blue Helmets—had been stationed in the former Yugoslavia since the 1990s. In UN parlance, they'd been known as the Kosovo Force, or KFOR.

"What do you know about him?"

"Major. Corrupt bastard. Lining his own pockets, of course, but the pockets of his men, too, so they're fiercely loyal to him. S'posed to be a good feckin' soldier. From what I hear."

"We think he's part of an underground railroad kidnapping Middle Eastern children and selling them to brothels. But one thing doesn't track … Kosovo's a Muslim country, isn't it? You'd think they'd find someone else to abuse."

"It's split," McTavish said. "Country's got Islam, got

Catholicism, got Eastern Orthodox, yeah? The northern region of the country is ethnically Serbian. This Basha, he runs an elite unit out of Operating Base Šar, which is in that Serbian region. And his unit's entirely Eastern Ortho. There's a faction in the government wanted it that way. Not everyone's happy about it, but there it is."

McTavish paused to glug his beer and wiped his mustache with the back of his hand. He managed not to emote any moral outrage at the concept of child prostitution. He earned a living selling his gunhand, which made it problematic to be judgmental of others.

"What should I know about the Kosovo Security Force?" Fiero asked.

"As good an' as bad as any man's army. Train some damn good soldiers. Major Basha's unit, I'm reliably told, is stocked with good fighters, with good discipline. Ye'll not be facing weekend warriors with the likes of them. Go up against Basha, and ye'll see some true soldiers."

Fiero considered the situation. She sipped her beer. It was vile, warm, and flat. McTavish drained and refilled his again.

"Are your men available?"

"Will be. Heading to the Sudan tomorrow. Hired to get some petroleum boffins in an' out of the Nuba Mountains."

"Good luck with that."

"Won't need luck." He flashed a smile and two gold teeth. "Won't turn it down, it comes my way. But I never count on it."

"Wise lad. When are you done in Sudan?"

"Two weeks. Maybe three."

Fiero reached into the beat-up leather satchel she'd carried into the bar and withdrew a buff envelope so fat that the red drawstring barely reached the metal grommet. She shoved it across the bar. It soaked up spilled beer as it went.

"Don't take any commissions once you get done with the petroleum boys," she said. "I've a feeling we may need you."

"We go up against them Kosovo fuckers, we'll want one an' a half our regular rates. They got arms, got training, got discipline. Plus, Major Basha's linin' their pockets. Gives a man incentive to fight well, that."

Fiero said, "Done."

McTavish raised his glass and she raised hers, and his glass slopped over as he caromed them against each other.

She caught a glimpse of a tattoo on McTavish's bulging biceps. *Irrimabo illis non accepere iocus.*

Her Latin was rusty, but she was pretty sure it meant: *Fuck 'em if they can't take a joke.*

C18

Major Driton Basha had just cleared his own checkpoint, his Jeep rolling into the dusty, flat territory of Kosovo, when his satphone blinked to life. He pulled over and checked the incoming scroll. It was his unit captain, Stevan Sorak.

Basha checked to see if the encryption button was lit up, then responded. "Go."

"News on the buyers, sir?"

"He said six of one flavor, four of the other."

Sorak had been with the operation since it started, and there was no need to translate *flavor*. Lazar Aleksić had lined up buyers for six girls and four boys.

"We're hearing rumors of suicide bombers on this side of the Aegean," Sorak said. "It could mean quite the influx of product. You know what they say about blood on the street."

When there's blood on the street, there's profit to be made. "Tell Lieutenant Krasniqi to concentrate on six and four, for now. But yes, round up as many as he likes. We can, ah, *bank* them. In case anything happens with our buyers."

Driton Basha and Stevan Sorak both had concerns about their longtime reliance on Lazar Aleksić. The youth was just too volatile for their tastes.

"Understood. One other thing, sir."

"Go ahead."

"I've got some men running the trap lines in Syria, Jordan, and Lebanon. Making sure none of the, ah, stock, gets noticed. You know?"

Basha put the Jeep in gear and pulled back onto the dusty road. "Go on."

"The men are in Tel Aviv now. Said a merc named McTavish was asking about you."

"About me?" Alarmed, Basha had never been in Israel.

"Yes, sir."

"What about me?"

"Dunno, sir. Just inquiring."

"What do you know about this McTavish?"

"Old-school merc, sir. Worked in every hot spot on the globe. Just a gun-for-hire."

"A gun-for-hire inquiring about me."

"Sir."

Basha considered this news, driving one-handed, chewing his lower lip. He didn't like it. Not at all.

"Find out all you can about this McTavish. Find out if he's got regular clients; who his friends are; who he works for."

"Sir," Captain Sorak said.

Basha disconnected without a word and underhanded the sat-phone into the passenger seat.

C|9

Finnigan got back to Serbia before Fiero—who had farther to travel—and decided to look into the unfinished high-rise building on Kneza Miloša, where they'd last seen the sleazy boy wonder, Lazar Aleksić, after he'd left the disco. The guards outside the garage entrance and in the lobby suggested that Aleksić and his partners controlled the whole building. That made it of interest.

Belgrade is a working-class city, leaning more toward industry and commerce than tourism. The Stari Grad, or old town itself, featured a lovely cliffside castle, but history buffs looking for crenellated Old World walls, or Roman ruins, or the onion domes of Eastern Orthodoxy, come away disappointed. The iconic images of Old Town Belgrade were McDonald's, Sephora, and Abercrombie & Fitch.

He again noticed that the trucks all bore Cyrillic advertising and logos; very few seemed to have English or German writing on them. The truck traffic in Croatia, on the other hand, had featured every language in Europe. He went online to figure out why.

Later, he walked a four-block-by-four-block perimeter, with the high-rise in the center, discretely taking cell phone photos from every angle. He stopped at every open door and asked if the proprietors spoke English. If they did, he engaged them in some basic banter, eventually rolling around to the subject of the unfinished building in their neighborhood.

Over the course of a late morning and a full afternoon, Finnigan discovered that the building had been four-fifths finished for well over two years. The signs advertising imminent move-in opportunities had been adjusted several times to keep the dates in the future. People didn't know for sure why the buildings had remained unfinished, but everyone had an opinion: the Americans, City Hall, Jews, Bosnians, the United Nations, the Russian Mafia, Romanians …

As the afternoon morphed into evening, he picked up a tail. Two guys, both young and both physically fit.

After hitting a mobile-phone shop, Finnigan reversed course and returned to a sporting-goods store he'd walked into hours earlier. The entire front half of the shop was dedicated to soccer. Not surprising in this part of the world. He wandered a bit, finding sections dedicated to outdoor activities such as fishing and archery, plus a section of cricket equipment, then track-and-field wear, and finally, to his surprise, a darkened corner with a short shelf of baseball equipment.

He found a college student behind the checkout counter and asked if he spoke English. The kid stuck a pencil behind his ear, dragged his head out of a biology textbook, and nodded.

"I gotta ask: Why baseball? Does anyone play baseball in Serbia?"

The student shrugged. "Some. Not much. We don't sell shit from that section."

Finnigan said, "Your lucky day, then." And handed the kid a wad of Serbian dinars and an aluminum baseball bat.

The staff sergeant on security detail at the Ragusa Logistics tower got a call from a local merchant, saying someone had been asking questions. The merchant had been paid to make this call in the event that anyone came sniffing around.

They weren't worried about Belgrade Police. Lazar Aleksić had bought and paid for the inspector who ran Belgrade's Major Crimes Unit.

Anyway, today's snoop appeared to be American, the merchant said.

The staff sergeant sent down two of his five men on duty: a corporal and a private. The men were dressed as civilians, like everyone on the detail. Major's orders, while working in Belgrade.

It didn't take the men long to find the snoop. It was an unshaven guy with wavy hair that hung over his collar. He wasn't large—maybe five-eight and wiry. They followed him from a sandwich shop to a mobile-phone store, and from there to a sporting-goods outlet. The clerk in the sandwich shop identified the man as an American and described him as friendly and chatty. They'd spoken about nothing in particular.

"Did he ask about the office building over there?" the corporal asked.

"Yes, that, but also lots of things."

The men got the same story from the mobile-phone place.

When the American didn't emerge from the sporting-goods store, the soldiers entered and looked around. They checked every aisle. When they didn't find the man, they asked the long-haired kid behind the counter. The kid had his nose buried in a book, his fingers yellow from highlighter pens. "American? Yeah. A few minutes ago."

"He left?" the corporal asked.

"I guess. Everyone leaves."

They asked about a back door and were told there was one, but it was always locked. They checked it out: unlocked and partially open.

They stepped out into an alley. A mountain of broken-down cardboard boxes towered over them. Several old-style, corrugated aluminum garbage cans stood about, half with their lids missing. They could hear the thrum of traffic on Kneza Miloša, fifty meters away.

"You go left. I'll—"

The corporal's leg exploded in pain.

He collapsed, blacking out for a moment, coming too with his forehead in a muddy puddle on the ground. His eyes opened to see the private fly into the mountain of cardboard, which created an avalanche, partially covering his body.

Electric pain jolted from his knee up through his hip into his spine. He found that he was holding his knee but didn't remember doing so.

A pair of legs appeared before his eyes. Plus an American-style baseball bat.

The corporal tried to roll over and the baseball bat disappeared. A flash of pain hit him near his kidney, and his long muscles locked in spasm.

He felt hands on his hips. Felt his gun leave his holster and his wallet leave his trousers.

He blacked out again and, when he opened his eyes, saw the American crouching by the pile of cardboard boxes, deftly disassembling a handgun. The corporal noticed his own broken-down Glock 17 lying in the puddle near his face.

Inhaling felt like trying to swallow tarmac. He lay there, groaning. Even that hurt.

The American crouched, his back to the corporal, and stuffed two wallets in his coat pocket. He used the private's own shirt to wipe down the baseball bat, then tossed it into one of the garbage cans.

The man stood and sauntered away, with the rolling, bandy-legged strut of a sailor.

The corporal wasn't sure, but he thought the American was whistling.

C20

THESSALY, Greece—A displaced persons camp on the Greek coast north of Athens was rocked Thursday when a suicide bomber detonated a vest of explosives at a Red Crescent medical tent. Officials say the death toll stands at fifteen, but is expected to rise. Scores of people were injured; mostly Syrians fleeing the fighting back home ...

Jane Koury huddled behind the chassis of an overturned Hyundai truck. The left rear wheel continued to turn, driven by an engine that, miraculously, hadn't stalled when the vehicle flipped on its side.

She held Mohamed and Amira Bakour tight against her. Both kids were crying, and so was Jane. The ringing in her ears was painful, and rose and fell in waves.

She peered through the thick smoke, looking for Tamer Awad.

At some point, someone yanked on her arm, hard, trying to

make her stand. Jane peered up and realized it was Mohamed. The fifteen-year-old stood, holding her arm in both of his small hands.

"We have to go!" he shouted.

The ringing had diminished. Amira stood, too, tears pouring down her cheeks. Jane realized she'd passed out.

"Are … you all right?" she asked.

"There are trucks leaving. We have to go." The boy tugged at her arm. Jane may have been petite, but he couldn't budge her from leaning back against the oil-smeared chassis of the truck.

"We … you have cousins here. We need to … where's Tamer."

"Jinan!" Mohamed shouted, planted his feet, and yanked.

"Ow!" She started to stand up straight. The earth spun. She fell, shook her head, and began again.

"Where's Tamer?"

"I don't know. Jinan, I saw the boy who … the killer. I saw him!"

She stared at Mohamed, who was doing his level best to—as her friends would have said back home—*man up*.

"The boy with … with the backpack …" She'd seen him, too, heading purposefully into the Red Crescent tent, wearing a quilted jacket too large and warm for the weather.

"I saw him," Mohamed said. "He wasn't alone. Jinan, he was with others. Come on!"

She stumbled to her feet, gripped Amira close to her chest. The girl's entire body shook with sobs and she held her right arm tight against her abdomen.

"Come on," Jane said, and began circling the smashed truck. "We … come on."

She was speaking English now, but didn't realize it. Mohamed understood, and together they led his little sister away from the dead and the injured.

Jane stepped over a smoldering bag in the dirt and part of a human arm still entwined in the shoulder strap. She saw soldiers with UN blue caps waving them forward. She joined the throng, holding the little girl against her side as if to stanch the flow of blood from an imaginary wound. Mohamed clung to her, too.

She'd gone almost thirty steps before her brain registered the arm and smoldering bag in the dirt.

The ratty canvas camera bag with the duct tape around the shoulder strap that she'd come to know so well.

C21

The partners convened over steaks and *pomme frites*, and a good pinot noir, at a little restaurant off avenue Hebrangova and not far from Finnigan's favorite weird roadside attraction in all of Southern Europe: the Museum of Broken Relationships. During dinner Finnigan did a thing unusual for him: he kept his smart phone out of his pocket, face down next to his plate, and checked it every few minutes.

"You know why Little Aleksić keeps his business headquartered here, while he's in Serbia?"

Fiero shook her head.

"The trucks here in Croatia come from every part of Europe. But the trucks we saw there—"

"Cyrillic," she jumped ahead of him. "Not so international at all. Why?"

"It's called the Schengen Agreement. I looked it up. Nations within the Schengen Area can travel from country to country without security checks. Free trade for everyone."

She said, "Croatia is within this Schengen Area and Serbia isn't?"

"Winner, winner, chicken dinner. Aleksić keeps his trucks registered here because they can travel anywhere."

Fiero informed him that Driton Basha was a major in the Kosovo Security Force, proving that the blond playboy, Aleksić, was bringing refugees up through Kosovo. She added that Basha apparently ran some sort of no-Muslims-allowed unit within the KSF, based in the ethnically Serbian and Eastern Orthodox region of the country.

"Kosovo was a Serbian province until it declared independence in 2008," Finnigan said.

"Serbia took that well, did they?"

"Oh yeah. Sheet cake, balloons …" He checked his phone. "McTavish?"

"He and his boys could be available in two or three weeks if we need them."

Finnigan squinted in her direction; the sun sparkling off the hotel windows overlooking the avenue. "There's gonna come a day …"

"… when the opposition hires McTavish before we do. Then we'll be the ones looking down the barrels of his boys' rifles. I know, Michael."

"None of this is personal for him. It's business. I'm just saying, we shouldn't ever mistake him for a friend."

She smiled. "Unlike Ways & Means?"

Finnigan laughed. "I don't know why ol' Gunther likes us, but for some creepy reason, he does. I think we're the equivalent of reality TV for him. He's living our adventures vicariously by helping fund them."

"What else did you find out in Belgrade?"

Finnigan laid out the two wallets he'd taken from the soldiers in the alley.

"These are …?"

"They belonged to two of the soldiers on duty in Belgrade."

She studied her partner for a second, forehead creasing. "You got into a fight with them?"

"I *provoked* a fight with them so I could get proof about who we're facing."

She shrugged. "Not bad."

The IDs in the wallet listed them as residents of Pristina, the capital of Kosovo, and soldiers in the Kosovo Security Force, or KSF. Fiero shook her head in dismay. "By all the saints in heaven. They carried legitimate identification into the field?"

"They didn't figure they had anything to fear from a nice Irish boy out for a stroll." Finnigan grinned, eating steak, as he always did, with his fork curved toward him as if he'd just roasted a dead animal over a campfire. He checked his smart phone; set it back down.

Fiero drew her own phone and brought up a Google Earth image, and handed it over. Finnigan manipulated the image—zooming in and pulling out—as his partner spoke.

"KSF Operating Base Šar. I asked Bridget to dig around. It looks like a single unit of KSF Military Intelligence is assigned there. About thirty soldiers, total. The rest of the place is deserted."

The base itself was shaped like a kidney and hugged a civilian road. It consisted of one major street, with five white, one-story barrack buildings to the east side of the road, plus a two-story building in the middle. "Admin?" Finnigan asked.

"Admin, hospital, and mess."

To the west of the road sat an exercise yard too green to be real grass, a shooting range, a clay heliport, and a building that appeared to be a post exchange store. The building also featured an array of radio aerials and sweeping radar dishes. To the far south of the base stood a largish garage with jeeps and trucks parked out front, plus three gasoline pumps to the side. That would be the motor pool.

The whole base was barely half a mile long and could have housed three hundred soldiers. "Just thirty guys?" he asked.

Fiero shrugged.

"Okay, as for Ways & Means, he's going to see if he can figure out who's buying sex slaves by following the Serbian dinars on the currency market. It's good. If he gets anywhere, we can maybe locate the buyer, or the brokers. Then pose as buyers ourselves and ask for some kids fresh off the boat."

Fiero stole a fry off Finnigan's plate, having finished hers. "That could help us place Aleksić with his victims."

"Wrap him up in a bow. Hand him over to the judge."

"I like it." She wiped her lips with her linen napkin. "Are you ordering dessert?"

"Thinking about it. You?"

"I'm watching my figure."

"Well, everyone else is watching your figure, so ..."

The waiter took their orders: Pie and coffee. And two forks. Finnigan checked his phone. He looked up to see her smiling.

"My old man."

Their coffee came. "He's all right?"

Finnigan shrugged. "I think ... there's this district attorney who works on corruption cases. I've been asking around a little. The guy might be investigating my dad."

"I thought your dad wore a tracking bracelet. Anyway, he's retired."

Finnigan said, "Yeah."

Fiero gave him a moment. When he didn't volunteer more, she changed the subject. "So the soldiers in Belgrade know that an American is running around, asking questions. They know this American can handle himself in a fight."

"Couldn't be helped. I—"

She smiled mischievously. "I know. I'm impressed. We know more now than we did before."

Finnigan told her that he'd already sent along copies of the corporals' IDs to Shan Greyson. "They'll start building a case linking Aleksić and the Kosovar soldiers."

"Then we need to figure out how to lure Aleksić out of his cocoon."

They finished dining and paid up, then stepped out into the flow of tourists. The night was crisp and both of them wore jackets. They wended their way down toward Ban Jelačić, following the cavalcade of boulevardiers. They got to the Dolac Market, the public farmers market that sat on a rise over the town square. The tables and their white umbrellas were still there, but the food and craft items had long since been stowed for the night. On the historic old stairs that led down to Jelačić Square, Fiero stopped walking. She sat on the wide stone balustrade and watched tourists flow by. Finnigan sat down next to her, his feet dangling.

He knew what she was struggling with, and he waited. Fiero didn't share her feelings often. And, he'd noted, she only shared them with him.

"They get robbed of their childhood by bombs and guns," she said, not making eye contact with him, watching the faces of the passersby. "They lose their families, their schools, their homes. They make it past fanatics and government kill squads. Get to Turkey, get to Greece, get to the Balkans. And then this."

Fiero, the good soldier, often did a fine job of hiding her outrage. But not always.

"I'm going to walk a bit," she said. "I'll see you back at the flat."

When Finnigan got back to the apartment, his phone vibrated. He recognized the false number: Gunther Kessler, their dark-world banker, asking for a call back. Finnigan used a voice-over-internet site out of Thailand, with a spaghetti of security overlays, and dialed the man back at his hideout in Varenna.

"Michael?" Ways & Means whispered, "I've found something that I think you'll need to see."

Finnigan caught the nuance: *need* to see, not *want* to see. "Something bad?"

"Well, I try not to be judgmental of my fellow man."

"Sure. Because you're corrupt absolutely."

"Thank you. But, ah, there's within the pale and there's beyond the pale. And, ah … it's best if I show you."

Finnigan waited.

"I was asking around about your Serbian purveyor. A client of mine has a client of his own, who suggested an investment opportunity. I agreed to take a look, thinking it might be of some value to you."

"Okay."

"It's a website, Michael. But it's encrypted. There's a video. I cannot be sure, but this client-of-a-client might have used one of those—what's the Americanism? Nanny-cams, to tape your Serbian making a sales pitch. This client-of-a-client wanted to invest in … this. And thought others might, too."

Now Finnigan felt nervous. Ways & Means would have invested money in an escape zeppelin for Adolph and Eva if the return on investment had been high enough. Whatever this was, the banker sounded almost nauseated.

He gave Finnigan a website, but not a traditional alias: no www and no dot-whatever suffix. Just a series of digits and periods. He also provided an eighteen-digit password containing letters, numbers, an underscore, and a backslash.

"Michael. After you see this ..." Ways & Means hesitated. "... if you need funds for this endeavor, you'll let me know?"

"Sure. If we do, we can pay you back after we get—"

"No," the German cut in. "To stop this, if you need funds, you'll have them. No questions asked. No exceptions. You understand, Michael?"

Finnigan felt his skin prickle. "Sure, man. I understand."

"Good. Contact me if I can help."

Ways & Means hung up.

Fiero returned from her walk looking depressed and skittish. She paced the cottage, draping her leather biker jacket carelessly over one chair, swiping her open palms through her hair, knotting her mane up atop her head, only to let it rain back down as an obsidian curtain.

Finnigan handed her a glass of scotch and said, "Sit. Watch this."

Fiero eyed him a moment, then sat at the dining table. Finnigan poured himself a whiskey, then opened their laptop and carefully input the complicated web address and password.

A video icon arose.

Finnigan hit PLAY and sat back.

The video showed two people talking. They sat on facing couches in an elegantly appointed den, in what appeared to be a private house. Blurred images on the edges of the video suggested the camera had been hidden, possibly on a shelf and surrounded by objects.

One of the men had his back to the camera.

The other was only partially in frame. They could see his left leg and left arm up to his shoulder, and occasionally a flash of blond hair. He held a cognac in a magnificent bowl. He made his pitch in English.

Fiero thought she recognized the hair. "Is that Lazar Aleksić?"

"I think so. Listen."

When the video ended, Finnigan closed the laptop and refilled their glasses.

He waited.

After a while, Fiero said, "So. It's not just ... selling children into ... *that*. This is, somehow, even more vile."

"Yeah."

"His pitch ..." she was talking to herself, he realized, working it out. "Do I understand this? His pitch is: These children are the sons and daughters of al-Qaeda, or ISIS. So ... doing such horrible things to them is, in its way ..."

Finnigan drained his glass. "Patriotic. Almost a duty."

"It's not enough that they ... it's not just defiling children. It's about them being *Muslim* children. It's ..." Her voice faded again.

They drank.

She said, "He wants his pedophiles to feel ... good about what they've done. To feel ... heroic."

"Striking out against the terrorists by ... yeah. That." Finnigan studied the cast of her jaw, the dark, metallic glint in her eye.

He said, "Look, this doesn't change the bottom line for us. We knew he was a shit, right? He's *more* of a shit than we thought possible. But we're not going to just kill him. We're going to gather the evidence, and take it to the International Court."

Fiero drank her whiskey.

Finnigan said, "Right?"

She sat and drank some more.

Finnigan crafted emails to his parents. He asked his mom about Nicole, wishing that his sister hadn't written him off after Michael abandoned the NYPD (read, *abandoned Dad).*

He checked the *New York Times* website, then reread a couple chapters of an old Elmore Leonard before calling it a night. He turned off the light around 1:00 a.m.

Fiero knocked quietly on his door around 1:03 a.m. She walked in, limned from behind by streetlights that shone into the living room window. She wore a faded, stretched-out T-shirt and panties.

She said, "I hate these people."

"I know."

She stood for a few more seconds. Finnigan waited.

He said, "We should get some sleep."

She stepped back out and closed the door behind her.

That didn't happen often. About twice a year, give or take, Fiero let it be known that she would consider sleeping with Michael.

He knew it was because she'd spent most of her adult life living lies and shooting people. She'd never had a decent, normal relationship. A Spanish spymaster named Hugo Llorente had taken an insanely talented teenager, an athletic academic who'd come to hate terrorists and terrorism, and crafted her into the *Oscura Sicaria*. And she'd come to accept that as a normal job; a normal part of life.

She knew she was beautiful. Everyone around her had told her that her whole life. And Hugo Llorente of the Centro Nacional de Inteligencia had taught her how to use it; to weaponize it.

With Finnigan, she couldn't help wondering if sex would make their partnership more … well, normal. Not because she was needy. But because she just didn't have a base of understanding for how humans interact without weapons.

Finnigan had had about two dozen girlfriends over the years. Sometimes for as long as three months (his personal best). His problem was the exact opposite of hers. He knew that sex between them would change everything. Not immediately. But eventually.

And right then, their partnership was about the only stable thing in his life.

Some of their colleagues assumed they were constant lovers. Some assumed they were far too incompatible to be lovers.

The truth, like most truths, lay somewhere in the middle.

C22

Major Driton Basha had an office at an isolated operating base southeast of the capital, Pristina, and on the far side of a long, arid strip of high-desert country. Nobody joins the military because they love paperwork, and venturing into the headquarters building meant taking care of the mountains of details that made up 90 percent of his job. Basha hated it.

The base itself hugged a civilian road. It consisted of one curved street with five one-story barrack buildings to the east of the road, plus an admin building that also held supply, kitchen, and mess. The base also had an exercise yard, a shooting range, a heliport, and a building that housed both the modest post store and a radar station to monitor the nation's airspace. The whole thing was barely half a mile long but could have housed hundreds of soldiers. As it was, Basha's unit had the run of the place, and they were only thirty soldiers deep. Four of the five barrack buildings sat completely empty.

The reason for that had to do with politics. And with covert operations.

The composition of the federal government in Kosovo was easy enough for anyone to follow. The country had a prime minister, a first deputy prime minister, and a deputy prime minister. Beyond that lay an assortment of almost twenty lesser ministers overseeing every imaginable portfolio, from finances, to justice, to culture, youth, and sports.

The cabinet included a minister of security force. But it was not she who set up Driton Basha's exclusive unit at KSF Operating Base Šar. The unit's mentor was another member of the cabinet; a man with the prime minister's ear but without a designated portfolio of his own.

And it was that good, gray minister who'd arranged for the creation of a unit from the northern, Serbian-domination region of the country; completely devoid of practicing Muslims. A few of the soldiers at Šar had come from Muslim families, but none of them practiced Islam.

The Republika Kosovo was proud of its reputation for inclusivity and pluralism. Its official languages were Serbian and Albanian. Its 2.2 million people included Serbs and Albanians, of course, but also Bosniaks, Gorani, Turks, and Roma. And it's acknowledged religions were Catholicism, Islam, and Eastern Orthodoxy.

But the language at Operating Base Šar was exclusively Serbian, and the faith—real or convenient—was Eastern Orthodox. The unit featured only thirty men, and those thirty were loyal to a quiet faction within the government that had sided with the Serbs and with the Bosnian Serbs during the civil war.

Driton Basha sat at his desk in the administration building, listening to men marching down the base's only road as he winnowed down the pile of horseshit in the in-basket, when a thundering boom made his door shake. Captain Stevan Sorak always knocked as if trying to beat out a fire.

"Come!"

Sorak entered smartly. He was a handsome man, not large, with sandy red hair and a clean cheek and jaw—the kind of man who can skip a shave some mornings and no one's the wiser. He was a favorite of the ladies, and the barracks were always filled with tales of his conquests. He stood at parade rest while his major scribbled his signature on forms he had no intention of reading.

"News on the product?" Basha asked.

"I've got Akil Krasniqi on the Macedonian border. We should be hearing soon. Also, I heard back from Tel Aviv. This McTavish is a merc, like we'd heard. He works for anyone with a checkbook."

Basha glowered up from the paperwork. "Did you hear about Belgrade?"

"No, sir?"

"An American was asking questions about Aleksić and his office tower. Two of our men went to find him. He took a cricket bat to them. One man with a broken knee, one with broken ribs. The American took their wallets."

Basha waited.

His captain turned beet red, his hands on his hips. "Holy shit."

"Yes. Holy shit indeed, Captain."

"They were carrying ID in the field?"

Basha nodded.

"When they get back here, they'll think back on the broken knee and broken ribs as the good old days. I'll ream them both new assholes."

"Good."

Captain Sorak frowned. "Are they sure it was an American? A cricket bat doesn't seem likely."

Basha waved it off. "Yes, they're sure he's American. No, I'm not sure it was a cricket bat. I was told a *bat*. What do we know about the Scotsman? Does he work for the Americans?"

"Possibly, sir. One of my men said McTavish is known to work for some bounty hunters, who may or may not be Americans. I'll look into it."

"Good."

"Is Aleksić going to be a problem, sir?"

Basha snorted an unkind laugh. "The party boy is a problem for sure, Captain. I've never met a weaker man in my life. But we need him."

He glanced at the paperwork in front of him, then snorted again, lifted it wholesale, and dumped it back into the in-box.

"Aleksić has been useful because of his contacts. If Americans are hunting him, maybe he'll be good for something else, too."

C23

The plan came together quickly.

Ways & Means found a corrupt attorney in Paris who was moving Serbian dinars—a commodity not widely traded in France. The attorney had alleged ties to French organized crime.

Fiero contacted her old friends in Spanish Intelligence, at the Centro Nacional de Inteligencia, and was informed that a *wardrobe* could be outfitted for her in a matter of hours. In the parlance of European intelligence circles, a *wardrobe* is a false identify, fully papered, that can be crafted to meet an agent's specific needs—in this case, a discredited Spanish attorney representing a rich buyer with a craving for illegal sexual conquests.

Once Fiero informed the higher-ups in the CNI about the target they were chasing, everyone agreed to move heaven and earth to help her. The grand majority of their resources were tied up fighting militant Islamists these days. They couldn't spare any agents—France wouldn't have permitted it anyway—but they were only too happy to help St. Nicholas Salvage & Wrecking take down an international human trafficking ring.

Wearing the online *wardrobe* of Solicitor Elisabet Falcón of Madrid, Fiero set up a meeting with a go-between in Amboise, France, a small town in the Loire Valley.

On board the de Havilland, Lachlan Sumner used the PA system to let his bosses know he was about to put them down on the Loire River outside Tours, France. Finnigan buckled in and made contact with their unofficial liaison with the International Criminal Court, Shan Greyson, to let him know that they'd reached the next link in the chain connecting Lazar Aleksić and the trafficking ring.

Amboise was a picturesque little village overlooking the Loire, with a castle looming over a bridge across the river, and a pedestrian-friendly main street of peak-roofed houses that stretched perpendicular to the river, with awnings over every shop and restaurant, and madly overstuffed flower baskets on every upper-floor balcony. To Fiero's eye, it looked like a Disney soundstage version of a Loire Valley town and not a real place.

There'd been no argument about which of the partners would wear the *wardrobe* of Spanish Intelligence. Finnigan's language skills weren't stellar. Fiero had once observed, *even his English isn't all that good.*

Fiero dressed for the part in a fitted black jacket and pencil skirt, low heels, white blouse, and pearls around her neck and in her earlobes. She parted her hair in the middle, Spanish-style, and put it up in a chignon that clung to her long neck. She carried an expensive satchel of the creamiest nutmeg brown leather. She looked every inch the professional Madrileña.

The meeting was set for a coffee shop only two blocks from a home once owned by Leonardo da Vinci. The person she was meeting was Guy Lacazette, a private investigator in the employ of a solicitor from Paris.

Fiero contacted Monsieur Lacazette at the last minute and asked if the meeting could be moved one building down from the coffee shop, to a storefront now vacant and with signs in the window advertising it for sale. It was the kind of move a person made in order to foil a police sting operation. It made Fiero appear to be fearful of a setup.

Bridget had contacted the real estate agent the night before and had paid a hefty sum for the opportunity to set up in the closed shop for that Thursday morning. With no sale imminent, the agent had readily agreed.

C24

Guy Lacazette had hated almost everything about his time in the French Army. But the year and a half he'd spent under the United Nations banner as part of KFOR, or the Kosovo Forces, had proven profitable. That's where he'd met Captain Stevan Sorak.

Lacazette was a thickly built man with slicked-back hair and a widow's peak, who always looked like he was one sideways glance away from taking offense and throwing a punch. He arrived for the meeting at 7:00 a.m., an hour early, and peered into the little shop, cupping his hands over the FOR-LET sign in the window. He stuffed his hands in his pockets and wandered down Place Michel-Debré, the main north-south pedestrian street, walking under the shadow of the royal château, enjoying the slow pace of the hilly little town nudged up against the verdant Loire River. He scanned windows and rooftops as he sauntered. He watched for lurkers. Satisfied, he returned to the shop and jiggled the doorknob. The door creaked open.

He walked the ground floor—it had been a confectionary shop, barely twenty paces by twenty paces—and found nothing amiss. The power was off, but he didn't want to be shining any lights, anyway. He located the door to the second floor—unlocked. He ran up the stairs, hands on the butt of his .32, and found a space with the exact same dimensions as the shop below, but empty except for dust and one rolled-up old carpet.

He walked back downstairs and waited.

Fiero, dressed as Señora Elisabet Falcón, arrived fifteen minutes before their appointment and slipped in furtively. She wore a somber suit and low heels. She'd spotted Lacazette but pretended she hadn't, and took the opportunity to look startled when he spoke from the shadows. "You're early."

She jumped, let the strap of her stylish bag slip off her shoulder. She caught it with her elbow, looking off-balance. She put a hand to her heart. "You're … ah, I'm the person who contacted you."

She spoke Spanish and Lacazette replied in French. "I know who you are. Sit down." He indicated two chairs; the only two that weren't upside down and atop tables.

"I don't speak French, I'm afraid. Could we …?"

"You're in France," he said, stepping up to one of the chairs and pulling it out. He sat.

"Do you speak English, perhaps?"

He shrugged.

Fiero sat, her bag by her heels. She placed a leather-bound pad and a capped pen on the table before her, then appeared to reconsider and slid them both away. "Thank you for seeing me," she said in English.

His eyes raked her form.

She cleared her throat. "I represent a man … a person. This person owns a sort of club in … a city in Spain. This person is looking for a specific kind of employee."

Lacazette dug a packet of filtered Gauloises and a book of matches out of his jacket pocket. He lit up and huffed a laugh. "Employee?"

She blushed. "Well, no. Not, ah, employees in the sense of … This person is looking for a … commodity."

"For his club."

"I didn't say it was a *he*."

Lacazette smiled with the cigarette between his lips. "You did, actually. So. Attorney, are you?"

"Yes. My client is looking for—"

"Still? An attorney?"

She paused. "Señor … sir?"

"It's *monsieur*, love. And you're still an attorney, are you?" He smiled.

As Elisabet Falcón, she blushed and shifted in her chair. Fiero's former maestro in Spanish Intelligence, Hugo Llorente, had assured her that this private investigator had bribed a clerk to get access to the cover story. The cover was designed to make Fiero look desperate: it included a conviction for bribing a judge and her temporary disbarment. It would put her in a weakened position for negotiating, which is where Fiero liked her opponent to be; she was counting on that false sense of security.

Lacazette drew on his cigarette, burning it down to the filter. He tapped another out of the packet, held one in each hand, and used the burning one to light the next. He dropped the butt by the feet of his chair.

Fiero said, "That unfortunate misunderstanding has nothing to do with my client's needs. Can we talk business? I am told you have arranged for this commodity—"

"Not employee?" He grinned and winked. "Want to make sure I'm clear about this."

"Ah, no. This *commodity*, for other clubs?"

He nodded.

"I may take that as a *yes*?"

"Not cheap," he said and picked tobacco off his tongue.

"Of course not."

He drew smoke, let it waft out through his nostrils. "Fifty thousand euros."

"That is quite a lot of money."

"Is it?"

She moistened her lips and shifted in her chair. "It is, monsieur."

"The price is the price."

"Ah. Is there a discount for quantity?"

He said, "The price is the price."

"Perhaps a twenty percent discount for a dozen? That doesn't seem—"

Lacazette's hand froze, the cigarette an inch from his lips. "A dozen?"

"For now, yes. To begin with, I mean. We are talking a great deal of money. More than half a million euros. A discount doesn't seem out of the question."

Lacazette's brain reeled. He'd been brokering the sale of these filthy little immigrants for over a year now. The largest sale he'd brokered was for three of the vermin! A dozen? *For now?*

"The price is the price. If you care to go elsewhere for this commodity …"

They talked a bit more but Lacazette just sat and smiled and smoked and repeated his words. "The price is the price."

Fiero let herself look frustrated, as if she had no other options. He shrugged and said, "It's not as if these little Muslim shits were five-a-penny at Franprix."

Eventually, she agreed to relay the price to her employer. "We can meet again, the day after tomorrow, at—"

"Call me by noon today," he said. He tossed the matchbook onto the table, and it bounced against her forearm. "Call with a *yes*. Then meet me at this address at eight tonight."

She looked at the address. "What is this place?"

"It's an office," he said, and strolled out.

She read the address again. It wasn't an office, she knew. It was a cottage.

Michael Finnigan was there right now and—as he worded it—casing the joint.

Captain Stevan Sorak of the Kosovo Security Force waited in an empty lot, three blocks from the confectionary shop. He waited and smoked until Guy Lacazette walked around the corner, almost dancing with glee.

Keeping his voice low, Lacazette beamed as he said, "The Spanish bitch offered to buy twelve—*twelve!*—of the dirty little bastards. *For starters!* She wanted a discount, like she was buying cheese or something! I told her, 'The price is the price.' I have to say, the slut was all but drooling over me. You could see it in her eyes. I'd have had her in two seconds flat. Will, when this is done. Show her a thing or two."

Stevan Sorak drew a smart phone out of his pocket and showed the investigator an image. "Is this her?"

Lacazette squinted. The image was a little blurry and showed a tall woman in tan-and-olive fatigues, her hair back in a braid. She carried an M16 over one shoulder. Lacazette recognized those cheekbones and the slightly pointed ears.

"Jesus! Yes, but my God, the mouse I met was no soldier! She—"

"When are you meeting her?"

"Eight. At the cottage. She's to call by noon to confirm. But—"

"Thank you." Sorak tucked the phone away. "Go back to your hotel. Wait for her to call. I'll join you in a while."

When the private investigator was gone, Sorak called on the satellite phone and got Major Driton Basha, still in his office at company HQ, southeast of Pristina.

"The detective identified her. It's one of the people behind this St. Nicholas Salvage & Wrecking," the captain said. "They're the ones who have hired the Scottish mercenary in the past. They're allegedly in the marine salvage business, out of Cyprus. But I'm told they're really bounty hunters."

The major fumed. "St. Nicholas? What kind of joke is that? Never mind. You know what to do."

Basha disconnected.

Fiero leaned against the bumper of her rental car in one of the town's municipal lots. She called and said her client would be willing to pay the six hundred thousand euros for twelve of the *commodity*. But that she wanted to meet the seller, face-to-face.

She could tell Guy Lacazette had her on speakerphone, which meant someone else was listening in. She and Lacazette agreed to meet at 8:00 p.m. and hung up.

She opened the car door and climbed in, dug her other phone out from underneath the driver's seat, and called Finnigan.

She said, "We're not going to lure Lazar Aleksić out of his spider hole, are we."

"Yeah," Finnigan said. "I'm getting the same feeling."

"The cottage?"

He laid out the basics for her.

"Well," she sighed. "Time to cry havoc, I suppose."

C25

Every good army has an intelligence wing, and that's true for the Kosovo Security Forces as well. The research that the brains in Pristina came up with indicated that the *fugitive recovery* firm was for real. St. Nicholas Salvage & Wrecking had a reputation and was known to have bagged several well-known criminals.

Captain Stevan Sorak put together a six-man team for the intercept: five of his soldiers from the KSF and the former French soldier turned investigator, Guy Lacazette.

So far, there'd been no sign of the other principal of St. Nicholas, an American, but Sorak assumed the man was lurking about. He also asked about the Scottish mercenary sometimes employed by the Spaniard and the American, but was assured that Brodie McTavish was escorting petroleum engineers through the mountains of South Sudan.

The house in Amboise was perfect for an ambush. It sat atop a belt-high retaining wall. The property sloped abruptly uphill from there and was thick with shrubbery. The house itself wasn't just set back and elevated, but constructed slightly off-center of the property lines, providing good privacy and making it difficult to see in through the few windows. Sorak's unit had purchased the property months earlier, assuming that at some point, someone would connect them to their broker, Lacazette, and come snooping. The house, and all of Amboise, had been established earlier that winter as the perfect kill zone.

Sorak suffered from a lack of imagination. He codenamed his team One through Five, plus Lacazette. Sorak's own call sign was One.

Lacazette's job was to meet the Spanish woman and to escort her in.

Captain Sorak would be inside the cottage with Soldiers Two and Three.

Soldier Four was stationed in a bakery van, parked across the narrow street and down two doors. He had top-of-the-line surveillance equipment, was monitoring police bands, and could see the only route by which the bounty hunters could approach, either in a vehicle or by foot. The van also stuck out enough that no one could barrel down the lane, going the wrong direction, and catch the team unawares.

Soldier Five stayed back to watch for the approach of Lacazette and the woman and to make sure they wouldn't be followed.

Sorak bet Soldier Two a hundred euros that they'd get through the whole mission without shots being fired.

Fiero wore a fitted jacket and skirt, her hair up in a Spanish chignon. She'd switched to riding boots. She tucked her leather satchel with the shoulder strap tight between her torso and her elbow. She was once again Señora Elisabet Falcón, the disgraced Madrileña.

She'd programmed the address of the cottage into her iPhone and started walking uphill, away from the downtown core.

Two blocks from the rendezvous, Guy Lacazette surprised her by tooting the horn of a Renault and waving from behind the steering wheel.

Fiero crossed the road and climbed into the passenger side. "Monsieur Lacazette. I thought we were—"

"Yes, yes." The private investigator nodded. "The seller is inside the house. But he's the paranoid type. Not like me. He's afraid of cops, don't you see?"

He reached for the Renault's glove box, his wrist brushing her bare knee. He produced a scanner baton, used to detect EM fields. "Do you mind?"

He ran the baton from her boots, up her legs, and across her torso and arms. He held it decidedly closer than would be necessary to detect listening devices.

"Mind if I look in the satchel?"

She hesitated, then lifted the strap off her shoulder and set the bag in her lap. She unlatched the fold-over cover, opened it wide for him to peer inside. The bag carried her pocketbook, a matching leather portfolio stuffed with documents, and a fat buff envelope.

Lacazette removed the last item, undid the red twine, and peered inside. It was stuffed with euros. He redid the twine and slid the envelope into his blazer pocket.

"I haven't—" She reached for the bundle and her bag slipped off her lap and landed near her feet.

"There, there." He patted her knee. "Dangerous, a pretty woman walking the streets with so much cash. I'll keep it safe. Shall we?"

He opened the driver's-side door and stepped out.

"Aren't we driving somewhere?"

"Did I say we were?"

Fiero sighed and climbed back out of the car.

"This way, please."

Lacazette led her uphill toward the cottage.

Stevan Sorak stood in the bedroom, facing the only window in the cottage with a half-decent view of the street. His radio thrummed and the readout said FIVE: the soldier on foot, waiting for the arrival. *"I see Lacazette and the girl. Over."*

"Confirmed." Sorak said. "Four?"

The soldier in the bakery truck responded quickly. *"Not yet, sir. I … No, there they are."*

Fiero and Guy Lacazette passed Soldier Five, who stood in the shadows and kept an eye on the likely approach to the cottage.

They reached their destination: a small house elevated on a hillock behind a retaining wall. The Frenchman unlatched the gate, which led to eight steps, then an S-shaped walkway of river stones, and then the front door. He said, "After you."

Fiero's eyes shot wide and she halted so quickly that Lacazette stumbled. "My bag. Where's my bag?"

She had left it on the floor of his car.

She turned to go back. Lacazette caught her arm and restrained her. "The car is locked. We'll get it when we return."

"I need it." Her voice rose slightly, insistent. That caught his attention.

"Do you, now?"

"Yes, please. I need—"

He held her firm. "It's fine. We'll get it later. Promise. Shall we?"

"But—"

He gestured toward the stairs.

Fiero hesitated, then stepped forward.

Lacazette drew the phone that the Kosovars had given him and toggled the switch, calling Soldier Five. He spoke in French; a language he already knew she didn't speak. "The girl's bag, in the car. I think she brought a gun. Get it."

She pivoted back. "What was that?"

"Nothing, dear." He slid the phone away. "Shall we?"

Fiero hesitated, turning again to mount the stairs. Lacazette watched her ass and legs, then followed.

Before they reached the door, he said, "The air-conditioning is shit, I'm afraid. Hot as a sauna in there. May I take your jacket?"

She turned to him. "I'll be fine."

"I insist."

She paused, studying his eyes. Fiero reached for the single done button on the jacket and slid out of it, handing it over.

Lacazette held it by the collar and ran his other hand over the material, feeling for anything suspicious and finding nothing.

He stepped to the door, laying a sweaty hand on the small of her back, just above her skirt. He felt nothing to indicate a gun, or a knife or a radio, under the crisp white blouse.

Lacazette rapped three times on the door—*all clear*—and turned the knob. The door opened. "My dear?"

Fiero stepped into the cottage and faced a squat, powerfully built man in a blazer.

Lacazette entered behind her and locked the door. He grinned. "Ah. Here we are!"

For the sake of appearances, Soldier Two sat in the living room of the cottage wearing a blazer and nice trousers and dress shoes. His job was to keep the Spanish woman calm until she was inside the house.

Once inside the house, and facing the front door, the kitchen stood to a person's left and the only bedroom to the right.

Soldier Three stood in the kitchen, his Glock 17 automatic pistol holstered.

Captain Sorak was in the bedroom with a Taser.

The optimum plan was to take the girl alive and find out who was paying her freight. And if she wouldn't talk, to use her as leverage to get her American partner to talk.

Sorak was hoping for the latter scenario.

C26

St. Nicholas had known in advance that the address on the Frenchman's matchbook would lead to a one-story cottage off an isolated lane. Bridget Sumner, their office manager and an experienced legal researcher, had done title searches throughout the Loire Valley, looking for any property linked to the Kosovo Army, Ragusa Logistics of Zagreb, the corrupt attorney in Paris, or his ex-soldier private investigator. It had once been said of Bridget Sumner had she could follow a paper trail in a Category 5 hurricane.

While Fiero met with the French PI for the first time, Finnigan had checked out the cottage. He picked the lock, scoped out the entire one-story cottage, and found the duffel bags of the Kosovar soldiers in the bedroom. He rooted through the bags and found plenty of ammunition, flash-bang grenades, ballistic vests, Tasers, and extra communications gear. He also found bondage essentials, necessary for detaining and questioning people against their will.

Any hope of luring Lazar Aleksić to France evaporated like dew.

He had the place to himself, and the time, so he disassembled the lock on the door that separated the kitchen from a short mudroom and, beyond, a thin sliver of backyard with a high fence and an umbrella-shaped clothesline on a standing metal pole. They'd likely need that egress later.

Before her rendezvous with Lacazette, Fiero called Finnigan for a debrief. He had the Kosovars under surveillance. "Five bravos," he whispered, using their usual code: Finnigan and Fiero, and any allies in the field, were *alpha*. Any opponent was *bravo*. "Soldiers, for sure. Three inside, two out. Plus the French creep, for a total of six. Figure they'll be watching your approach."

"All right," she said. "See you in ten."

Now, as Lacazette led the lamb to slaughter, Soldier Five returned to the Renault. He cupped his hands around his eyes and peered through the passenger window.

There was the girl's tote bag, on the floor near the emergency brake.

Even before Lacazette called in the information, Soldier Five had overhead the conversation from the shadows, less than half a block away. The girl had been determined to get the bag. Even though the money had been removed.

Why?

Lacazette assumed she'd brought a gun. Soldier Five figured it was either that, or a radio for her partner. Either way, he decided to pick the lock, get into the car, and find out what she was hiding.

While lurking outside, Finnigan had peered through the windows. He clocked a bravo in the bedroom with all the duffel bags, and another in the front room. He knew Fiero would be with the Frenchman, plus the soldier riding drag. Another one waited in the bakery truck out front. Six on two. And Fiero was unarmed.

A fair fight.

As Fiero and Lacazette approached the cottage, Finnigan snuck into the kitchen via the mudroom. A soldier waited in the kitchen with an automatic in a hip holster. Finnigan recognized the Glock 17—among the most common guns in use for law enforcement and military around the globe—although this one looked different. He didn't have time to figure out why. He snuck up behind the soldier, clipped the guy behind the ear with a lead-and-leather sap that an uncle had given him when he graduated from the NYPD academy. Finnigan caught him and eased him to the floor without a sound.

He listened to the front door swing open. He heard the Frenchman say, "Ah. Here we are!"

The front door closed again and the locking mechanism snicked.

Before everyone arrived, Finnigan had borrowed a flash-bang from the duffel of one of the soldiers and had rigged it behind the dresser in the bedroom.

Finnigan now held a wireless detonator in his left hand. He hit the button.

Guy Lacazette said, "Ah. Here we are! Signora, plea—"

He was surprised when the Spanish beauty covered her face in her arms. She was more frightened than he imagined.

Then the light of God, or perhaps of Satan, spat from the bedroom on his left, followed by the boom of thunder that shook the tiny house. Lacazette could feel the noise in his chest and his head as it reverberated around the room.

In the living room, Soldier Two yelped and ducked, arms flying over his head as if expecting shrapnel.

Finnigan stepped out of the kitchen and clobbered Soldier Two with his sap. The soldier folded like a road map.

That was Lacazette's last memory before Fiero's elbow snapped back into his nose. His head ricocheted off the door and he slumped to the floor.

Finnigan knelt and drew the downed soldier's holstered handgun. He whistled high-low and underhanded the auto in a soft arc toward Fiero.

She turned and caught it one-handed.

Fiero identified it as an Austrian-made Glock 17, but retrofitted with the longer, thirty-three-round mag, not the traditional seventeen-mag. She ejected it, checked to see it was full, and slapped it back home. She pulled back the slide an inch to confirm a bullet already in the pipe and released the tension.

She stepped to the bedroom door and kicked it open. Or rather, kicked it about ten inches. The door bounced off the top of the head of a man who knelt, hands over his ears, eyes screwed shut, all but catatonic with pain from the flash-bang that had gone off just a few feet from his body. Fiero shouldered open the door and noticed that a chest of drawers had been turned into kindling, and the room's window was blown out.

Finnigan raced back into the kitchen, one hand over his left ear, listening to the radio that they'd secreted inside Fiero's satchel. He heard a rattle as the car's door was jimmied open.

Finnigan set down the remove detonator he'd borrowed from the soldiers and reached into his jacket for a second remote.

Soldier Five sat in the driver's seat and reached across the emergency brake handle for the tote bag, just as another flash-bang, sewn into the lining, erupted.

The noise shattered both eardrums and the light scarred his eyes. He threw his hands over his face and slid out of the car, onto the grass, screaming in pain.

Finnigan emerged from the kitchen, dragging an unconscious soldier in his wake. "Sounds like we got one more by the car. That's five."

Fiero dragged out the stunned man from the bedroom and dumped him on the floor with Lacazette and the man in the jacket and dress shoes.

Finnigan searched the soldiers, then Lacazette. The private investigator had carried a small ziplock bag of cocaine. Finnigan studied it and grinned. He opened the pouch and knelt, dusting the guns and the hands of the fallen soldiers with the white powder.

"Ooooh," Fiero smiled. "Nice touch."

"It's the little details that count." Finnigan winked at her. "No chance the neighbors missed this racket. Did you see the ..."

"... bakery truck?" Fiero finished the sentence.

"Here." He tossed her a Taser from the soldiers' duffel bags. "Through the back, round to the left. There's a latched gate. Have fun."

Fiero whisked off her white blouse and dropped it on the floor. The camisole beneath was matte black; the better for skulking. Skulking was also the reason she'd switched from low heels, earlier in the day, to riding boots. She slipped through the kitchen door, into the narrow backyard, and heard neighbors muttering on the far side of the high fence. Despite what she had told Guy Lacazette, Fiero's French was quite good. The neighbors had heard explosions; two of them, one from down the hill by the main street, and another from the cottage owned by the strange foreigners.

Fiero assumed the flash-bang in the Renault would occupy the town police first—it was nearer the town's only police station.

In the meantime, she opened the latch, snuck around the left side of the cottage, and emerged on the street behind the bakery truck. She saw the silhouette of a man sitting on the driver's side. She cut behind and around the van, and tried the door. Unlocked.

The man was on his radio, shouting in what Fiero assumed was Serbian or Albanian; the primary languages of Kosovo. She whisked open the door, stuck the Taser against his flank, and pulled the trigger. He flopped over like a fish.

Earlier that day, Captain Stevan Sorak had bet a hundred euros that the takedown would proceed without a single shot being fired.

As it turned out, he was right.

C27

Moving quickly, Finnigan and Fiero took the soldiers' duffel bags and any ID with them, plus their communications gear, and piled them into the bakery truck. They shoved the unconscious soldier into the back.

It was Fiero's idea to take the soldier from the truck with them. He appeared to be the youngest of the lot. She figured they might get him to talk.

They found a cheap, blue-and-white striped shirt in the back of the truck with *Andre* stenciled over the breast. Fiero slipped it on, put the van in gear, and rolled downhill. Finnigan stayed in back with the unconscious soldier. At the bottom of the narrow lane, she came upon a police car, three officers, and the Renault parked amid a halo of shattered glass. One of the Kosovars lay on the lawn, temporarily blind and deaf, howling in agony, hands cuffed behind his back.

The cops were pointing uphill, toward the cottage, where neighbors must have reported hearing another explosion. There, they'd find four unconscious men, fully armed and with evidence of narcotics use, in a country where the police don't take lightly armed gangs selling drugs.

It would be the town's biggest, strangest arrest in decades, and the authorities would be talking about it forever. The officers on duty that night could be forgiven for urging a bakery truck to get out of the way.

At the downtown core, Finnigan hopped out, grabbed the rental car, and followed Fiero across the city bridge to Lesser Amboise. They ditched the twice-stolen bakery truck a kilometer from town in a secluded turnout, and wiped it down. They transferred the duffel bags to the back seat and the soldier, hogtied and Tasered again, to the trunk.

They drove westward toward Tours, the de Havilland, and Lachlan Sumner.

It was going on midnight by the time they carried the soldier aboard the de Havilland. Lachlan watched for trouble as the partners secured the soldier in the aft storage hold, handcuffing him to the D-ring restraints bolted into the deck. The hold was fully ventilated but soundproof; this wasn't the first guy they'd held back there.

They decided to let him stew. Lachlan would sleep on board in a hammock that took up most of the amidships cabin. Finnigan and Fiero walked to a hotel a quarter mile from the marina, where they'd earlier rented a room.

They slept side by side. Like many a trained soldier, Katalin Fiero slept like the dead immediately following a field operation. She stripped down to a tank and boy shorts and fell asleep as soon as her head hit the pillow.

Finnigan stayed up an hour with a gun in his lap, near the

window, where he could keep an eye on the seaplane in the marina. When it became clear that nobody had followed them, he stripped to his boxers, lay beside his partner, and drifted off.

He woke in the morning when he heard Fiero turn off the shower. Finnigan rolled out of bed, groaning, and checked his watch. Then he called Shan Greyson.

"We were hoping to get Aleksić here, with evidence that he's trafficking humans. No dice. We failed."

"Failed?" the Englishman laughed. Fiero stepped out of the bathroom, wearing a towel and drying her hair with another. Finnigan put the Englishman on speaker.

"You had six-to-two odds and bested them! You have solid proof that the Kosovo soldiers are involved in the trafficking. Send me their IDs and we'll find out if they all come from the same unit. We identify their commanding officer, and we'll be that much closer to shutting down their trafficking. How is this a bloody failure?"

Finnigan ran a hand through his unruly hair, sitting on the edge of the bed in his boxers. "Dude. Our goal was to get Aleksić next to the victims, so we could make the case and haul him in. We didn't do that. Alternatively, we hoped to get the son of a bitch away from his babysitters in Belgrade. We didn't do that, either."

"You're alive," Shan replied. "We'll call this one a win."

Finnigan disconnected and tossed the phone onto the nightstand. Fiero sat on the corner of the bed, toweling her hair dry.

"They obviously knew who we are," she said. "They wouldn't have had a six-man team otherwise."

"Well. We provoked a reaction, all right."

"It's the next reaction I'm afraid of. If the Kosovars are

anywhere near as good as they appeared, the smart play would be to kill every child currently in the pipeline and shut down the trafficking operation until the heat cools down."

Finnigan and Fiero sat on the bed, staring at each other.

C28

"Oh, I say. Director Aleksić?"

The Dutch National Opera was offering that season's rendition of *Medea*. During the intermission, Thomas Shannon Greyson found himself shouldering through well-heeled patrons and ran directly into the director of the Levant Crisis Group of the United Nations High Commission for Refugees.

"Ah, Greyson."

Shan pivoted to his left. "May I introduce Judge Hélene Betancourt of the International Criminal Court? Don't believe you've met."

The three of them were jostled by the river of fans walking to, and returning from, the bar in the second-floor lobby of the Dutch National Opera & Ballet. Aleksić made his own complementary pivot as his wife drew up to them, creating a foursome. "Judge Betancourt, Mr. Greyson, allow me to introduce my wife, Marija."

"How do you do?" said his wife, though it was clear that, amid the din, she hadn't caught either name. She looked a bit lost, egg-shaped and smiling blandly. She blinked myopically about, not the least bit perturbed. She had lived sixty well-sheltered years of joining conversations without knowing who was speaking to or on what topic. She was most at home in the dark. *Is she wearing a fox fur, or is the fox fur wearing her?* Greyson wondered unkindly.

Director Aleksić and Shan Greyson were much of a kind. Both men were slender and impeccably dressed in tuxedos. Both were habitués of The Hague and Brussels, the lifeblood of New Europe. There was an ineffable *Europeness* about Shan's casual wealth and style, and a similar *Britishness* to the Serbian diplomat's restrained smile and body language. There are men who are born to the role, as if, in the delivery room, a hotel concierge had leaned over their cradles and murmured, "Would M'sieu require anything else?" And thus imprinted, they traveled through the world waiting to be asked that very question.

Hélene Betancourt stood in extreme contrast to the tall, slim men. Scoliosis meant she no longer stood five feet tall. She walked slowly and painfully, with the help of a cane. Her thick lenses made her look perpetually shocked.

Director Miloš Aleksić greeted the senior-most judge of the International Criminal Court. The director chose French. "This is a great honor, madam. I have, of course, followed your career from afar."

"Too kind, M'sieu Director." Aleksić had to step closer to hear her over the din of the opera fans. "How goes your work for the refugees?"

Aleksić grimaced. "Most difficult. Perhaps more even than I initially supposed. Germany is doing its part, of course, but the rest of Europe ..." He shook his head in disappointment.

The stalactite chandeliers of the utterly modern opera house sparkled against Judge Betancourt's far-oversized eyeglasses, and she peered up owlishly at the director. "And Turkey?"

The director glanced at the bar and the Champagne, which

had been their original destination. He cast a questioning smile at Shan Greyson, who apparently missed it altogether.

"Ah. Turkey. Madam, Turkey is too busy fighting the Kurds to be of assistance. The Kurds are fighting ISIS. ISIS is fighting the American-backed rebels. The American-backed rebels are fighting Bashar al-Assad's government forces. The government forces are finding new and creative ways to bomb hospitals and mosques. And Russia appears to be standing on the sidelines, throwing shoes into the gears, hoping to gum it all up."

"Yes, indeed." Betancourt nodded. "Well, at least Iran is behaving."

Aleksić wondered if the old woman was naive or senile, but Shan Greyson belted out a laugh to show which it was.

"Indeed, madam. Well said." Aleksić began making his excuses, tugging gently on the elbow of his wife and plotting a route to the Champagne.

"I am concerned about the rumors of trafficking through Kosovo," Judge Betancourt said.

Her voice hardly carried in the great hall. Aleksić favored her with a smile. "Madame?"

"Kosovo, Director Aleksić. Reports of Muslim youth being hijacked into the slave trade."

Marija Aleksić looked aghast. "Such atrocities! Most of these stories are wildly inaccurate, one assumes, but even if a fraction are true ..."

Her husband nodded solemnly. "Prostitution is a crisis we have been dealing with since the times of the Old Testament. One wishes there were easy solutions, of course."

"*Prostitution*," said the judge, looking neither aghast nor solemn, but resolute, "is a term the legal community prefers to *slave trade*. It is a term which, like *victimless crime*, reflects only dimly the horrific nature of the human rights violations."

Miloš Aleksić began to respond as the overhead lights flickered, signaling the end of the interval. "Ah. Perhaps we should—"

"I shall be counting on the High Commission's assistance in rooting out any trafficking in the Balkans, Director. I speak for the Court when I say this is of the utmost importance."

He favored the small woman with a critical, calculated smile. "I trust this has nothing to do with your position regarding Serbians, Madame Betancourt."

"My position …?"

"Your sentencing of the former Serbian leaders could be seen, by some, as, ah, more strident than justice demands. That's not my opinion, of course. But one hears talk …"

"Those cases were adjudicated more than a decade ago, Mr. Director, and have nothing to do with trafficking today."

"Naturally. Trafficking in minors is horrendous. Of course, the problem lies in Hungary and Italy as much as the former Yugoslavia."

His wife sniffed. "The *Italians!* I mean, after all …" She smiled as if those words had formed a sentence.

Judge Betancourt peered up at the director. "Are you aware of large-scale human trafficking, involving underage Muslim victims in Hungary and Italy, M'sieu Director?"

He blinked down at her. "Cross-border prostitution is a crisis for all of the Schengen signatory nations, Your Honor."

"Yes, but you mention Hungary and Italy specifically, M'sieu. I cannot help but wonder if perhaps you are already focused on this crisis and if I am, once again, preaching to the choir."

"Indeed, madam." Aleksić glanced in the direction of the Champagne like a man crawling through sand toward a mirage. The house lights flickered again, and the flow of bodies moved decidedly back toward the theater doors with their brocaded curtains.

Shan Greyson turned to the judge. "Shall we head back in?"

"I am fatigued, Shan. Perhaps we could persuade Medea to carry on with her poisoned cloak without us?"

"Of course, madam."

She offered Miloš Aleksić a hand misshapen by arthritis, with knuckles as gnarled as the thorns of an ancient grapevine. He held her hand, rather than squeeze it or shake it. Holding it seemed dangerous enough for such a frail person.

Shan, touching her elbow and leading the judge slightly, began wading against the inbound crowd.

They reached the edge of the balcony-level lobby and two beefy security guards stepped to the left and to the right of the judge. One of them spoke into a wrist mic; downstairs, a driver began bringing around her armored sedan.

Hélene Betancourt's driver picked them up at the streetcar stop near the Stadhuis-Muziektheater, and Shan helped her into the car. He'd had a small, black-painted box installed on the left-hand side of the rear seat so that, when the judge sat there, her feet would rest on something solid. Sitting was terrible for her spine, and traveling even short distances was an agony.

One guard rode shotgun. Another climbed into the follow-car behind them. The route home would be selected randomly by the head of that night's security detail; they never picked the same route twice in a row.

The car pulled out and Shan raised the privacy barrier behind the driver. "Think Aleksić knows?"

"About his son?" The judge began removing her antique opal earrings. "I don't know. That bit about Hungary and Italy might have been misdirection, to save us asking about his son. Or it might have been national pride, after I pointed a finger at the Balkans specifically."

"I can't tell if he's the villain or a compete bore," Shan said, yawning.

"St. Nicholas?"

He flashed her his satyric smile. She had never met the principals of St. Nicholas Salvage & Wrecking, and God willing, never would. The streetlights of Herengracht threw oily rainbow colors across the upholstery of the seatbacks before them. "They've linked Aleksić the Younger to a unit of the Kosovo Security Force. But as for putting the bastard in a room with actual victims …"

"I want an arrest, Shan." She didn't have the lung capacity to emphasize the request, but then again, she never needed it. "I want a trial and a conviction."

"And if that proves impossible, madam? If Lazar Aleksić is too well-insulated or too smart for an arrest, and a trial, and a conviction?"

Betancourt stared out the window as Amsterdam rolled by. Each pothole sent a wave of pain through her back. She rolled the opal earrings in her palm as if they were dice. Or as if she were a sorceress, casting bird bones and hoping for a glimpse of the future.

When at last she spoke, it was directed at her own reflection in the left-hand window, and not Shan.

"The system is the system, Shan. I can bend it. On occasion. But not break it."

Greyson said, "Yes, ma'am."

They rode through the night, admiring the distinctive architecture of the historic city.

Major Driton Basha's satphone was tricked out with text capability, unlike the older models. And all texts came with a GPS indicator. He awoke the next morning to the chirp of a text.

He'd assumed it would be news from France. The team lead by Captain Sorak hadn't reported in yet, to Basha's surprise. Or, it might have been Lieutenant Akil Krasniqi, reporting from the Macedonian border, where he'd been assigned to pick up the merchandise.

Basha studied the readout on the satphone. It was from neither France nor Macedonia. The text originated in Amsterdam.

Drawing interest Judge Betancourt.
She's a problem. Must meet soon.

C29

The young medic checked Mohamed and Amira Bakour first, treating a nasty scrape on the boy's arm with disinfectant and a clean elastic wrap. Mohamed never blinked, his jaw set to take the pain.

Amira had broken her wrist, and the doctor applied a cast from just shy of her elbow to the web between her thumb and fingers. She cried, but tried not to.

Jane Koury plugged her cell phone into an adapter and took her turn with the medic. He confirmed what Jane feared: that her eardrum was damaged on the right side, her hearing cut in half, and the tinnitus that had affected her on the bus drive north through Macedonia wasn't going away any time soon. Jane also had sprained two fingers on her left hand, and the medic swapped out dirty tape for a smelly, yellow antibacterial scrub and new wrappings. She gave all three of them antibiotics.

"You are mother?" The medic was Greek, and attempts to communicate with them in Greek had failed. He fell back on stunted English.

"I'm British," Jane said. "I'm a journalist."

"Go," the aide said, and pointed to a checkpoint thirty meters on.

Jane started to rise and the medic pushed Mohamed forward. "Go." But this time, he pointed to another checkpoint in the opposite direction.

"We need to stick together," Jane said. "I'm responsible for—"

"Go English," the medic said, returning items to his Red Crescent backpack, casting his eyes about for the next patients. He waved vaguely to the first checkpoint, then to the second. "Go Muslims."

"We need to stick—"

But the young medic had moved on.

"What happens to us now?" Amira asked, tears in her large brown eyes. Her face was smudged with dirt, her pretty jumper grimy.

Jane pulled her into a hug. Her older brother stood vaguely apart.

"We get across the border," Jane said. "Come along."

Mohamed had added a guarded look to his worried brow. "But you're British. We cannot—"

Jane stuffed her passport into her shoulder bag, burying it deep beneath her palm-width reporter's notebook. She took Amira's unbroken hand and half dragged her toward the second checkpoint for the refugees. The queue was several hundred people deep and appeared not to be moving.

"Mohamed, come along!"

Once up to the checkpoint, Jane could see the gold-on-blue flag with six white stars. The flags were planted on the Kosovo side of the fence. She saw a mass of refugees, along with buses and military transport units. UN officials and Greek officials began separating the Syrian refugees from all others.

Jane identified herself as Jinan Koury and held the siblings close together.

"You are Syrian?" an aid worker asked.

"We are together," she replied in Arabic.

"These children, they are Syrian?"

"Yes," Jane said.

"And you are—"

"We are together."

The flow was too much; the aid worker stamped a sheet of paper, thrust it at Jane, and waved them through.

Together.

The journey through the checkpoints, and onto Kosovar soil, took another three hours. Someone brought water for the refugees, and the kids drank their fill. Someone provided sandwiches and woody, tasteless apples, and Jane Koury made sure her charges got fed, then stuffed two more of the prewrapped sandwiches into her bag. The ringing in her ears and the dull ache from her sprained fingers made every simple movement a challenge. The sun shone down bright, and the slow-moving refugees kicked up a cloud of dust.

Amira cried into her sleeve. From the way she held her right arm, she was in considerable pain.

Jane rummaged through her rucksack and found the flip phone that she and Tamer had purchased, the one she'd charged in the medic's tent. It was identical to the phone they'd left with Mohamed and Amira's parents.

Jane showed it to the girl. "When your mom and dad get through, they'll be able to reach us. Okay?"

Amira nodded, eyes large and glistening behind tears.

"I need to keep this safe. I have an idea." Jane took the slim phone and slid it into the space between the girl's cast and her skinny forearm. "There. Your job is to keep this safe. When your mother and your father call, we'll know just where it is. Okay?"

That seemed to make her smile.

Jane turned to see how Mohamed was holding up. The boy was peering over his shoulder. He turned back and bent close to Jane, speaking for her ears only.

"The other checkpoint has shorter lines," the boy said. "You'd have been through by now."

Jane squeezed his shoulder. "We'll be through soon enough."

An hour later, they were in Kosovo, amid more aid workers. Tents had been established. Food and water were distributed, along with salt tablets and used clothes. A Red Crescent tent provided a mobile surgical hospital. It was doing a brisk business.

The threesome sat under a tree and ate oranges and carrots, gulping water.

Jane excused herself and stepped behind a tree to puke, but brought up only froth. As she turned back to the siblings, a handsome young man in a military uniform approached them. He crouched low and smiled.

"You are Serbians? You are family?" he asked in stilted Arabic.

"We're together," Jane replied, stepping closer, wishing the ringing in her ear would subside.

"Who are you?"

"I'm Jinan. This is Mohamed and Amira. We're together." She kept to her mantra, now fearful that her British passport would serve as a wedge between herself and the children.

"You're so young!" the soldier said and smiled. Jane knew she looked like a teenager, even when she tried to dress stylishly in London. Now, in a dirt-stained hijab, long skirt, and trainers, she probably looked like she was eighteen.

"We've had a long journey. They … we have family waiting for us," she said.

The soldier said, "This lot won't get out of the camp until the day after tomorrow. I think I can get the three of you through faster. Come with me, I'll see if I can't expedite matters."

They stood. Jane damn near threw her arms around him and kissed him. "You are too kind!"

"Not at all. Give me a moment to contact my people."

He walked fifteen paces away, drawing his walkie-talkie.

"It's Krasniqi. Let Major Basha know: we have a new shipment."

C30

Finnigan unlocked the cargo hold of the de Havilland. He found their prisoner sitting up, glowering sullenly at them. He dogged the hatch and sat on the floor. His prisoner's left wrist cuffed to the iron tie-down D-ring in the floor. He was maybe twenty-five, Finnigan thought, and clearly a tough guy.

Finnigan had brought his iPad. He sat very close to the soldier; within striking distance. *That term goes both ways.* The soldier leaned a bit to his right, away from Finnigan. He said something in a Slavic language—*do your worst*, Finnigan figured, or some such cliché.

Finnigan set the iPad on an inverted box of photocopier sheets—the de Havilland served as a flying office, with all the accoutrements—and activated the video player. He sat back against the fuselage, cross-legged, eyes on the screen.

It showed a France 24 video of the arrests in Amboise. The news presenter bubbled excitedly about drugs and guns and organized crime. The editors had spliced together images of flashing red-and-blue dome lights, and the pistols dusted in cocaine, and the Kosovar soldiers, handcuffed, hunched and humbled, doing the perp walk to an armored paddy wagon in the scenic old town.

The next video was an al Jazeera report on the same arrests.

Finnigan pointed to the screen, to the automatic weapons and their light dusting of narcotics, and shook his head. "Cocaine. You know that word? Cocaine? We got it from Guy Lacazette. Fucker brought a dime bag to the hit. Can you believe this guy?" He shook his head in wonder.

Finnigan hadn't known whether the soldier spoke English but now he knew, from the way the guy's body language reacted to that little speech.

The video switched to a Reuters report on the arrests. Finnigan reached out to lower the audio. He leaned back against the curved surface of the fuselage and ran a palm over his stubble.

Five minutes passed. The videos, on a loop, returned to France 24.

The soldier spat on the floor. "Fuck you. I tell you nothing."

Now Fiero knew that the kid spoke English, too. She stood with Lachlan Sumner, on the far side of the aft hatch, listening via the Skype function on the iPad.

Finnigan said, "It's simple. You guys are kidnapping little kids—Muslim kids—and selling them to perverts. You know that word? Pervert?"

The soldier lacked even a rudimentary poker face. Of course he knew the word. He'd absently moved his right hand to brace his left flank, where Fiero had hit him with the Taser the night before.

"We want this little bitch Lazar Aleksić. He's a snot. A fucking stain on humanity. The World Court already has his number. It's, I don't know … a day? A week? Till they put this asshole away."

"Go to hall, you American bastard!" The soldier tried to growl the insult, but his tone was flecked with self-pity, and not a little pain. Plus, he hadn't peed in about a dozen hours, so that was bothering him. He sounded more defensive than angry; playing not to lose too badly, rather than playing to win.

Finnigan said, "*Hell.* Go to *hell.*"

The soldier tried spitting on the deck again.

"We do not care about the Kosovo Security Force." Finnigan stopped, gave it a beat, then repeated it with the exact same cadence and inflections. "We do not care about the Kosovo Security Force. You're an army. Do I look like an army? Me and Señora Falcón? We're cops. We arrest crooks. Like Aleksić. We don't arrest armies. What, we look stupid to you? Something about us leads you to think we're naive? I'm, like, a babe in the woods?"

He nudged the kid, elbow to elbow. "Huh?"

Despite himself, the soldier shook his head—just a little. Likely, he was totally unaware of the gesture. But he'd entered the dialogue now.

"Armies do terrible things, but cops don't arrest armies. It never happens. Not in the real world. Police arrest dumb shits like Lazar Aleksić. He's who we want. You understand?"

"Go to hail."

"Better. Short *e*. Listen, here's the thing. You've got no ID, no money, no comms, no weapons. The French police are looking for you. I've given them your photo. When you get out of here, you're going to want to get back to Kosovo. I get that. But if you don't get arrested, can you imagine the greeting you get when you stroll in on Major Basha?"

The kid flinched at the name *Basha.*

"Think about what I'm saying. Help me put the dumb shit in prison, and I'll owe you one. I can get you out of France; no muss, no fuss. Don't help me, and you've gotta walk the length and width of Europe to get back to the base, from which you are absent without leave. It'll take you weeks. I'll still arrest the dumb shit, but now it'll happen after you show up, outta the clear blue. What's Major Basha gonna think about that? Hmm? Think he'll be suspicious? Think he'll kiss you on both cheeks and give you a promotion?"

Finnigan sat forward and set aside the iPad. He untucked the four flaps of the photocopy paper back, and reached in, withdrawing a cheap flip phone.

"Know what this is?"

The soldier frowned. "Is phone."

"Right. This is programmed with my number, and my number only. You can reach me anytime. Help me out, I get you outta France. Free of charge."

He slid it into the soldier's breast pocket.

Finnigan reached into the box again.

"Know what this is?"

"Is Taser."

"Right," Finnigan said, then he tucked the tines under the kid's lowest rib, and fired.

They left the unconscious soldier sprawled out on the same motel bed they'd slept in the night before. Lachlan got the de Havilland revved up, and they were airborne long before the Kosovar awoke.

C31

While Lachlan Sumner flew south and east toward the Adriatic, the partners sat in two of the four bolted-down club chairs, circled around a low plastic table, and ate sandwiches and bags of chips and drank wine from a pouch. A soldier and a cop, they were well-used to eating prepackaged food with plastic utensils. Finnigan took food and bottled water up to Lachlan, then returned to his own lunch.

While they ate, he made a call to old friends and arranged for 24-7 surveillance of Lazar Aleksić and the Ragusa Logistics building in Belgrade. As he hung up, Fiero wiped her lips with a paper napkin and said, "The Black Harts?"

"Who better?"

St. Nicholas Salvage & Wrecking could subcontract out with a detective agency, presumably, but most such agencies are required to follow very specific laws in regards to their work. The Black Harts—a nickname culled from a pub they call home—were thieves. The arrangement was simple: St. Nicholas occasionally asked the Harts to help when personnel were required, and the

Harts helped themselves to stealing anything that didn't directly interfere with the mission.

But relying on the Black Harts was similar to relying on Brodie McTavish and his mercenaries. Thieves, like mercenaries, went where the profit was. You could rent their loyalty, but you couldn't own it.

She sipped her wine. It wasn't terribly good and, being a Spaniard, Fiero could tell the difference. She knew Finnigan couldn't. "This Basha. He sent men to do a job, and they failed. Spectacularly. Public arrests, the guns, the cocaine you found on Lacazette." She licked mustard off the pad of her thumb. "He lost personnel. He lost a head-to-head matchup with an opponent. He lost face."

"If he's figured out who we are, and he clearly has …"

Fiero reached for the intercom on the wall and toggled it. "Lachlan?"

"Go," the laconic Kiwi drawled from the flight deck.

"Have Bridget clear out of Kyrenia for a while. It's possible these people know—"

"Did it last night," the pilot interrupted. "I figured the same. She's checked into the Semeli in Nicosia."

"Good thinking. Thank you." She toggled the switch off and sat back. She selected a single potato chip from Finnigan's bag— she'd finished her own. "We have to shift focus. We need to work on Driton Basha."

"We're getting paid to take down Aleksić."

"Aleksić is a posturing adolescent. It's unlikely he'll kill any refugees currently in the pipeline, or who were recently sold, in order to cover his tracks. I'm afraid Major Basha will."

Finnigan poured a little more wine from the metallic sack into their plastic glasses. "The soldier kid we grabbed, he might help with that."

"Possible."

"So, how you wanna play this?"

"Throw a spanner into the works, see what happens."

"That might endanger the victims."

"Doing nothing might endanger the victims."

"Is Basha expecting us to come at him?"

"Not directly, I think." She favored her partner with a frosty smile. "He'll assume his soldiers failed in the field. He'll credit the outcome with their incompetence; he won't credit us for outfighting them. And he won't expect us to go on offense now."

"So is that what we do? Go on offense?"

Fiero's smile grew frostier.

C32

Major Driton Basha stood in his quarters with a glass of vodka in one hand and the TV remote in the other, watching Sky News, aghast.

Unbelievable.

One of his chief aides, Capt. Stevan Sorak, handcuffed and scowling at the cameras as he was led from an armored van to a prison outside Paris. Four good men with him. One man missing. The arrested men facing charges after being found with guns, and … cocaine?

Basha had a fairly good sense for which of his men were fuckups and which weren't. The men he'd sent to France were as good as any he had. There was no possibility of the operation *accidentally* becoming a drug-buy-gone-wrong. No, this was a message. It was a message directed at Basha himself. The bounty hunters with the stupid company name. They were sending a very loud, very public *fuck you* to Driton Basha.

He drained his glass, eyes locked on the screen. *If it's a war they want …*

C33

Lazar Aleksić had gone through stages of reaction after witnessing the murder of the girl he'd brought back from the club.

He had stood in the far corner of his penthouse living room as Kosovar soldiers brought up a body bag to dispose of the girl—who still wore Lazar's T-shirt. She'd bled under the coffee table, but not as much as he'd expected from someone stabbed in the heart by what amounts to an ice pick.

Lazar experienced pure, unalloyed horror at the sight of the murder. He'd vomited and more. A very large part of his conscious mind focused on the cadaver—the girl he'd picked up, the girl he'd screwed—while a smaller, but important, part of his conscious mind focused on his relief that the soldiers didn't realize he'd soiled himself.

After the horror came the slow, insane certainty that he and Major Basha would both be arrested for the murder. So very many people had seen Lazar with the girl—*what the hell was her name?*—the night before. They'd seen her leave with him; how could they not, her in her scarlet dress and acrylic platform shoes and improbable breasts? The witness list for the murder trial would go on for days.

The day continued and was followed by night—and so very, very much marijuana and coke and vodka and whiskey—which was followed by morning, and no police ever showed up.

Of course, the badly hungover Lazar Aleksić realized his new-found friends in the Kosovo Security Force had created a bubble of reality for him, based on the profits his enterprise was generating. They had the product, he had the buyers and the European distribution system, and together they had turned over a few million dollars in less than two years. With no end in sight. As such, he lived in a cocoon of an alternative reality, constructed and controlled by Major Basha.

And even before Basha, Lazar had purchased the controlling rights to the inspector who ran Belgrade's Major Crimes Unit. The police kept well clear of Lazar's business, and the top brass were well paid for that.

Lazar played the moment over and over and over and over in his mind. The girl. The look in her eye. The ice pick. The cool assuredness of Driton Basha. The slow-blooming circle of blood on that old T-shirt.

He had loved that T-shirt.

And after another day had turned into another night turned into another morning, and after shot after shot of liquor with coke with ecstasy, Lazar Aleksić had finally reached a final stage of reaction.

He wanted to try it.

He wanted to see if he could do what Basha had done. As coolly.

He told one of the Kosovar guards that he wanted a girl.

Someone who could go missing.

C34

The young Kosovar corporal—his name was Agon Llumnica—
awoke in a strange hotel room.

He'd been hit three times with the Taser, and his gut ached.
He rolled out of the bed and limped to the window, spotting a
sunny day and a grassy slope and a curving river that he thought
likely to be the same one he'd seen since arriving: the Loire.

He remembered sitting in the bakery truck listening over his
headset as chaos erupted inside the cottage. He remembered calling to Captain Sorak, or to anyone on the team. Then the driver's door had been ripped open and the tall, black-haired woman
appeared, as if from out of the mist.

He remembered waking up in a storage hold, handcuffed to
the floor. He could feel the floor rocking and decided that they
had him on some sort of barge on the river.

The American bastard had come in and showed him the video
of Captain Sorak's team being arrested. And charged with …
drug dealing?

Was that possible? Just barely.

The truth was, the major had first crossed paths with the blond party boy in Belgrade because the unit's own drug dealings intersected with his own. The unit had been making good money on the side selling cocaine and heroin imported up through Greece, until the wars in the Middle East interrupted that supply chain. Rather than panic, Major Basha had found a new—and decidedly more profitable—merchandise to sell, and Aleksić had provided the transportation and the clients. The unit still moved a considerable amount of cocaine, but it was an enterprise with some risks. With drugs, the unit had to rely on Chinese, Thai, or—worst of all—Mexicans for their supply. With refugees, the supply walked up to the door, knocked, and asked to come in!

In this case however, no … That wasn't what had happened here in France. Captain Sorak's team surely would have been happy dealing a bit of drugs on the side, but if so, the entire team would have been in on it. *No*, the soldier told himself, *this has to be a trick by that American fucker and the tall Spanish bitch.*

Llumnica reached into his shirt pocket and withdrew the cheap flip phone.

This is programmed with my number. You can reach me anytime. Help me out, I get you outta France. Free of charge.

Llumnica washed up in the hotel bathroom then snuck out into the parking lot. He marched to the highway and hitched a ride with some German tourist kids to an *aire de service*—one of the Shell Oil–affiliated motorway service areas that dot France's autoroutes. He waited until a lone businessman was washing his car—far from the dining crowd and the laughing children on the outdoor play set. Llumnica simply walked up to the businessman and plowed his fist into the man's stomach. The pudgy man folded like a Swiss Army knife. He took the man's wallet and keys and—why not?—his watch and wedding ring. Then he called headquarters.

He reported to his staff sergeant—who was in on Major Basha's cabal—exactly what had happened. The staff sergeant told the first sergeant, who told Lt. Akil Krasniqi, who reported up the ranks to Major Basha himself.

They arranged for Corporal Agon Llumnica to get to Le Mans-Arnage Airport, where a Ryanair ticket to Belgrade awaited him.

He palmed the cheap phone throughout the flight, deep-red murderous thoughts sloshing through his brain. The American has assumed that he, Agon Llumnica, would be disloyal. That he'd be easy to flip.

He would see. He most definitely would see.

C35

KOSOVO

An olive-colored truck with military stencils and a canvas roof over a metallic ribcage took nineteen of the refugee youths north toward Europe. Jane Koury, who looked like a teenager, huddled with Mohamed and Amira Bakour in the back, one arm around each. A fatigue overcame Mohamed, who slept almost the entire trip. Amira held her broken right wrist tight against her torso. She made herself as small as she could and absently played with the hem of Jane's kaffiyeh.

The humming in Jane's ear had subsided a bit.

It felt surreal, hearing the whoosh of fresh pavement under the tires and the sound of regular traffic on the highway. No more traveling by foot on sand and dirt. From time to time, wisps of loud music slipstreamed past her, surfing a Doppler curve. If Jane closed her eyes and ignored the thrumming in her ear, she could imagine driving the M20 to Dover.

Not all of the children were from Syria. Some were very dark, and Jane guessed they had escaped sub-Saharan Africa. Before he fell asleep, Mohamed pointed to a clique of very tired children in very dirty clothes and said, simply, "Afghan." Whether the fifteen-year-old knew or was guessing, Jane couldn't tell.

She, too, slept part of the way, stirring as the truck veered off the highway. She felt a terrible crick in her neck and her right arm, locked tight around Amira, had fallen asleep. Without waking the girl, she used her shoulder to wipe tears off her cheek. She'd been dreaming of Tamer Awad, of his camera bag and lenses and corny jokes.

Mohamed awoke and twisted around. The canvas top of the truck was battened down to the metal sides at iron grommets. He lifted the canvas between two grommets, creating a thin, vertical slit of bright light.

"Where are we?"

The boy was quiet for a time. The tires plowed into great pot-holes and crawled back out. "It's army," the boy said. "I think."

Amira was awake now and Jane unwound her arm from the girl's skinny shoulders. She tried not to groan like an old lady as she got around, onto her knees, and bent low to peer through the horizontal gap that Mohamed had created by holding up the canvas.

Their truck approached a long, high fence topped with razor wire, a gatehouse, and a long red-and-white striped barrier arm on a counter-lever. A guard with a machine gun, wearing newish fatigues and a black beret, strolled out of the guardhouse as the truck ground to a halt.

Jane looked for signs indicating the Red Cross or Red Crescent, or the United Nations. She saw none.

The blue-on-white sign over the barrier arm, in some Slavic script, but also in English, read: KOSOVO SECURITY FORCE—OPERATING BASE ŠAR.

The nineteen young people were ushered out of the back of the military truck. They were uniformly tired, dusty, scared, and quiet. Jane saw no aid workers and no media. Every adult within sight wore fatigues and berets, and all wore firearms on their hips. Some also carried machine guns.

Guards herded the refugees into a long, brown-and-white one-story wooden building. A large Arabic numeral 3 had been stenciled beside the door. Jane saw two identical buildings to her left and two more to her right, and the nearer was stenciled 2.

Inside, the building featured a large room with rows of army cots, each with one pillow and a coarse, brown blanket. A room off to the right, behind open double doors, showed cafeteria-style tables with benches. Doors off to the left appeared to lead to toilets.

The nineteen refugees were ushered by unsmiling soldiers into the cafeteria room. A large green plastic tray with prewrapped sandwiches sat on the nearest table. Jane recognized the tray as the kind used to slide dishes into an industrial dishwasher. Towers of upside-down plastic glasses stood next to the green tray.

"Arabic …? Greek …?" a guard chanted as the kids walked into the cafeteria. "English …? Arabic …?"

Jane thought back to the aid worker in Macedonia who had tried to separate her from the Bakour siblings because she carried a British passport. "English …?" the guard said as she entered, but she kept her head down and averted her eyes. Mohamed watched her, and Jane gave him the most tentative little head shake.

When all of the refugees were in the dingy hall, a soldier put two fingers between his lips and whistled shrilly. "Listen!" He spoke Arabic. "You are staying in the barracks. Toilets are that way. Water is from the sink, over there. You are not to leave the barracks! Is that understood?"

Jane, who stood near the tough plastic dishwasher tray of sandwiches, raised a tentative hand.

"What is it?"

She replied in Arabic. "There are nineteen of us. There are, um, a dozen sandwiches."

The soldier shrugged. "We'll get more, I'm sure. No one leaves the barracks! People caught outside the barracks will be considered spies and will be shot!"

Several of the younger children began crying.

The soldiers marched out.

Some of the older kids began scooping up the sandwiches. Even in times of horror, people who have known hunger will grab for food. Jane snagged one, which she planned to split between the Bakour kids until more food arrived.

Mohamed grabbed one of the upside-down glasses.

As they made their way to the queue in front of the kitchen sink, Jane heard the telltale sound of the barracks door being locked.

C36

Finnigan and Fiero met Shan Greyson at the apartment they'd turned into a makeshift operation command, over a bookstore on avenue Petra Berislavića. The shadow-diplomat stepped into the walk-up and immediately looked like he'd been born to the place, tossing his jacket over a dining room chair and slouching against the refrigerator that formed a de facto wall separating the kitchenette from the living room from the foyer. Finnigan had a flash-illusion that the floral, midseventies wallpaper perfectly matched the pattern in Shan's tie.

"How goes the good fight?" he drawled.

Finnigan stood in the kitchenette, breaking eggs one by one into a mixing bowl, a towel thrown over his shoulder. Fiero sat sideways on the couch in yoga leggings and a stretched-out Gypsy Kings T-shirt, her legs straight and crossed at the ankles. She'd draped a bath towel over the room's coffee table and had broken down a P226 SIG Sauer to its component parts, laid neatly on the towel along with a rag, wire brushes, and solvent. The bits of gun lay on the table in more or less geographic proximity to where they would be in a fully formed gun, like the bits and bones of a paleo-hominid in a museum case.

Finnigan threw away the eggshells. "Well, Aleksić is the link to organized crime in Europe. He's also the distribution. The Kosovo Security Force provides the victims and also the muscle."

"Or more precisely," Fiero broke in, running a thin brush through the disconnected barrel of the firearm, "a specific unit of the KSF, run by a Major Driton Basha. He used to be linked to Serbian right-wing death squads after the Yugoslav civil war."

Finnigan said, "Basha got promoted from being an asshole for a cause, to being an asshole for a paycheck."

Shan didn't even bother pretending he wasn't studying Fiero's long legs and tanned feet, or the curve of her shoulder where it emerged from the frayed collar. "Can you connect Aleksić the Younger with his victims?"

"Not yet." Finnigan nodded toward the cabinet over the sink, behind him. "You want breakfast?"

"Famished." Shan rolled up his sleeves and set about collecting all three plates from the cabinet, along with three forks and both knives and squares of quilted paper towel off the roll by the sink.

"So once upon a time," the Englishman murmured as he dithered about, "a junior attorney for the International Monetary Fund moved his family to Amsterdam in pursuit of his career. Said family included a sixteen-year-old daughter who fancied herself something of a victim in this move, bereft as she was of her friends and her favorite mall back home in Georgia."

Finnigan used a fork to froth the eggs, then poured them into a chipped pan. He turned and drew a plastic bag, filled with bread, from a cabinet.

Shan said, "What's this?"

"Big treat. I had a cousin ship it in from New York. You'll love it."

Shan studied the polka-dot wrapping on the loaf. "Wonder Bread?"

"Infinitely better than that baguette stuff you get here. Crazy! Buy a loaf in the morning, it's stale by noon. Who designed that? Wait and see. This stuff's great."

He popped two spongy slices into the toaster. Fiero kept her attention on the internal workings of the SIG.

Shan returned to his tale. "So anyway, the daughter decided to dress all in black—no offense, Katalin, my sweet—and to lurk in coffee shops, writing poetry and inscribing to future generations her suffering. She bought a secondhand Nikon with a zoom lens and fancied herself an artist. She read—as God is my witness—Kafka." He shuddered.

Finnigan stirred the eggs with the flat underside of the fork.

"Then, one day, the daughter of the junior attorney for the International Monetary Fund stumbled upon yet another urchin whose life was *actually* sad, as opposed to *artfully* sad. The girls started talking. The newcomer to this tale, whose name was Daisy, was a source of fascination for the young daughter, in that she wore a plaid microskirt and acrylic platform heels and a white blouse tied off above her midriff."

Fiero glanced up from her cleaning supplies.

"Rather than become fast friends after that first sharing of overpriced coffee and angst, Daisy's reaction was somewhat different. She slit her wrists."

The toast popped. Finnigan plucked out both and slid in

two more, then swiveled back to the eggs. Shan eyed the white bread nervously. "Ah. Interesting. You're sure about—"

"Dude, read this. What's it say?"

Shan peered at the packaging. "Helps build strong bodies twelve ways."

"Right. And in the States, they couldn't say it if it wasn't true."

Shan let it go. "Anyway, the junior attorney for the International Monetary Fund, and his beloved daughter, heard about the suicide attempt and dashed to the hospital. Daisy survived. And the surprises were as follows: Daisy was not Daisy at all, but Fatima. Daisy the Teenager wasn't a teenager at all, but twelve-going-on-forty. Daisy the exotic, anorexic beauty wasn't whiling away her time in a coffee shop reading Kafka. She was escaping a series of horrific sex crimes that no sane human should, or even could, imagine."

Finnigan said, "Sit."

Fiero unwound herself from the couch and disappeared to the bathroom to wash her hands. Shan Greyson poured coffee in three mismatched mugs and distributed them, along with a carton of milk and a half-empty box of sugar.

Finnigan split the eggs three ways onto plates. "You found the attorney, or the attorney found you?"

"Friend of a friend. I heard his tale and introduced myself to Daisy turned Fatima. Whence I learned several things: She was from Aleppo. She'd been separated from her family somewhere around Greece. She described Aleksić the Younger to a T, although she never heard his name. I showed her a picture of him, and she was too frightened to properly identify him. Anyway, she'd been sold to a businessman who should die with festering boils. Or better yet, should *live* with festering boils. I also believe that the incident in the canal was her first suicide attempt, but not likely her last."

They dug in.

Finnigan said, "We've got Aleksić under surveillance."

"Who's watching him?"

"Don't ask. Aleksić lives in a secure penthouse suite in Belgrade, under twenty-four seven security from the KSF. He parties in nightclubs, but always with an armed escort. So far, he's kept a clean distance between himself and his victims."

"Well, he needs to be stopped," Shan said, his eyes on his breakfast.

Fiero said, "Stopped." Just that. And kept eating.

They ate in silence, listening to the Zagreb traffic and the laughter of tourists.

Until the penny dropped.

Finnigan sat bolt upright, his fork halfway to his mouth, eyes going wide. He set down the fork, loaded with a mound of scrambled egg. He made the T-for-timeout symbol with both hands. "Whoa-whoa-whoa-whoa."

Fiero smiled up at him; she'd wondered how long it would take.

"Stopped? He needs to be *stopped*?"

"That," drawled Shan, "would be my vote. Fatima's, too, I suspect."

"And Judge Betancourt?"

Shan shrugged. "She is pure of heart, Michael. You know that."

Fiero set her knife and fork down on her empty plate, crossing them like the bones on a pirate flag.

Finnigan studied the Englishman. Then his partner. Then the Englishman.

He said, "We're not assassins."

Fiero said, quietly, "I have been."

"Yeah, but *we're* not. We're getting paid to get the evidence that leads to a conviction. We're getting paid to get that worthless shithead into custody, then into a courtroom."

Shan said, "Bounty hunting in Europe is illegal."

"We know that."

"But that won't stop me from making sure you get paid, fair and square, should you be successful."

Finnigan studied him. "Meaning what? Assassination's illegal, but we'd get paid anyway? You're equating the two?"

Finnigan wiped his lips on a paper napkin and brushed back his chair. His breakfast was half finished. He stood.

"I'm going for a walk. You,"—he pointed to Fiero—"contact the Harts. Tell 'em we need to get into that penthouse. Contact McTavish. Tell him to get his ass up here."

Finnigan collected his jacket and sunglasses and stormed toward the door.

"You," he said to Shan Greyson. "Dishes."

That night, Finnigan lay in bed, one arm behind his pillow, finishing the Elmore Leonard. Fiero tapped twice and slid the door open enough to peer in.

He looked at her over the top of the pages. "Hey."

She stood with her weight on one leg, shoulder against the jamb. She wore a long T-shirt that clung to the pronounced muscles in her shoulders and her long, straight torso.

"Is your father in trouble?"

Finnigan said, "I think maybe, yeah."

"Can you help him?"

"Probably not."

"You're not him, you know. You're not a good cop gone bad."

Finnigan didn't respond.

"We work outside the law. But we're doing good, for all that."

He shrugged. "Sure."

He lay there, staring at her. And she stood there, hip cocked, staring at him.

Finnigan said, "We're not assassinating this jackass."

Fiero said, "Certainly hope not."

And closed the door.

C37

They flew Corporal Agon Llumnica directly to Pristina, where an MP with the personality of a brick met him by a Humvee and whisked him south and east from the city, to the isolated operating base that served as HQ for Major Basha's unit.

Lt. Akil Krasniqi debriefed him and made Llumnica tell the story three times: the ambush in Amboise, France; the assistance of the corrupt French private investigator; the cottage selected for its strategic value; the six-on-two odds; and the moment Llumnica woke up in "some kind of barge on the river" with the American they'd earlier identified as Michael Patrick Finnigan.

When he finished the story, Lieutenant Krasniqi stared at the young corporal for a full sixty seconds.

"Explain it to me again."

Llumnica did.

"He gave me this." Llumnica held up the disposable flip phone, the kind available at a few hundred thousand shops throughout Europe. "Said it could call his number. He expected me to betray the unit."

"And did you?" Krasniqi scowled at the youth—although there were only eighteen months difference in their ages—and took a step closer. "You're not in some fucking cell in France. Correct? Captain Sorak is. The rest of the team is."

"I can't explain that!" The corporal stood at attention, sweaty palms flat against his thighs, back razor-straight. "The bastards took me. Hit me with a Taser. Three times. They expected me to—"

"Show me."

Llumnica drew up his shirt and undershirt and showed the lieutenant the vampire bite marks on his left side, and those on his right. They were inflamed and swollen.

"And you didn't talk?"

Llumnica's discipline broke. "I didn't tell them fuck-all, Akil!"

Krasniqi took another step into the young corporal's personal space. "I didn't tell them fuck-all, *sir*."

"I didn't!"

Krasniqi took the flip phone and checked its memory. One phone number was registered; an international number. He noted zero outgoing calls.

He chewed over the tale and decided it was too unlikely to make a plausible lie. Besides, Krasniqi imagined himself a good judge of his own soldiers. Agon Llumnica was a solid-enough fighter but nobody's version of a creative genius.

"All right. Go get some food. The major went north to talk to the little blond asshole. I just got back from the refugee checkpoint on the Macedonian border." He bunched his fingertips, touched them to his lips, and kissed them away. "Some lovely fruit, Agon. They are falling off the trees, and there's nobody but us to pick them."

The corporal relaxed, feeling the tension bleed from his bones. "Yes, sir!"

"Get some rest today. Oh eight hundred tomorrow, requisition a truck from the motor pool. Talk to none but Ristić! Get the keys from him, and him alone. You understand?"

"Sir!"

"I have the *product* in Barracks Three. We'll gather them at eight, and drive them to Belgrade. Understood?"

"Sir!"

The corporal saluted and turned smartly on his heels.

"And Agon? We get one chance to fuck up in this unit. Maybe you fucked up in France. Maybe you didn't. But don't let me down."

C38

Shan Greyson felt his phone vibrate. He'd arrived back from Zagreb less than forty minutes before, and now was speaking to a trade commissioner from Finland, nodding occasionally, making the appropriate *hmm* noises. Shan had no earthly idea what the topic was, but no doubt the apple-cheeked youth was passionate about it. As Madame Betancourt's unofficial minister without portfolio, Shan often found himself deep in conversations that he neither understood nor cared about. That way people could go back to their bosses or their constituents or their lovers and tell them, *Say what you will, at least the judge heard me out.*

The call was from the executive assistant to Miloš Aleksić, director for the Levant Crisis Group of the UN High Commission for Refugees.

The assistant informed him that Director Aleksić wished to speak to him on a matter of some importance, as soon as possible.

"Would it be possible for you to stop by the director's home tonight, Mr. Greyson? Perhaps for a quick drink?"

"Of course! When and where?"

But with a *ping*, a calendar item with time and address appeared, as if by magic, on his cell phone.

"Please tell the director, it will be my pleasure."

C39

Finnigan and Fiero flew into the shabby little airport at Sarajevo, made famous two decades earlier as an easy target for Serbian death squads, who could sit in the hills with rocket-propelled grenades and wait patiently for easy-picking incoming flights.

Bridget Sumner used Airbnb to find them a farmhouse outside of the city. The place looked rundown enough, and isolated enough, that they needn't worry about snooping neighbors. Bridget herself was hiding in the resort town of Paphos, on the far-western edge of Cyprus and among the expat Russian petro-luminati, but she had a laptop and a high-speed connection, which meant she could whistle up whatever the team needed, whenever they needed it, from the comfort of a chaise lounge working on her tan.

The Scots mercenary, Brodie McTavish, brought two men with whom the partners had worked before and one they hadn't. The newcomer was an Italian, wiry, sunburned, and stoic, with a crew cut and a tattoo of Venus on a half shell filling the inside of his right forearm. "This is Bianchi," the big Scotsman boomed, once everyone was safely ensconced in the old farmhouse. "He speaks Serbian, which, I'm told, is what most of the soldiers in the KSF speak. Bianchi, this here is Katalin. She's the shot-caller on this thing. You follow?"

The Italian nodded in her general direction but didn't make eye contact. Finnigan studied the newcomer, thinking possibly he was just shy—or maybe he just didn't like the idea of a woman issuing the orders. Finnigan decided it was the latter.

Fiero stood a bit apart, as was her poker-player's preference. She'd dressed in black and leather and was wearing her sunglasses, arms folded under her breasts, leaning against a rough-hewn wall with the sole of one boot against the rough pine, her knee thrust forward.

Exactly the same body language and wardrobe as the day Finnigan met her in Crimea.

McTavish continued the introductions. "This is Michael Finnigan. He's a civilian, an' he's a cop, and he's a taxpayer. Which makes him an honest man. Pay him no heed if he starts to pontificate regarding the sanctity of human life. But if he spots trouble: stop, drop, and roll. D'you follow me?"

Again, the Italian just nodded a bit to his left, more or less toward Finnigan.

The Scotsman turned to the partners, fixing both of them—one at a time—with a serious eye. "Bianchi's done a few jobs with me. He's fine in a fight."

That was good enough for the partners. *Fine in a fight* being the highest praise possible from Brodie McTavish.

The other two they knew.

Lo Kwan was a tough little fighter from Hong Kong who

liked knives for close-up work and explosives for the rest. After one memorable job, he also had gotten flamingly drunk in an Egyptian bar and ended up dancing the night away with Fiero, who towered over him. Lo, it turned out, was an outstanding ballroom dancer.

Fekadu, an Ethiopian, was a sniper. He liked long-distance work and had the vision, daylight or night, of a falcon. He didn't talk much to Finnigan, but he'd spent a couple of long-haul flights in unregistered Hercules aircraft quizzing Katalin Fiero Dahar about her mother's religion and her own lack of faith. He had purchased a copy of the Koran for her after one particularly fierce firefight in Oslo. Fiero put up with it because a good sniper is worth his weight in guilt.

Finnigan recovered slowly from the bear hug he'd received from Brodie McTavish, then asked how the hell he'd gotten a team together so fast. Fiero had called him only twenty-four hours earlier.

"The surveyors we was escorting around Sudan turned out to be pussies, them." McTavish hawked up a gob and spat it into the cold fireplace. "They heard a single gunshot, a quarter kilometer from a base camp. Some fucker firin' straight into the air, and what did they do? Pissed themselves and demanded we return 'em to Djibouti tout suite. It was babysitting duty, anyhow. Only so much backgammon I can play with Lo Kwan before I want to pinch his fackin' head off."

Finnigan said, "How do you know it was some fucker firing straight into the air and not trouble?"

McTavish belched a laugh. "Cause the fucker was me, wasn't it! Scared off the punters, let us take a real job instead. An' here we are."

Finnigan and Fiero exchanged smiles.

Finnigan distributed coffee and sandwiches for everyone,

then showed them the stack of photocopies he'd brought. "A unit of the Kosovo Security Force is kidnapping Syrian refugees coming up through the Greek Corridor. They take children and sell them, either to brothels or to private buyers. They work out of this joint."

He distributed aerial photos of KSF Operating Base Šar, kidney-shaped and bisected by its single road, which curved around a few buildings. To the east of the road, five white, one-story barrack buildings stood end-to-end, along with the two-story admin building. To the west of the road, they could see the exercise yard, shooting range, heliport, garage, and the combination PX and communications/radar. Finnigan had the layout memorized by now.

"Major Driton Basha's unit has the run of the place, and they're only thirty guys deep," Finnigan said.

"They sleep here." Fiero stepped away from the wall and pointed to the first two of the five barrack buildings. "Buildings Four and Five appear to be empty. From what we can tell, someone's staying in Building Three, and food gets delivered."

Lo Kwan picked up one of the photocopies. "These aren't Google Earth. These are US Milsat images."

"We have an employee who can get her hands on anything." Finnigan made it sound like no big deal but, to be honest, he and Fiero also had been stunned by the images Bridget Sumner had scrounged up for them.

Bianchi sipped his coffee. "US military satellite images. Are you CIA?"

Finnigan said, "Do we look like CIA?"

The Italian sighed into his cup. "They never do."

"They're not," McTavish slapped the man on the shoulder. "St. Nicholas is old mates. I know 'em."

Bianchi looked confused. "Which one's St. Nicholas?"

Finnigan said, "Long story." He turned back to the photos splayed around the kitchen table. He picked one out—a grainy, distant shot of a man with gray hair clipped close to his skull, with a bull's neck and a bony jaw. "This is Driton Basha. Major, Kosovo Security Force. He's in charge."

Finnigan pointed to another of the satellite photos. "This is his base. It's forty miles from Pristina, and a hundred and forty miles from the next regular army base."

Fekadu, the Ethiopian, scratched his head. "How do you know the traffickers are here?"

"We grabbed one of these schmucks in France, two days ago. He led us here."

McTavish said, "How?"

"Tracker in a phone I gave him. Another tracker sewn into the hem of his jacket. The phone's also jinxed to send audio signals even when nobody's making a call. The guy we released is there."

"As well as victims," Fiero added.

"Yeah. We taped a conversation we got off the phone. Our office manager had it translated. They just got a supply of victims from the Macedonian border. The kids were transported up here. Probably in Barracks Three, right in the middle of the camp, here. They'll be moved out by truck at 8:00 a.m. tomorrow. Destination: Belgrade."

McTavish checked his diver's watch. It was going on 5:00 p.m. local time. "Tight."

Fiero nodded from behind her opaque sunglasses.

Fekadu pointed to one of the high-res photocopies. "Easier to hit the truck when it gets away from the camp?"

"Don't think so." Finnigan pointed as well. "They get out of camp and, two minutes later, they're on a heavily congested highway to Serbia. It's filled with military and civilian vehicles. It'd be a nightmare. It also puts too many civilians in the crosshairs."

The quiet Italian gave a small shrug. The partners ignored him.

"Here's the tough part," Finnigan said. "We want to separate the vics from the soldiers at the base camp. But we don't want them to warn their CO, Major Basha, who's up in Belgrade with the guy who runs the organized-crime end of this thing."

Lo Kwan cast him a scowl. "No time for reconnaissance. Outmanned, outgunned, on their home turf. And you want it done quiet?"

Fiero said, "Well, initially we wanted a team that could pull this off poorly and loudly, but they were busy. We had to settle for you."

McTavish howled with laughter. Bianchi scowled. McTavish noticed and tapped him on the shoulder.

"'Fore you ask, lad, St. Nicholas has paid the freight. In full. Plus bonus money for taking on a feckin' army base, thank you very much. So that's that, and that's *all* that's that. You follow? What's left is the deed itself. Then it's rum and true religion."

Fekadu said, "Rules of engagement?"

Fiero spoke, again from outside the cluster, with her eyes hidden by the shades, her shoulders and the sole of one boot against the wall. "This lot signed on to be soldiers for their country, and instead are making a fortune stealing children and selling them to monsters. They called the tune. They don't get to be picky about how we play it."

"Yeah, but …" Finnigan jumped in. "If we can do this quiet and stealthy, that's better. That's preferred."

After that, the mercs peppered them with questions. "Number of refugees in the camp?"

Finnigan shrugged. "Unknown."

"Transport?"

"Figured we'd use theirs."

"What do we do when we have them?"

"A friend who has contacts in high places. He's actually the bank for this caper. Also the UN. He's going to have an escort waiting at the Serbian border to get us through."

"And the Kosovar CO in Belgrade?"

Fiero said, "He's ours. Everyone else worry about the rescue."

McTavish laughed. "A lark, then."

C40

Director Miloš Aleksić lived a few kilometers outside the government city on a spit of land overlooking the North Sea. The house was an icon of 1970s architecture, and looked more like an outdated notion of a flying saucer than an actual home. But the view was splendid. It was perched on a rocky outcropping, surrounded by a massive sloping lawn and a formidable stone wall on three sides, with the cliff—and a sheer drop-off—and the North Sea on the fourth side. Curved floor-to-ceiling windows in the UFO building provided about 200 degrees of sea view from every room. And while it appeared to be a two-story building, lower floors and basements had been dug into the hard rock to both anchor the saucer-shaped top floors, and to provide more space within.

The lawn was rolling, a deep, unnatural green, and bisected by a winding driveway paved with crushed white shells that led to a five-car garage.

As his car pulled up to the turnabout before the vast garage,

Shan Greyson looked out at the house and its land and said, "Well, I'm here now."

On the other end of his phone, Judge Hélene Betancourt made a *tsk* sound. "I'm not sanguine about this at all. It's going on midnight."

"I believe you spooked him when you spoke at the opera. He's fishing, to find out what, if anything, you know. With a bit of luck, we'll soon know if Aleksić the Elder is aware that Aleksić the Twisted is a trafficker."

"You know what I say about luck, Shan."

He promised to be careful and rang off. As he reached for the door handle, Heinrich, his longtime driver, turned in his seat. "I'm with the judge. You yell if there's trouble."

Shan knew that Heinrich carried a sidearm. "Trust me. You'll hear me shriek pathetically if I so much as smell a problem."

He stepped out and jogged up the steps toward the curvature of the house, securing the middle button of his fitted black jacket. His white shirt was far too crisp for anyone making a midnight call. He had eschewed a tie.

The director's wife, Marija, answered Shan's single knock. "Mister, ah …"

"Thomas Shannon Greyson." He smiled brightly. "Mrs. Aleksić, my deepest apologies for calling at this ungodly hour."

She simpered. "Oh, not at all, Mr. Grenville. My husband is a night owl. We've visitors at all hours. Do, please, come in."

She escorted Shan to a sunken living room featuring a Japanese-inspired indoor garden with a bamboo waterfall and a stacked-stone fireplace opposite the seaside windows. *There's an avocado-colored organic open space in hell for modernist architects,* Shan thought. The lights of oil derricks and cargo ships glistened on the horizon.

"Right in here. Please, make yourself at home, Mr. Greenland.

My husband is on a call to America. Won't be a moment. Would a drink be appropriate at this hour? I can brew tea, of course. You work for that judge, Madame Bonneville, yes? She seems to have it in for Serbians, I understand. Of course, such prejudices date back generations."

"Judge *Betancourt* holds the people of all nations in high regard," he smiled, correcting her name gently, not bothering with his own. "And I'll have a scotch, if that's at all possible."

"I would ask you to help yourself. The bar is just there. I shall let Miloš know you're here, shall I? Please, please. Sit anywhere."

She flitted about, adjusting a pillow here, straightening a curtain there.

"Miloš might be under the impression that the judge does not like the Balkan countries, Mr. Greyville. There is, perhaps, a bit of prejudice still to be found in Europe, when it comes to the people of the former Yugoslavia? I hope that I do not offend."

Shan had made no move toward the wet bar. "Not in the least. Judge Betancourt is quite fond of the former Yugoslavia. She welcomes the diversity that the region brings to the European Union."

"Pleased to hear it!" The booming voice from the stairs startled him.

Miloš Aleksić descended down a curved, open staircase, wearing a cardigan and driving moccasins with his pressed trousers and starched shirt. He'd helped himself to a clean shave, as evidenced by the pink sheen of his under-chin and the whiff of menthol. He shot out a hand to shake. The silver hair over his ears exactly matched his pewter cuff links. *Can one wear cuff links with a cardigan?* Shan asked himself, and quickly responded: *Indeed not.*

"If you were walking in the direction of the scotch, kindly bring back two, will you?" Aleksić turned to his wife and bent at the waist to buss her cheek. For a second, she reminded Shan of one of those stackable Russian dolls. "Can't find my blue shirt, the one from Paris."

"I know where it is, dear." She toddled off.

Shan brought a heavy tumbler of good, amber single malt to the director, who took it with a sideways smile. "Damn good of you, Greyson. Shall we?"

He moved the conversation to a dark-brown sofa.

There is a rhythm to the conversation of diplomats. Those not adept in the art can get confused or bored, but Shan was very much the adept. So as he settled into the expensive leather couch, they spoke of the weather and of a recalcitrant American Congress. They spoke of by-elections in England and of the growing clout of the anti-Europe caucus and the *Brexit* of the UK from the EU. Shan let slip the fact that he recognized the hand of the tailor who'd crafted the suit Aleksić wore to the opera the other night. Aleksić laughed and they told anecdotes of the crotchety, ninety-year-old tailor who had once, it was said, hemmed the trousers of Hermann Göring.

Miloš Aleksić eventually wended his way toward the subject of human trafficking and his assumption that *the learned judge* knew fully well that the problem of abuse of refugees could be found across the board. Of the various routes now in play for the Middle Eastern flow of refugees, tales of the sex trade were rampant everywhere. As, indeed, they always had been.

"It was true of displaced persons after World War II," Aleksić said. "It was true of displaced persons when the Iron Curtain rose. It was true during the Prague Spring and in Hungary in fifty-six. And of course it was true when my beloved Yugoslavia fell apart after the death of Tito."

"Precisely," Shan said. "Truly a terrible and universal truth. Someone will always exploit those most in need of the world's protection. It was ever thus."

Aleksić nodded sagely and repeated the line, as if Shan had coined it himself. "It was ever thus. Exactly. May I …?"

He refilled their glasses from the wet bar. A North Sea squall began to block out the lights of tankers and oil platforms, the weather moving north, or left to right from Shan's perspective.

"How is your son?"

Aleksić paused over the bottle and the fine, heavy glasses, if only for a second. "My son?"

"Laurent, was it? We met at a fund-raiser for … oh, dear. Don't remember. Oxfam? Possibly. He's an entrepreneur, I believe? Businessman?"

Aleksić brought him his refreshed drink. "Lazar, actually. Yes. He works out of Zagreb. Trucking."

"I adore Zagreb."

"Cheers." They *tinked* glasses and the older man sat again. "Funny you should mention him."

"Hmm?"

"Lazar. Funny you should mention him. He's had this idea for the refugees. He's collecting used dental equipment from the United States and Canada, getting it into the hands of refugee aid agencies in Turkey and Greece."

"Really? Splendid idea!"

"Apparently, there's a dire need for dental hygiene for those escaping the wars. Anyway, Lazar saw a need and …" Aleksić waved his glass as if it were a wand. "Voila."

"Excellent. There are those who doubt Europeans have the entrepreneurial gene, but of course that's nonsense. Proof positive. *Salut.*"

"*Salut.*"

They spoke more, and in the meandering way of diplomats. The conversation was a bit like sailing a boat near, but not too near, a rocky shoal. Aleksić would dip close to the subject—was

Judge Betancourt prejudiced against the Slavic people?—without being so gauche as to actually raise the question. And Shan, for his part, steered them toward the harrowing reports of underage trafficking coming out of Serbia. Without, of course, ever pointing any accusing fingers.

Forty minutes later, the men stood at the doorway to the flying saucer house and shook hands vigorously. *So good of you ... and ... grateful for your insight ... and ... Pleasant journeys ...* and all the rest. Big smiles. Sage nods.

Shan walked toward his car, smiling to himself.

He thought it likely he had the answer the judge needed.

He tapped the roof of the limo twice and slid into the back. "To Amsterdam, please."

He pulled out his mobile and checked his emails and messages. No word from Katalin Fiero or Michael Finnigan, but then again, they'd warned him they were about to go dark. He wondered if that meant they were moving against the younger Aleksić.

He glanced up, noticing that the car hadn't moved. Heinrich hadn't even turned over the engine.

He leaned forward. "Heinrich?"

His driver leaned against the window.

Dead.

C41

For radio communications, they decided on the following call signs: Fiero would be Sweeper, and Finnigan would be Keeper. McTavish was Defender. That left Bianchi as Wing Back, Lo Kwan as Midfielder, and Fekadu as Striker.

Finnigan had to write it all down on the web of skin between his thumb and forefinger, just to remember the silly call signs. God knows he tried to instill a little civilization to the group. "Or, we could go with point guard, shooting guard, high and low post, center … Yeah? Anyone? No?"

They blinked at him like he was speaking Etruscan.

"Fine. Whatever. What's a sweeper?"

They drove from the farmhouse outside Sarajevo in the back of a boxy, top-heavy Renault Trafic, painted to resemble a laundry truck, which Bridget Sumner had scrounged up from her chaise lounge with parasol, overlooking the bright blue Med.

Fiero took the wheel. She chose back roads, the provenance of which was provided by the same military satellite photos that Bridget had procured for KSF Operating Base Šar. They didn't rely on the GPS device in the truck—chucked it out the window, in fact, because if the truck fell into the wrong hands, a GPS device with its backed-up memory storage can become a liability. Fiero drove the laundry truck within two kilometers of Šar and parked it under a cluster of pine trees, well back from prying eyes.

The team checked their equipment. Everyone wore black fatigue pants and lace-up boots, plus black undershirts and light ballistic vests. They also wore radios clipped to the back of their vests, with ear jacks and voice wands.

Finnigan and Fiero carried their own handguns: A fifth-generation Glock 17 for him, chambered for 9mm bullets, which, for his money, was second to none in performance and durability. Fiero also preferred a 9-mil, but she liked the SIG-Sauer P226 Tactical Operations gun. Many women prefer a smaller gun for smaller hands, but Fiero had crewed racing yachts and had excelled in archery in college; her wrists and hands were strong enough for the full-size weapon. To compensate for the size, she favored the lighter-weight anodized alloy frame. Fiero wore hers slung low to her long thigh because she'd trained as a kickboxer and disliked a holster that limited her ability to pivot and strike.

A cop from a cop's family, Finnigan also carried a Halligan bar—a door-breaching tool that looked part pry bar, part hatchet, part tire iron. The thing could open virtually any door, if you didn't mind leaving a smashed doorframe in your wake.

The four soldiers-for-hire favored the Browning Fabrique Nationale GP35 handgun, for its pure stopping power.

Fiero, McTavish, and Bianchi carried Canadian-made C8 assault carbines; the standard assault weapon for Fiero, and the heavier C8SWF for the guys, with its longer, heavier barrel and under-slung grenade launcher. McTavish had been trained in the British Special Air Service, where he'd first been introduced to the C8 and its curved, thirty-round box magazine. He adored his gun. He'd never given it a name, because to McTavish, that was a fetish only slightly less weird than guys who have a nickname for their penis.

Beyond his Browning auto, chambered for .357 SIG ammunition, Lo Kwan also carried a wide array of knives and a small machete. He looked absurdly bulky under both a ballistic vest and the kind of fisherman's vest favored by photojournalists, his Velcro-secured pockets bulging with explosives, triggers, timers, and det cord.

Fekadu, the distance-shooter, strapped an Accuracy International AW50 to his back. His kit included a long, state-of-the-art sound suppressor, and he chose subsonic rounds so he could shoot from afar with a minimum of noise. The AW50 was as reliable as the traditional L96A1 sniper rifle, but designed to take out armored vehicles. With the use of an infrared scope, it could even eliminate targets inside bunkers by shooting straight through walls. The recoil was ferocious, but Fekadu figured the rotator cuff damage was a price worth paying for a gun that could essentially kill a Buick.

Geared up and carrying rucksacks, the six of them took off from the cluster of trees at 0100 hours. They hiked east through a field of barley, then up a craggy hill, down a steep and rocky slope, and up the next hillside. They did this two more times. At the top of the final hill, McTavish spotted a felled tree that would make good cover, and they hunkered down. The tree was backlit from the glow of KSF Operating Base Šar, less than a kilometer away.

Lo Kwan pulled binoculars out of his backpack and scanned the scene. "One ... sorry, two guards at the gate," he whispered. "Guard in the tower by that training field. Helipad but no helicopter. Lights in the admin building. Lights in Barracks One, Two, and Three. No lights, Barracks Four and Five. Also, one armed guard outside Barracks Three.

Finnigan said, "The refugees."

McTavish stuffed chewing tobacco into his cheek. "We play by Mighty Quinn rules."

Finnigan glanced at Fiero.

She nestled close to him, her hair up in a French braid. "Mighty Quinn: *All without, or all within.* Either we do this quietly and kill nobody, or we shoot every target we see."

He said, "The former's better."

She said, "Sure," and turned to the mercenaries. She tapped Lo Kwan on the shoulder. "Can you take the guard in the tower quietly?"

"Of course."

She turned to Fekadu. "If Lo Kwan can get you the tower, can you control the whole base?"

The Ethiopian nodded. "Much of it."

She nodded, turned to McTavish. "Midfielder and Striker take the tower. Keeper goes for the motor pool …"

Finnigan checked the writing on his hand, thinking, *Oh, right, that's me.*

"… while you, me, and Wing Back take Barrack Three. Clear?"

Brodie McTavish spat tobacco into the roots of the felled tree. "Now that,"—he grinned—"sounds like a feckin' plan."

C42

The guard outside the Ragusa Logistics high-rise called inside to alert everyone that Major Basha had arrived.

The major rolled his Explorer down the ramp and into the hundred-unit parking garage that stored Lazar Aleksić's ever-growing classic car collection, including the Escalade, Stingray, Jaguar, and a gold-plate Humvee so ugly and useless it made Basha's head swim. The rest of the garage was echoic and empty, without even proper oil stains on the poured concrete floor.

Basha buttoned his suit jacket and strode up to the guard at the elevator, who called upstairs to have the lift sent down.

He rode up to the penthouse alone, reminding himself not to pistol-whip the stupid young gangster-wannabe, with his insipid blond highlights and his cocaine habit. Idiot, Aleksić might be, but not so dumb that Basha had unfettered access to the kid's trucking company, or his organized-crime connections throughout Europe. The youth was still useful, and he knew it.

The elevator car was still four floors from the penthouse when Basha began to hear the reverberant backbeat of hip-hop music.

He stepped out of the elevator and faced the night-shift sergeant, a soldier who'd been with Basha for three years and who had a good head on his shoulders. "The boy?"

They spoke up to be heard over the rap music.

"Clubbing for a while, sir. Came back early. I think he's waiting up for you."

Basha checked his watch. It was just a bit past 1:00 a.m.

He rolled his eyes—the sergeant nodded and smiled—and strode into the living room.

Lazar Aleksić stood, playing a classic arcade pinball game and drinking Dom Pérignon out of a Big Gulp cup with a clear plastic dome and a fat red straw. He wore an Oakland Raiders jersey and, around his neck, braided gold chains as thick as rattlesnakes. His back was to Basha, his attention thoroughly on the pinball game.

Basha strode to the sound system and shut it off.

"Who the fuck—" Aleksić spun and realized who it was, cutting off his response in midsnarl. "Hey, ah … Major."

Basha scanned the expansive room with its view of Old Town and the Slava and Danube rivers. Belgrade sparkled at night.

"We have several refugees at our base," he said. "You promised buyers for six girls and four boys."

Aleksić took a long sip of Champagne through the plastic straw. "Uh huh. Yeah. Sure do. You said France is shut down?"

"It is," Basha said, without explaining why they could not sell any slaves via the French route.

"No problem, no problem. I have a broker in Krakow; he'll take them. Honestly, I have a buyer right here in Belgrade. He wants two. We could move them today."

Basha said, "Two of what?"

Aleksić shrugged. "I don't think he's all that picky."

Basha didn't want details about the perversions of the buyers. He just wanted to count their money. He nodded.

"So that's twelve, total," the young man said, nodding quickly. His eyes were wildly dilated. Basha noticed that his hair now had coppery red highlights, along with the blonde. That annoyed the major even more. "And, ah, let's make it lucky thirteen."

"You have a thirteenth buyer?" Basha was thinking. Lt. Akil Krasniqi had reported that nineteen youths had just been transferred up from the refugee camp in Macedonia. Depending on what happened with the St. Nicholas fools and the International Criminal Court, these nineteen might be the last of the commodity for weeks or even months to come. Any of them that Aleksić could sell, they ought to. Any he couldn't … well, digging ditches is a time-honored make-work project for soldiers. And ditches aren't that different from graves.

"I'm …" the youth wet his lips. He slurped more Champagne, his cheeks caving. His eyes glanced toward the buttery leather couch and the low, glass-topped coffee table. "I want one of them. The Muslims. For me."

Basha checked his watch. He had a plane to catch. "Why?"

Aleksić hesitated.

"What is it?"

The kid wiped his sweaty palms on the sides of his too-long Raiders jersey. "I just want one. Okay. I don't need to explain why. I've got the trucks, and I've got the buyers, right? And we've got more of the little freaks than we do buyers. At least for now. We can afford for me to … use one."

Basha shook his head. "You're not happy fucking every tart in heels at the clubs, that's none of my business. If you—"

"Don't want to fuck 'em," Lazar Aleksić said. His eyes glanced toward the coffee table again.

The table, under which one of his whores had bled to death.

Basha began to see. "You want a girl who …"

"… no one will miss, right. Yes. Like … her." Aleksić didn't know the name of the girl he'd picked up at Club Obsidian. He hadn't known then, and he hadn't known when Basha shoved an ice pick into her heart. "You know … the girl you …?"

Basha nodded. "I know."

"Well?"

It was a tricky question. If Basha's unit was moving heroin, and if their distributor was using the product overly much, Basha would simply have him killed and move to a different distributor. But slave trafficking was a tougher—if more lucrative—prospect. The distributors weren't exactly falling from the trees. And it wasn't quite the same as dealing with a junkie to sell junk. That was inherently stupid. This was just … risky.

He said, "How old?"

Aleksić shrugged. Nerves made him stutter. "I don't know. Doesn't matter. Older, I suppose. Yes. Older."

Basha drew his mobile phone, the one with the security encryption built in. He placed a call to the officer of the day at KSF Operating Base Šar. Basha wasn't worried that it was 0130 hours. Soldiers work when the work is needed.

A voice answered after three rings. "Sir."

"Major Basha," he barked. "Krasniqi?"

"Yes, sir. I have the watch." The lieutenant tried not to sound like he was struggling awake.

"The nineteen," Basha said, not using specific—criminally actionable—nouns, despite the encryption software. "Are they all of the same age?"

"Ah …" He could hear Krasniqi gulp water, trying to wake up. "Yes, sir. More or less."

The younger they were, the higher the price they could demand among the most disturbed buyers. "Are there any that are older?"

"Ah … one sir. A girl, Syrian, I think. She looks … I don't know, eighteen maybe? Nineteen?"

Basha said, "Get three of them up here tonight. The older girl, plus one boy and one girl. Bring the other ten up tomorrow. Understood?"

"Sir."

"Good. Any problems there?"

Krasniqi said, "None whatsoever, sir."

"Good. Out."

Basha hung up. "Ten for your buyer in Poland. Two for your buyer here. And ah … let's call it a sales bonus. Shall we?"

Lazar Aleksić grinned. He slurped Champagne.

Earlier in the day, he'd sent one of his *posse*—that was the American term—to nick a brand-new ice pick from a restaurant supply store, without explaining why he wanted it.

He was ready.

C43

KOSOVO SECURITY FORCE OPERATING BASE ŠAR

No more food was coming. Mohamed Bakour was sure of it. He decided the time had come to act.

Jinan Koury had brought them this far. She didn't even know Mohamed's family, not really, and he knew for a fact that she'd had several opportunities to leave Mohamed and his little sister, Amira. Nobody would have blamed her if she'd left after her friend, the photojournalist, died. She could have left them at the last checkpoint, too.

But she hadn't.

And now, the wise and worldly Jinan—who was so different from any girl Mohamed had ever imagined back home!—was as lost as they were. She had no idea where they were. She didn't know a way out. They were prisoners, along with sixteen other refugees. These soldiers had no intention of getting them to the freedom of Europe. They were in enemy hands—as doomed as if they'd fallen into the clutches of President Assad's forces or, worse yet, Daesh.

So it was time for Mohamed to act like the man he was.

First, no more food was coming. That was clear. They'd given Amira half of the one tasteless sandwich they'd had for the three of them—all wilted lettuce and mystery meat. Jinan had given Mohamed the other half, but he insisted on eating only a quarter and shoved the rest back into Jinan's hands.

The exotic English girl had looked so grateful.

Mohamed had come to understand that he was madly in love with Jinan, even though she was ancient; at least twenty-five. Didn't matter. She'd captured Mohamed's heart, and he'd do anything to show her that he was man enough to protect her and Amira.

One of the other Syrian kids had a wristwatch with a plastic strap and numbers that glowed in the dark. Mohamed squinted at it and realized it was well after one in the morning. No more food was coming, but probably no more guards, either. At least not until morning.

Mohamed threw off the scratchy blanket and sat up. His wood-and-canvas cot groaned a little. Like the others, he slept in his clothes. He slipped on his Adidas sneakers and crept to the toilet room. He'd seen it before, when he'd needed to go. It smelled of mildew and men. The grout between the tiles was black with grit or green with fungus—it was hard to tell in the low light. He'd spotted windows earlier, and now he stood on one of the lidless toilets to see if the nearest one would open.

It wouldn't. From what Mohamed could tell, it hadn't been designed to open, ever.

He climbed down, listened for trouble, then checked two more windows. They were the same.

He crept out of the bathroom and walked softly across the barracks room. At one of the windows he glanced out and saw the glow of a cigarette from the guard outside the one and only door. The glow reflected off the barrel of a rifle slung over the guard's shoulder.

Mohamed snuck into the cafeteria room next, walked

between its rows of tables and benches. He spotted more of the small, square windows, the same as he'd seen in the toilet room.

No hinges, no sliders. No hope.

He crept farther into the room, into the dishwashing area with the large fridge—empty and unplugged; the stench of old milk wafted out when he checked.

Would the guard outside smell it? *The dead would smell that,* Mohamed thought.

He found a door that led outside, but with a padlock bigger than Mohamed's fist.

He jostled one of three big, plastic garbage cans with his hip. Something caught his eye.

He shoved the can away from the wall. A square hatch had been cut into the wooden wall on the same side of the barracks building as the side door, facing Barracks Two. The access hatch was more or less the same size as the thick, gray plastic garbage bins.

Fill them up, shove them outside to be collected by … whoever, whenever.

The hatch was a door on tracks, above and below. It also had a small metal hasp, L-shaped, and another padlock. The hasp screwed into the wooden wall and was held in place by only one screw, although it had holes for two more. Mohamed touched the L-shaped bit of metal and jostled it a little with the tip of his finger.

He returned to the cupboards beyond the empty fridge and the big double sinks. He opened them one at a time. In the fourth drawer, he found an old can and bottle opener, the size of a stick of gum, both ends angled up, one end squared off and the other pointed like an arrowhead. He'd seen his mother open bottles of Coke with the flat end and cans of soup with the arrowhead end.

His father had taught him about Archimedes. *Give me a lever long enough and a fulcrum on which to place it, and I shall move the world.* His father had called Archimedes a great Arabic thinker.

A teacher at school said he was Greek, but Mohamed figured the teacher just got it mixed up.

He took the opener back to the hatch in the wall. He gently shoved aside all three garbage bins. He knelt and fit the arrowhead end of the opener between the wooden lip of the wall and the metal hasp.

He slowly, slowly applied pressure. The hasp strained against the single screw head.

The screw began to move.

C44

The team spotted two guards on roving duty. They walked in a pair, clockwise, chatting softly. It took them about thirty-five minutes to make one loop of the perimeter. The team watched them make the loop twice.

It was after 0200 hours when Fiero gave a signal. She and Brodie McTavish moved downhill, creeping quickly. Finnigan watched them until Fiero seemed to disappear. Then he just watched McTavish. Since he'd met her, he'd known Fiero could move in such a way that she was difficult to track. He called it *ghosting* or, just to annoy her, *that crazy ninja shit you do.*

McTavish got to the fence and found it neither electrified nor well lit. He carried bolt cutters in his rucksack and snipped open a vertical access point.

Once they were done, Finnigan and the other three mercenaries scuttled downhill and crouched through, into the grounds of Operating Base Šar. McTavish then used simple black twist ties to secure the sides of the fence again, using them almost like sutures.

The vertical slit wouldn't be visible from a distance, but it could be reopened in a heartbeat.

Fiero appeared out of nowhere, touched Finnigan's thigh and pointed south. He nodded and followed the perimeter fence toward the motor pool garage.

She tapped Lo Kwan and Fekadu on their shoulders, pointed toward the exercise field and the twenty-five-foot guard tower. The duo moved north and disappeared from sight after a dozen paces.

Fiero, McTavish, and the laconic Italian, Bianchi, moved toward the heart of the base and the row of barracks.

Lt. Akil Krasniqi had hoped to get back to sleep after the major called from Belgrade. But now he needed to organize a night run north into Serbia.

Krasniqi had nineteen of the grubby little Muslim beggars in Barracks Three. Major Basha wanted thirteen of them transferred to Belgrade. Would they hold onto the last six or dump them in the forest? Krasniqi would follow his orders, either way. For now, his plan was to move while the prisoners were asleep and groggy. Rouse them, get them up and startled, and separate them fast. Move three tonight and let the rest go back to sleep. Wake them up before dawn—the lack of sustained sleep helped keep them off-balance—and move thirteen more north.

He'd keep them calm by telling them the United Nations can only process so many refugees at a time, and that they'd be reunited by lunchtime.

Krasniqi rolled out of bed, reaching for his fatigue jacket and his walkie-talkie.

C45

Finnigan stole his first car at age twelve. He remained proud of that to this day. In his Long Island neighborhood, the median age for a first Grand Theft Auto was fifteen; maybe fifteen and a half.

He'd gotten caught, of course, and his mother had screamed at him for a week.

Detective Patrick Finnigan, upon hearing about it, waited until his wife was celebrating Mass, then took his son out to the garage, to the Charger he'd been rebuilding, and said, "Show me."

The two of them laid out on the front seats of the Charger and Michael showed his dad how to find the appropriate wires from within the steering column.

"What the hell is this?" his dad had asked. "That's not the way you do it. Who showed you this?"

"I … I can't tell you."

His father had snorted something that might have been an appreciative laugh. "Look at me. You looking at me?"

His son nodded.

"Never, ever, ever get caught stealing another car. Or anything. Just don't. Okay?"

His son nodded.

"See this? This is the ignition wire. Now, watch and learn …"

The two guards on perimeter duty around KSF Operating Base Šar strolled counterclockwise. Finnigan headed the same direction, in their wake. The land around the fence included several rough drainage ditches and a couple of oil tanks, so the going and the sneaking were easy. But getting caught meant getting shot, so Finnigan took it slow.

The base motor pool was a classic auto garage, with one rolling bay door and room inside for maybe a dozen vehicles, including trucks. From the first window he came to, Finnigan spotted a lube/oil/filter pit for basic maintenance, partially occluded by a late-model Jeep. Maybe a quarter of the vehicles within were in some state of disassembly and repair. The rest were just parked.

He circled the garage, checking every window. No lights shone. He sketched the building's geometry in his head and determined that there were no hidden rooms within. He also caught no signs of any security wiring. Who steals a truck from inside a military base out in the middle of Kosovo's version of the ass-end of nowhere? Nobody—and the security precautions reflected that theory.

He spotted two doors and picked the one farthest from the well-lit admin building. He placed the Halligan bar against the doorjamb, brace hand near the wood, pressure hand out at the far end of the handle, and applied the slightest pressure. Then slightly more.

He watched as the tongue of the lock slid free of the doorjamb. Once it was out, the door swung open with no significant damage or noise.

There was no way of knowing how many refugees they'd be driving out. Once inside, Finnigan moved toward the largest supply truck he could find, a massive diesel Scania with a detachable canvas top stretched over steel ribs. He drew his penlight and shone it across the truck's canvas side. He did the same for two more trucks.

He glanced at an oil barrel, standing upright, between the tops. Something lay across the top, looking a bit like laminated place mats you might find in a diner.

Finnigan moved closer and ran his light over them.

They were magnetized, rubber logos, the kind that can be adhered to the door of a truck, then easily peeled off.

They bore the logo of Ragusa Logistics.

Lo Kwan reached the wooden guard tower first. It stood twenty-five-feet tall with four sturdy legs and a simple wooden box with a hip-high support wall and a roof over it—like every guard tower ever built at every army base on earth.

The mercenary preferred to work with his hands free, so he didn't bother carrying a rifle. He tested the lowest rung of the tower ladder and found it well constructed and sufficiently nailed. It made no noise as he applied weight to it. He glanced around again and saw no one close, although he thought he saw more lights on, inside the admin building, than he'd noticed before. Could be an illusion, he told himself.

He glanced back over his shoulder. The sniper, Fekadu, nodded. *Clear.*

Lo began climbing. He tested every rung before trusting it. He worked slowly. Quick movements will catch a person's peripheral vision, especially at night, in ways that a slow and steady motion won't.

He heard floorboards creak overhead. The guard in the tower, ambling slowly from side to side, partly to keep an eye on the base below but partly to keep awake. Lo had done his fair share of late-night sentry duties, and he knew what every good soldier knows: Gen. Boredom and Gen. Fatigue undermine more campaigns than the finest strategists.

He reached the point at which his head was almost level with the underside of the floorboards. He paused and listened. The highway, only a kilometer away, provided a regular swoosh of late-night traffic. An air-conditioning system atop the admin building chugged. Crickets chirped in the fields around the base, and bats flitted in and out of the small forest to the east.

He heard an outer door of the admin building swing open and slam shut on springs. He heard the low murmur of voices speaking a Slavic tongue.

The guard in the tower moved in that direction to see what was going on.

Lo Kwan took the last two rungs. He spotted the sentry, his back to him, wearing fatigues and lace-up boots. The sentry held his carbine, rather than slinging it over his shoulder (*Good on you, soldier*, Lo thought). The man was average in size, with a buzz cut and a black beret cocked at a fuck-you angle.

Lo stepped up and onto the platform, moved behind the sentry. He reached up and swept the man's beret forward, covering his mouth with it. He locked his other forearm around the man's throat, tight. He swung his legs around the man's hips, leaned, and tipped them both onto their backs. Lo's rucksack took the brunt of the fall.

The sentry reached for the thing that was being pushed into his mouth. Naturally, that meant dropping his rifle, which, like all well-maintained carbines, did not discharge on impact.

On their backs, Lo's legs locking up the sentry's legs, his arm crushing the man's carotid artery, jamming the black beret further into his mouth. The man struggled but had no leverage. He tried kicking at the hip-high retaining wall but Lo minimized his leg movements.

The brain focuses on suffocation before all else: the real threat was the pinched-off carotid, but the wool cap in the man's mouth, and the panicky tightness when he tried to draw a breath, kept the sentry's hands busy scrambling for his own face, and not reaching back for Lo's eyes.

It would have been much, much easier for a knife artist to kill the sentry, but Katalin Fiero and Michael Finnigan called the tune: *All without, or all within.* Kill nobody if you can help it but, if the plan goes pear-shaped, kill whomever you come upon. They were still in the kill-nobody phase, but that could change swiftly.

It took less than sixty seconds for the sentry to slump. Lo had done this enough to know; he waited to feel the man's thigh muscles, under his own thigh muscles, relax. That was the true sign that he was out and not faking.

Lo Kwan rolled the man onto his stomach. He reached for the zip ties he carried in a pouch on his belt, secured the man's wrists behind his back and his ankles to his wrist. He kept the beret stuffed in the sentry's mouth but cleared his nose.

He moved back to the ladder, digging a red-filtered penlight out of his rucksack, and flicked in on and off, three times.

He saw Fekadu sprint from out of a drainage ditch and jump onto the ladder, his sniper rifle bobbing on his shoulder.

C46

Fiero heard the telltale chirp of activation from her ear jack.

"Striker has eyes."

Fekadu, the sniper, announcing that he'd taken up position atop the guard tower.

Fiero tapped her ear jack—everyone would hear the confirmation chirp. No need to comment further.

Fiero, McTavish, and Bianchi were hunkered down next to Barracks Four, which appeared to be empty. A cluster of old oil barrels had been left to the side of the barrack and made for a good duck blind.

The big Scotsman made a gesture in the direction of the admin building. They'd all heard the door opening and swinging shut, and the sound of men talking, but too far away for Bianchi to interpret.

The Italian tensed up and Fiero made a no-go gesture. He settled back down.

The plan still relied on stealth. The Kosovars were committing major, international crimes from this base. If the team could steal a truck, get the kids on board, and hit the gate—the guards, like all military base guards, would be on the lookout for someone breaking *in*—they could get to the highway in under a minute. And the troops involved in human trafficking likely would hesitate before getting into a running gun battle on an international highway.

That was Plan A.

The chatter continued. The bad news: more soldiers were awake and moving about than they'd hoped for. The good news: the chatter sounded casual; the soldiers weren't awake and moving about because of St. Nicholas and the mercs.

Something thumped behind the barracks. McTavish and Bianchi, both down on one knee, twisted in that direction. The Italian rose and crept to the southeast corner of Barracks Four; farther from the light and chatter, close to the forest-side perimeter fence.

Fiero covered her mouth with her palm, pushing her voice wand closer to her lips. "Striker: eyes on the men by admin?"

Fekadu replied softly. *"Affirm."*

"How many."

"Three."

She heard another soft thump from somewhere behind the barracks. Were they being distracted by soldiers talking loud at the well-lit admin building while someone moved up on their flank? Bianchi, at the right rear corner of the building, brought his automatic rifle up to his shoulder, elbow on his knee, eyes on the raised rear sight.

"Hold fire," Fiero whispered for the sake of everyone, but mostly for the Italian.

Bianchi shot her a look. She stared him down.

He put his good eye back on his rifle sight.

Mohamed let the garbage hatch thump shut, wincing at the noise, and duckwalked from Barracks Three to a high chain-link fence, beyond which lay a forest. He knelt, further ripping out the knees of the only jeans that still remained from the beginning of the family's odyssey. For the first time in his fifteen years, he smelled moldering pine needles and rich brown earth and the sweet decay of dead birds and squirrels. The potpourri of it made him dizzy. The forest was loud, too. Why had no one ever told him that forests were loud with frogs and cicadas and owls?

He took a moment to take in the darkened base. It seemed huge to him, with lights atop tall poles, and wooden buildings with metal roofs. The road through the camp—what he could see of it—was well-paved and smooth. Mohamed had seen well-paved roads only on important government streets, and he subconsciously associated fresh tarmac with power. He wondered what country he was in that had such wealth, that they could pave the roads in the army base.

He had no doubt they were prisoners. The military types of Syria had been hardened and bitter but didn't care about the refugees. The military types of Turkey and Greece had been overwhelmed and stunningly disorganized—even from the perspective of a fifteen-year-old—and hadn't particularly cared about the individual refugees, seeing them only as a river of people that needed to keep flowing, in order to save themselves from drowning in it.

But the soldiers of this unnamed country *cared* about the refugees. And, Mohamed realized with terror, they seemed to care for all the worst reasons.

He had excellent night vision and watched as three men slipped out of the two-story wooden building, about mid-center of the camp, talking and lighting up cigarettes. A fourth soldier joined them, but quickly jogged away. He was gobbled up by the night, only to emerge in the cone of light under one of the poles, twenty yards down.

Mohamed didn't want Amira to wake up and find him gone. Or the exotic English adventurer, Jinan, for that matter. He rose and turned, but quickly fell to his knees among the reeds.

A man appeared at the next low building to Mohamed's left. The man knelt at the corner, one elbow on his raised knee, and aimed a rifle down the length of the rear side of the barracks buildings.

The path to the garbage hatch in Barracks Three, and Mohamed's way back to his sister, intersected perfectly with the sights of that ominously long gun.

Finnigan got the housing off the steering column of the great Scania truck and separated the wires by color, using a penlight held in his teeth for illumination. His ear jack chirped.

The languid, almost musical voice of the Ethiopian shooter, Fekadu, whispered to him. *"Keeper has a Bravo heading his way."*

Finnigan twisted the penlight to shine on the webbing between his thumb and fingers. Bravos were the bad guys. That one he knew. *Keeper: that's me. Right.*

He heard gravel crunch. He lay sideways on the elevated driver's seat, his legs dangling horizontally in midair, and slid out of the truck, quietly closed the door.

With a rumble, the big garage door began to rise, a narrow rectangle of dim light emerging on the cement and growing oblong.

Finnigan dashed across the garage toward an older-model Jeep. He saw a pair of legs and boots outside the rising door. He slid to one hip like a runner stealing second, gliding under the Jeep, landing inside the lube/oil/filter pit.

C47

Lt. Akil Krasniqi smoked down one cigarette and waited for the private to retrieve one of the trucks. Each of the Ragusa Logistics vehicles had the necessary bumper stickers to get through the borders of Schengen Agreement countries without stopping to be searched. He shook a cigarette free of the pack and handed it to Corporal Agon Llumnica, who accepted it and a light.

"The major wants three of the cattle heading north tonight. The oldest girl we've got, and two others; boy and a girl," the lieutenant said. "I'll take them."

"Yes, sir." Llumnica drew on his cigarette.

"You're the duty officer, soon as I leave."

Llumnica straightened up. "Yes, sir!"

They heard a revving engine from the direction of the motor pool. Llumnica and the private with them finished their smokes, and Lieutenant Krasniqi led them toward the barracks. The truck would meet them there. The man guarding the barracks snapped to attention as they approached.

The lieutenant made a gesture with his chin and the guard shouldered his rifle, digging keys out of his fatigue jacket.

Krasniqi led his two men inside, leaving the guard where he was. The private hit the lights, and refugee children began stirring on their cots. As they sat up, rubbing sleep from their eyes, Krasniqi looked at them.

"Her," he gestured toward a girl who was maybe twenty, or maybe a little older. "And two others. One each. Don't care who."

The private spoke fluent Arabic but with a Riyadh accent. He stepped forward and spoke slowly, keeping his orders rudimentary. "Attention, please. The United Nations checkpoint is overrun with refugees. They need to start getting people through as quickly as possible. We need to take three of you now. Everyone will be reunited at a British camp over the border."

Jane Koury was still half asleep. The ringing in her ear had faded but her head still ached. Three soldiers entered the barracks, threw on the lights, and were talking, but their accents were weird and she was having trouble following.

Something about a British camp over the border?

There were no British camps anywhere near the Balkans, Jane knew. She must have misheard.

The soldier who spoke pointed to her and made a get-up gesture. Maybe he'd figured out she was English?

She tried standing and felt her gorge rise. *You're concussed, you daft cow,* she chided herself. The room spun.

Amira was standing, too, so Jane put an arm around the girl's shoulder. Another refugee boy, one of the Afghans, stepped forward after toeing on his ragged Chuck Taylor trainers.

The soldiers moved to escort them toward the door.

Amira pulled back. She grabbed Jane's hand and yelled, which set off the spinning in the room and the dental-drill headache over her right eye.

Amira said something. What …

Mohamed!

One of the guards scooped Amira as if she were a rolled-up sleeping bag and made for the door.

Another grabbed Jane by the upper arm.

"No wait …" She tried to clear her head. "Wait, we—"

The guard shoved her toward the door.

"No! I can't. Mohamed, he's—"

The guard cuffed her on the back of her head.

Jane went to one knee and dry-heaved.

Amira screamed as the soldier carried her under one arm out the door.

Jane was lifted to her feet and escorted roughly.

"Wait … we're with a boy …"

The soldier who spoke Arabic said, "I understand. You'll be reunited. It's okay."

A small truck pulled up in front of the barracks. The Afghan boy and Amira were ushered, none too gently, into the back.

"No, wait! Mohamed! I have—"

The guard put hands under Jane's armpits and hefted her easily into the back of the truck.

Amira screamed.

The soldier raised the tailgate of the truck, then whacked the brace twice with an open hand.

The driver put the truck in gear.

C48

Fiero hissed, "We hold."

A small truck with the logo of Ragusa Logistics had pulled up in front of Barracks Three. Soldiers had entered the building and now emerged with three of the children; two girls and a boy, all dusty and disheveled. The younger girl with her arm in a cast howled in fear. They were hustled into the small truck and two soldiers joined them. A third soldier and the original guard remained.

Fiero peered into the night and recognized the soldier. It was their old pal Llumnica, the same guy they'd captured in the Loire Valley in France.

The truck spat gravel, heading back onto the main road.

Agon Llumnica held a walkie-talkie to his lips and spoke in Serbian or Armenian; Fiero couldn't tell the difference. Didn't matter: he was calling ahead to the gate to alert them that the truck was heading their way.

Fiero grinned wolfishly. She touched her ear jack. "Keeper: Good to go?"

Finnigan said, *"Give me sixty."*

"Change of plan. We're taking the barracks now. Striker: subdue the base, please."

Fekadu said, *"Confirmed."*

"Midfielder: deaf and blind, please."

Lo Kwan spoke from elsewhere in the base. *"Confirmed."*

Fiero made a come-here gesture to the men behind the oil drums. McTavish moved forward quick-like. Bianchi did not. McTavish started to repeat the gesture but Fiero stopped him. Her message was clear: either the Italian followed orders or he didn't, but he didn't get to pick whose orders he followed.

After a beat, the Italian dropped his rifle to his side and squat-walked to join them.

Fiero covered her voice wand, speaking only to the two of them. "Corporal with walkie. We need him. Guy at the door is expendable. McTavish has him."

Bianchi hissed. "I thought I saw someone back—"

She said, "Try not to piss yourself. Let's go."

She swung her carbine over her shoulder, the strap cross-body, and drew her SIG. She stepped around the corner of the barracks and advanced, the guys behind her. They were now only five paces from the soldiers, who were chatting with each other. The guard laughed. Corporal Agon Llumnica spotted Fiero, and his brain took a moment to realize who he was seeing, here at his nice-and-safe base. She stepped past the guard and jammed her SIG into Llumnica's face, barely two inches from his nose.

She heard McTavish deck the guard a pace behind her. The man's head ricocheted off the barracks wall and he bounced into McTavish's arms, as limp as a rag doll.

Fiero had been watching the keys in the guard's hand; they hadn't gotten around to relocking the barracks.

She used her free hand to reopen the door. Corporal Llumnica started to speak and she used the gun to bop him on the bridge of his nose—not hard, just enough to shut him up. She grabbed his lapel and shoved him into the barracks. Then, following as he stumbled inside, Fiero drove the sole of her boot into the side of his knee. Llumnica crumpled.

McTavish hauled the unconscious guard in her wake and dumped him on the floor.

Bianchi scooped up the man's fallen rifle and entered, closing the door behind them.

Fiero went to her haunches and took Llumnica's gun and walkie-talkie. The refugee kids were awake, most of them sitting on cots or standing next to them, eyes wide.

"Be calm." Fiero spoke Arabic. "We're not here to harm you. Please stay calm."

A girl with a patch over one eye, who was all of fourteen, said, "Who are you?"

Fiero offered the girl a warm smile, aware that she wore all-black fatigues and carried firearms. "We're here to get you out. Tell everyone else, would you please?"

She turned to Agon Llumnica. "Hi. Remember me?"

"How the fuck did—"

She clocked him in the ear with the side of her gun, just enough to get his attention. "I'd like nothing more than to shoot your cock off, Corporal. Do as I say, and you'll rob me of that joy. You understand?"

He nodded, eyes wide.

"Good. We're stealing your refugees. Why should your corrupt major make all the profit? Our commander wants a slice of this sweet pie, too. Money enough to go around. Yes?"

It had been Finnigan's idea to play the role of the competitor. Appear to be an invading force, and the soldiers of Operating Base Šar might suffer from an onset of late-stage patriotism. Appear to be criminals ripping them off, and they'd be less likely to risk their own hides in an all-out battle.

The corporal glared at her. "Fucking bitch. The whole thing in France—"

"That's right. We needed the Serbian kids' buyers. Now, we're—"

Something rattled in the mess hall, like a pan on a cabinet. A shadow flitted across the double doors.

Bianchi raised his silenced carbine.

McTavish reached him first, a hand the size of a catcher's mitt shoving the gun an inch to the left.

Bianchi fired. The sound suppressor huffed.

The bullet blew a hole as big as a bagel through one of the dining hall doors, six inches from the head of Mohamed Bakour.

C49

The guy who jogged into the motor pool and grabbed the small truck hadn't bothered calling anyone on his walkie-talkie. He'd just hopped in and rolled out. Finnigan took that as a good sign.

He pulled himself out of the lube/oil/filter pit. The soldier had veered toward the back of the shop and Finnigan headed that way now, finding what he'd missed first: a pegboard with keys. He grabbed the one that matched the Scania with the Ragusa Logistics logo. He dashed to the big door and hit the red button. The door began to rise. He climbed into the truck, turned over the ignition, and saw the fuel gauge bob over to FULL.

He rolled out of the garage without a care in the world. New York boys don't know the ins and outs of human trafficking and white slavery. But stealing a car? Bitch, please.

He tooled up to the row of barracks. A guard had been posted at Barracks Three, but now wasn't. Fiero and the guys were inside. He let the truck roll to a halt with only a light tap of the brakes; no way of knowing how squeaky the brake pads were on this big boy.

He halted beside Barracks Three.

The door didn't open.

Fiero grabbed Mohamed by both shoulders. He looked like he was a breath away from having a heart attack.

"It's all right. He didn't mean to. You're okay."

The kid looked around at the wakeful refugee children, and the strange soldiers. He peered at two of the bunks, empty except for a backpack. "Where's Amira?"

"Amira?"

If anything, the boy's eyes grew wider. "Where's Amira? Where's my sister?"

Fiero cursed herself. She'd sacrificed three of the refugees to separate the enemy. The sister likely was among them.

"Listen. The soldiers took three of the children. Are you listening to me?"

The boy nodded. She could see him working to master his fear, even though his body was rigid with it. *Impressive kid.*

"We know where they're going. Okay? We'll get you all out of here. We'll catch up to them. Okay?"

The boy gulped but then nodded once more. "We are from Homs. Amira and me. We do not know where our parents are. They were with us but …" He shrugged. "We are traveling with a British girl."

Fiero frowned. "British?"

Mohamed said. "*Woman.* British *woman.* Jinan. She is very brave. She is gone, too. I think she is protecting Amira. I went to find food. I left them."

"You did good," Fiero said and gripped his shoulders tighter. "Do you hear me? You did good."

Mohamed raised one skinny arm and pointed at Bianchi. "That man tried to shoot me."

"That's because he's not a very good soldier. But the big man with the beard is."

"He's your leader?"

"I'm *his* leader," Fiero said. "We're going to get everyone out. Are you ready to help me?"

Finnigan drummed on the steering wheel. He checked his watch.

He heard the squeak of a door hinge, well off to his left. A Kosovar soldier stepped out of the admin building, an unlit cigarette to his lips, lighter halfway there. He saw the idling truck.

Finnegan casually reached down and wrapped his hand around the grip of his 9 mill.

The soldier threw the cigarette into the dirt and marched his way. He swung a carbine off his shoulder, the gun rotating like the pendulum of a clock. He made it another three steps and shuddered, went to one knee, and landed on his chest. He made no effort to block his fall, his cheek flopping into the dirt.

In his earpiece, Finnigan heard the Ethiopian in the guard tower. *"Bravo down, inner courtyard."*

Fiero's voice answered. *"Copy that. Coming out."*

The barracks door opened and McTavish led the way. He popped open the canopy in the back of the truck.

Fiero came next, escorting very young and very frightened children. Two by two, McTavish and Fiero helped them into the truck, the teenagers in turn helping the younger ones get settled. They just kept coming: two by two by two. Everyone remained quiet.

Fiero touched her ear jack. "Striker, give us thirty, then evac."
Fekadu said, *"Roger."*

Bianchi emerged from the barracks last, gun to his shoulder, leading with it, checking left and right and rotating gracefully on his lead foot.

Someone, somewhere, shouted. The voice was Slavic and a little panicky. Finnigan couldn't tell where it came from.

"Musliman deca! Oni—"

The voice stopped abruptly.

Fekadu said, *"Second Bravo down. He came from the perimeter fence. Lights coming on in the admin building."*

Fiero climbed into the passenger seat next to Finnigan and spoke into her mic. "Striker, evac now." She turned to Finnigan. "Go."

More men were yelling. More windows lit up. Fiero rolled down her window. McTavish popped one of the stays on the side of the truck, creating an aperture under the tarp on the driver's side. Bianchi took up position at the rear.

The windshield directly in front of Finnigan's face cracked in a starburst pattern. He instinctively ducked but kept driving, upshifting from first to second.

Fiero said, "You drive like my grandmother." Finnigan grunted and hauled on the wheel. "My mother's mother," she amended. "You know. The one who's been dead for five years."

McTavish fired a single shot to the left. Bianchi let loose a rapid blast on full auto, straight back.

Finnigan vectored for the gate. The red-and-white-striped barrier arm remained down. A bullet pinged off the door frame, inches from his shoulder.

McTavish responded on full auto.

They curved around the communications building and Finnigan jammed on the brakes. The kids screamed in horror.

Lo Kwan dashed from the building and, with Bianchi's help,

hurdled onto the tailgate and landed in the back. Fiero said, "Got him."

Soldiers came running around the building, firing.

Finnigan gunned the engine.

The cell tower atop the communications building exploded, the shock-flash of light sending monster shadows throughout the courtyard. The coming soldiers ducked, throwing arms up over their heads, fearing an aerial assault.

The cell tower began collapsing, one leg disintegrated. Fiero had asked for *deaf and blind, please.* Lo Kwan had delivered.

The truck's rpm climbed near the red zone as Finnigan smashed the Scania through the blocker arm at the gate.

Fiero, McTavish, and Bianchi laid down suppression fire as the truck roared into the night.

Fiero turned to Finnigan and nodded. She touched her ear jack. "Striker?"

Fekadu sounded out of breath. "*I've reached our truck. Rendezvous on the highway.*"

"Well done," she said and turned to say something reassuring to one of the Muslim boys behind her. The kid appeared to be about fifteen and was the least panicked of the refugees. He and Fiero spoke in Arabic, then the boy turned and spoke to the other children. They began to calm down.

Fiero sat forward in her seat. "Nice driving."

"How many did we get?"

She did a quick headcount. "Sixteen. And three to go."

"Sorry?"

She had removed her rucksack and thrust it into the space between her long legs. She withdrew their satphone and tapped in the unlock code. "Three others were taken. My young assistant here is Mohamed. His sister and an English girl are among the missing. They'll be heading to Belgrade."

Finnigan blinked at the road through the star-shaped crack in the windshield. "English?"

Fiero shrugged.

"We were heading to Belgrade anyway," he said. "Guess we just have to get there faster."

"I'm calling Shan now."

Finnigan drove. Behind them, they could hear Mohamed calming the other children. Now that they were on the highway, McTavish and Bianchi stowed their weapons out of sight.

With a single honk, the stolen laundry truck from Sarajevo pulled up next to them. Fekadu waved from behind the wheel, then fell back and tucked in behind the Scania.

Throughout, Fiero kept the satphone to her ear. A kilometer passed under their wheels. She made eye contact with Finnigan.

"No Shan?"

She shook her head. "That's a complication. He was going to get a World Court envoy to get us across the border."

A sign drew closer. In both English and Cyrillic, it announced fifteen kilometers to the Serbian border.

C50

The smaller Ragusa Logistics truck pulled up to the border crossing and picked the northernmost gatehouse, the one designated for military vehicles, police, and other first responders.

Lieutenant Krasniqi climbed into the back and drew his Glock sidearm. He showed it to Jane, Amira, and the Afghan boy. "Shhhhhh …"

They sat huddled together, their eyes on the slow-boil smile of the lieutenant. Jane's headache had dropped to tolerable levels. She noticed for the first time that her backpack was missing. And, with it, her British identification and her passport.

She wasn't sure if that was a good thing or a bad thing.

It was going on 3:00 a.m. and a Kosovar border guard jogged slowly out of the office toward the gate. He recognized the Ragusa Logistics logo. He circled around to the driver's side, where the private handed him an envelope of euros.

"Have a pleasant journey!" he laughed, and unlocked the gatehouse, hitting the switch and raising the barrier.

The truck rolled into Serbia.

One hundred yards ahead lay identical gates and gatehouses, staffed by Serbian soldiers.

The private reached for the second envelope of euros. He'd made the trip enough times to separate the money for the matching guards—on both the Kosovar and Serbian sides—before arriving.

Lieutenant Krasniqi waited until they were past the second barrier and picking up speed. He reholstered his weapon and shouldered his way through the hatch, back to the cab.

Jane squeezed Amira's shoulder very tight. The girl trembled. "I want Mohamed. Where's Mohamed?"

"I know, love." She let her fingertips trace the pulpy edge of the girl's forearm cast. "Amira? Do you still have the phone I gave you?"

They were wasting time and everyone on the team knew it.

The stolen Ragusa truck and the Bosnian laundry truck pulled into a broken-down warehouse. Bianchi got out and cut through a chain to open the gate, and the trucks rumbled over pitted tarmac that had broken up into large chunks, like a melting ice cap, between seas of reedy grass. Fiero and Fekadu, who spoke Arabic, assured the children that the stop was necessary, and Fekadu escorted the children, two by two and by gender, to a locked and darkened water closet to relieve themselves by the glow of flashlights.

Nobody could help the Afghan children to understand, but Mohamed Bakour took it upon himself to keep them calm.

The St. Nicholas partners gathered with McTavish's mercenaries around the hood of the laundry truck to go over the situation. Finnigan said, "Our contact was supposed to have clerks of the International Criminal Court, and UN observers, at the

Serbian border. They were to take the kids and get them safe. But also, get them on camera; start building a case against the guys running this shit-show."

"No contact?" McTavish fussed with his massive beard. The partners shook their heads.

"We have to assume the worst," Finnigan said. "Our contact is compromised, and we're working illegally in Kosovo without a lifeline. The border is off limits. At least, as far as these kids are concerned."

McTavish made a sword of his hand and thrust it westward. "Then we get them out the way we got in: overland into Bosnia, into Sarajevo."

Finnigan considered the plan. "Taking out the cell tower and the radio tower at the base only bought us so much time. We can get these sixteen kids out the way you say, but not the three who left in the first truck. So we split up. McTavish and the guys get these kids to Sarajevo. Get them to the US embassy there. We'll go after the others in Belgrade."

"And Lazar Aleksić," Fiero added.

"Most definitely."

It was agreed. Fekadu would switch to the big truck, with Lo Kwan driving. They'd reverse course and take the goat trails back over the hills, just as they'd entered. But it was already going on 0400 hours, and they wanted to get across before the sun rose. Time wasn't their friend.

Mohamed was bringing the final group of Afghan boys back from the bathroom. Fiero nodded him over and explained the plan. "Your job is to keep the youths calm on the drive to Sarajevo," she said.

And he replied, simply, "I'm coming with you."

"You can't. I need you to—"

"I'm coming with you."

She looked him sternly in the eye. "Mohamed, you have to be the man now. I need you—"

"No." He didn't sound scared or angry. Only resolute. He maintained eye contact and his emotions. "My father and mother might be in Turkey. Or Greece. I don't know, and they do not know where we are. My sister is in the hands of monsters. I am the only family left who can save Amira. And when we reach her, I'm the one she'll listen to and believe. You'll just be more Westerners with more guns."

Fiero opened her mouth to counter and Mohamed didn't wait.

"You need me to be a man? In my family, right now, I am the man."

Finnigan circled the laundry truck but kept his distance. He pretended to watch the stars.

Fiero rose and turned to him. "He's coming with us."

C51

The smaller Ragusa Logistics truck carrying the kidnapped Muslims joined the E75 heading north, making great time in the predawn hours, and rolled into the city, turning off the freeway virtually within sight of the great Eastern Orthodox Temple of Saint Sava. The morning traffic was still light, with only service trucks and a few cars on the streets. Lieutenant Krasniqi allowed himself to drift to sleep intermittently, secure in the knowledge that the three urchins in back wouldn't make any trouble. The soldiers had made this run often enough that they had become inured to the danger.

As they left the freeway and vectored onto the main street of Kneza Miloša, he drew his prepaid cell phone and called the Ragusa building to alert them.

"The garage will be open as you roll up, sir," the graveyard shift soldier told him.

"Put coffee on. Is the major there?"

"Negative, sir. He flew north. To the Netherlands."

That was odd. Krasniqi wondered why.

Blue lights began flickering in the rearview mirror. The soldiers glanced back and saw a Belgrade police officer on a motorbike, urging them to pull over.

Krasniqi said, "Hold. We'll get there shortly," and hung up.

They pulled over just shy of embassy row. Belgrade was safe territory for the Kosovars, but being this close to so many international diplomats still seemed risky.

The motorcycle officer doffed his helmet and approached on the passenger's side, which was unusual for a traffic stop.

Krasniqi rolled down his window. "Help you?"

The traffic cop looked more than a little ill, even under the harsh early morning streetlights. "I need you to stay here, sir."

"You really don't. We're fully permitted."

The kid—he was all of twenty-three, Krasniqi thought—wet his lips. "I'm sorry, sir. I just got orders to detain your vehicle. Please stay inside the vehicle. Please turn off the engine and remain here."

Krasniqi smiled benevolently. "Do you know Inspector Marco Petrovic? In your Major Crimes Division? Check with him. He'll see you done right."

Krasniqi was confident. The inspector's palm had been well greased for exactly this reason.

The traffic cop said, "I am under orders from Inspector Petrovic. Please remain in your vehicle."

He walked back to his motorcycle.

The corporal looked at his lieutenant, then cast a glance back toward the rear of the truck.

It was a hell of a cargo to sit with, this close to the embassies of the world.

Jane could hear the police officer speaking outside the truck, but the words were muffled, and she didn't speak the language. She knew they were in a major city because the ambient urban noises had become evident over the past several minutes. She wasn't even sure the man speaking outside the truck was a cop.

But she suspected he was.

Thanks to the phone call she'd made with the last of the charge left in the mobile hidden in Amira's arm cast.

C52

A French long-haul truck driver pulled into a rest stop just shy of the Serbian border. He would have liked to have made it through before dawn, but the demands of his bladder were not to be denied.

He relieved himself and stepped out of the bathroom and found a woman leaning against the cinder block with only her shoulder blades and the sole of one boot touching the rough wall. She was at least five-ten, with pitch-black hair worn down. She was dressed in black canvas trousers with many pockets, like a soldier, and a black T-backed undershirt.

"I need a lift into Serbia," she said, picking French—the truck driver didn't know how she'd tumbled onto his nationality.

He humphed. "Well, I need five hundred euros and a blow job."

She said, "Done," and disconnected herself from the wall by shoving with her foot. She produced a wad of euros and stuffed them into his hand. "Shall we?"

He led her around to the parking area. A bit after five in the morning, and it was mostly empty. As they drew abreast of his big, Russian-made truck-and-trailer rig, he spotted a gangly boy in ripped jeans and a grimy hooded sweatshirt. Also, a wiry man with messy hair and several-days' growth of beard. He, too, wore fatigue pants, boots, and a black T-shirt. He grinned in the manner of congenital idiots and Americans.

The trucker said, "What's this?"

"My lover," the tall woman gestured to the smiling man. "We're running away to Belgrade. Papa doesn't like him."

"Your papa may be on to something there."

"Would another five hundred euros help?" She handed him another wad of money, then reached up for the passenger-side handle and climbed up on the wheel covering. She turned to the smiling man.

"Oh, darling. Our driver would like a blow job. D'you mind?"

The trucker sighed wearily. "*Comédienne ...*"

The St. Nicholas team and Mohamed sat in back, cross-legged among boxes of auto parts. They'd shown the French driver more stacks of euros and felt confident he'd get them across the border.

Mohamed closed his eyes—it was a wonder he'd stayed awake, given the past week of his life. Finnigan, speaking English, nonetheless kept his voice low. "We're too late."

"I know."

"Blowing the comms tower delayed them calling out for help. But as soon as a single one of them drives into range of the next cell tower, they'll call Aleksić, and he'll have the kids killed. Including You-Know-Who's sister."

Fiero knew her partner liked to think out loud to sort the facts in his own head, so she let him prattle on.

"If they had a satphone at the base, they wouldn't even need to get to a cell tower."

She nodded.

The truck hit a bump, and Mohamed's eyes shot open, glaring around. Fight or flight. Finnigan offered him a stick of gum and an easy smile.

They rode in silence. Mohamed's eyes dropped again and he rested his head on one of the boxes.

Finnigan said, "Mission one is to rescue the kids. Mission two is to get the evidence for a conviction."

Fiero closed her eyes and also rested her head back on the box.

"We are not—*not*—going to Belgrade to assassinate Lazar Aleksić," Finnigan spoke softly.

Fiero nodded to the youth half asleep next to them. "Tell him that."

"Okay." Finnigan leaned forward and tapped the kid on the knee. Mohamed raised his head and opened his eyes.

"Translate for me."

Fiero said, "This isn't—"

"Please."

She hesitated, then nodded.

"Mohamed. I'm Michael. This is Katalin."

Fiero translated.

"I'm a police officer. Katalin is a soldier. But the good kind; not like the guys who kidnapped you."

The boy listened to the near-instantaneous translation and nodded. "Can you save Amira? And Jinan?"

Fiero repeated the question in English.

Finnigan kept his eyes locked on the kid. "Maybe. I'm not gonna lie to you; it won't be easy. We'll try as hard as we can. If we don't, we'll arrest the men responsible and we'll make sure they go to prison."

He was speaking to the boy, for sure, but also to his partner.

Mohamed frowned. "If these people hurt my sister, I want them to die."

"Yeah, I get that. Sure. But I'm a policeman and Katalin is a soldier," he repeated. "We can mete out justice, not vengeance. Only God can do that. And God would want us to do our best, and to be true to our calling. You understand?"

Mohamed spoke. After a moment, Fiero said, "Yes, I understand. But I don't like it."

And Finnigan knew she wasn't just translating.

"I know," he said. To them both.

C53

Inspector Marco Petrovic of the Belgrade Police Department's Special Crimes Division believed that the worst ways to wake up were (*a*) with a gun pointed at you, (*b*) with your wife in some other man's bed, and (*c*) with calls from the media.

Possibly, he'd switch *b* and *c*. It was close.

He'd received word from his night watch commanders that the *Irish Times* had called saying one of their freelance journalists had uncovered a plot by Kosovar soldiers to sell underage refugees on the slave market in Belgrade. Worse, the reporter was actually with some of the victims, and some of the smugglers, and reporting in real time from the Serbian capital.

After the *Times* called, Reuters called. Then Al Jazeera. Then Sky News. Then the BBC. The time between each call was diminishing, so that they essentially were tying up every phone line on the night shift of police headquarters.

Petrovic told his officers to stall and lie. He wasn't exactly the Napoleon of media strategies; it was the best option he could come up with at five in the morning.

He dressed and put on his coat and waddled out to the back-yard, digging through his pile of firewood for a sealed sandwich bag and a disposable mobile phone that he wanted his wife never to find. He called his contact at Ragusa Logistics, in the mostly finished office building on Kneza Miloša. He got some wet-be-hind-the-ears junior officer, who was under orders to work with Petrovic whenever he called. After all, Petrovic kept all of the cops away from Lazar Aleksić, and had since the kid arrived on the scene a few years earlier.

"Do you have a truck coming in from Kosovo?" he demanded.

"Ah … yes, sir."

"For the love of Jesus, do you know how much shit is hitting the fan right this second?"

The youth said, "Ah … No sir. No, I … shit, sir?"

"By Joseph and Blessed Mary! Get the truck to your building. Do it now! I'm on my way. Who's in charge there?"

"Lieutenant Krasniqi, sir."

"Have him meet me there. And son …?"

"Sir?"

"Tell your lieutenant that, if he's ever felt a shortage of ass-holes, not to worry. He's about to get himself a brand-new one."

The French trucker dropped the partners and Mohamed off at an Autogrill on the Serbian side, took his money, and resumed his route.

Finnigan spied a couple of guys dressed as highway con-struction workers park a Jeep Wrangler near the children's play structure and head into the restaurant. "That looks juicy."

"I'll explain to Mohamed that the nice police officer likes to steal cars."

Finnigan waggled his finger at Mohamed but spoke to Fiero. "Steal a car for a man, and he'll drive for a day. But teach a man to steal a car, and he'll drive for life."

They drove the Wrangler into Belgrade just as their watches hit 6:00 a.m. Mohamed eyed the big city with fear in his eyes. "We have to find Amira in *this?*"

"We know where she is," Fiero told him and turned to Finnigan. "Remember our friend Agon Llumnica, from France? I found him at the barracks with the refugees."

"Poor dumb bastard," Finnigan said.

"We had a heart-to-heart. He says to say hi." She smiled. "He said the front doors of the office tower are chained, and the only access is through the parking garage. The elevators are controlled by soldiers on the penthouse level."

Finnigan nodded. They both knew that the lieutenant and his three hostages had at least an hour head start on them by now. The chances of getting to the hostages in time—in that tower— were diminishing quickly.

He pulled the Jeep off the highway and headed toward the office tower, Fiero riding shotgun, and Mohamed in back.

"Slowly," she said. "I want to see how many guards they—"

"Amira!"

Mohamed almost ripped open the rear door and leaped out of the moving vehicle. Fiero restrained him.

A BMW X5 sat outside the Ragusa Logistics building with police flashers embedded in the grille, the engine running. Three men stood around the vehicle; two who looked like soldiers were being yelled at by an obese civilian with a magnificent mustache. In the back of the SUV, three young people sat shoulder-to-shoulder: a boy and two girls.

"It's Amira and Jane! You found them!"

Finnigan said, "Shhhh ..." and kept rolling.

Fiero watched the scene as they drove past. The big man with the medicine-ball belly had a finger in the face of the lead soldier, chewing him out. The three Middle Eastern youths sat in the back of the SUV, looking petrified. The few pedestrians out at that hour were giving the melee a wide berth.

"How the hell did we make up so much time?" Finnigan wondered, hitting his turn indicator and drifting to his left.

"No idea. But gift horses ..."

"So, Aleksić has bent cops. That was predictable." He pulled into an alley perpendicular with the main drag. He knew this alley well; he'd taken a baseball bat to two soldiers here, not long ago.

"We have to go back!" Mohamed wailed.

"We will," Fiero calmed him. "Mohamed, we have to do this smart. Yes? Those men have guns, and they have your sister."

The boy was all but bouncing in his seat.

Finnigan took the next left, routing them back in the direction they'd come. The next alley over would dump out onto Kneza Miloša again. Finnigan said, "Translate, will you?"

He took the next left and slowed to a halt.

"Kid, climb out here. Run up to that corner, okay? There could be more bad guys, and I need you to alert us if you see them. Here ..." He drew his cell and held it over his shoulder. Mohamed reached for it. "Speed Dial Number One is Katalin. You know how to use it?"

"Of course," he told the woman translating.

"Good. Go."

He climbed out and dashed, all knees and elbows, toward the street ahead of them.

"Good kid," Finnigan said, and threw the Jeep into gear. They slow-rolled forward.

"The garage door's closed," Fiero said.

"They gotta get the kids inside."

"Last time we passed by here, we saw a ramp leading to the basement."

Fiero smiled. "Gravity's our friend."

"Roll cages on those BMWs are sweet."

"Shall we?"

Fiero reached for her door handle and climbed out of the car.

Finnigan adjusted his seat belt.

54

Lt. Akil Krasniqi stood his ground, unwilling to capitulate to the crooked head of the Belgrade Police Department's Major Crimes Unit. "I understand, sir, but—"

"Half of the fucking journalists on earth are screeching at us for answers, Lieutenant! The *New York Times*! The London *Times*! The *Washington Post*!" The man vibrated, his jowls and belly shaking. "The fucking *Montreal*-fucking-*Gazette*! All because you idiots captured a fucking journalist!"

Inspector Petrovic pointed a nicotine-yellowed finger back at his BMW X5 and the three heads barely visible behind the seatbacks.

"Get rid of them, Lieutenant! Don't do it in Belgrade, and don't do it in Serbia. Take your mongrels back to Kosovo and cook them, for all I care! Then tell Major Basha that our deal is being renegotiated! Am I making myself clear, Lieutenant?"

Krasniqi saw no advantage in continuing the argument, here on the pavement, with the sun rising and the traffic picking up. He had every intention of contacting Major Basha as soon as he could get this confrontation inside the building and off the street.

Krasniqi had heard from KSF Operating Base Šar, of course. He knew that armed insurgents had stolen his other sixteen refugees. According to Corporal Agon Llumnica, the insurgents represented another army unit that wanted in on their profits. That meant any deal cut with the Belgrade Police was now suspect. It was time, the lieutenant thought, for their forces to regroup and reconsider their options. That meant killing everyone currently connected to their operation: the stolen kids, the crooked cops—even Lazar Aleksić.

"Take them into the garage," he told the inspector, avoiding the use of *sir* or the man's title. "We'll transfer them to our vehicle." He drew his walkie-talkie. "Open the door."

The garage door began rolling upward on well-oiled tracks.

Inspector Petrovic marched around to the passenger side of the BMW and damn near sprang the door hinges before climbing in, the shocks wobbling under his girth. He growled at his driver. "Get them inside."

The driver checked to see that the garage door was sufficiently high, then put the car into gear. He turned ninety degrees, the front tires reaching the lip of the ramp. The BMW's nose dipped.

Finnigan swerved the stolen Wrangler out of the morning traffic on Kneza Miloša and slammed into the rear of the Beemer.

Petrovic, the driver, Jane Koury, Amira, and the Afghan boy—everyone's head snapped back. Finnigan gunned it, and the two cars began rolling down the concrete ramp.

Petrovic's driver screamed and stomped on the brakes. The BMW began to glide sideways, relative to the ramp.

Finnigan tapped his own brakes, creating a little air between them. As the left side of the BMW came around, he punched it again, slamming back into the car, which now screeched sideways down the ramp, tires belching blue smoke. Finnigan saw the driver and the children in back, screaming in shock.

The BMW, now acting like a snowplow in front of the Jeep, rumbled downhill, tires bursting, rims screeching, and slammed sideways into a support pillar.

Up top, Lieutenant Krasniqi and his corporal stood on the sidewalk, gawking, shocked. Neither even noticed as Fiero strolled up the sidewalk toward them. Krasniqi drew his gun and began moving downhill.

As she drew abreast of the corporal, Fiero swung her elbow and clocked him in the temple. The man's eyes rolled up in his skull. Before he could fall, she grabbed him by the lapels and hip-checked him down the ramp. His body bowled into the back of Krasniqi's heels like they were tenpins. The lieutenant had been picking up speed and was off-balance to begin with. He stumbled, falling, trying to arrest his impact by letting go of his sidearm. But he was too late, and his wrist broke badly as he hit the concrete.

In the Jeep, Finnigan coughed talcum and shoved away the deflated airbag. Having rolled down all the windows prior to hitting the SUV, he undid his seatbelt and climbed out through his window, sliding onto the crumpled hood of the Jeep and bracing his boots on either side of the busted-out driver's window. He reached through, between his own legs, and hauled out the police driver. The man's head lolled. Finnigan clocked him once, just to be sure, and dumped him over the side of the Jeep's hood. The man slid over the edge but one foot got tangled in his seatbelt, and he hung off the side like a landed fish.

The fat man with the walrus mustache leaned forward, blood pouring out of his nose, his eyes closed.

In back, the children looked petrified but largely unhurt. *The BMW is a marvel of safety*, Finnigan thought.

He glanced back and saw Fiero march down the ramp, stepping over two unconscious soldiers.

He looked around. The garage could hold a hundred cars,

maybe, but today housed only a handful of hot, expensive, and pristinely washed cars, including a Jag and a gold Hummer. Somebody once said that crime doesn't pay. Finnigan thought that person was full of shit.

Fiero reached the bottom of the ramp and drew her SIG.

A soldier came running from the direction of the elevators, and she shot him once in the chest. The man stumbled, falling forward. He wore body armor but a .45 is a .45, and the hydrostatic shock of the hit likely broke some ribs. She looked back the way they'd come. No pedestrians had stopped. Traffic on Kneza Miloša continued as if nothing had happened.

A moment later, Mohamed's expressive face appeared at the garage door.

Fiero whistled and signaled him down.

She turned and marched over the guy she'd shot, stopping long enough to clock him behind the ear with the butt of her gun. She rose and headed to the three-car elevator bank. She found the controls for the garage door and hit DOWN.

Mohamed, still near the top of the ramp, stood with his eyes and mouth forming an almost perfect circle. Finnigan could guess what he was thinking: *Muslim women in Europe aren't what I expected!*

But then the sight of Amira climbing out of the BMW caught the boy's eyes, and he sprinted downhill.

Jane Koury climbed out as well as she could with her wrists cuffed behind her back. So did the Afghan boy who'd been taken with them.

Finnigan retrieved a handcuff key from the cop he'd KO'd and got the three refugees freed. Mohamed, Amira, and Jane hugged and wept. There was much crying and rapid-fire Arabic, so Finnigan backed off the scrum.

Fiero came his way. "Elevator's locked out, as we were told."

Finnigan jutted his chin at the lieutenant, halfway up the

ramp, who held his broken wrist and rocked onto his back, moaning. "Think he'll help?"

"We can ask nice."

Jane broke free of the group hugs and came to them. Tears streamed down her grubby face, and her hair was askew. She spoke English. "Excuse me, please. Who are you?"

Finnigan produced a packet of Kleenex from his cargo pocket and handed it to her. "St. Nicholas Salvage & Wrecking."

She blew her nose. "I don't even know what that means. I'm Jane Koury. I'm a reporter for … I'm an independent reporter. You're Americans?"

Fiero said, "He is," and headed uphill toward Lieutenant Krasniqi.

"I can't thank you enough. These kids, they're my responsibility. I was trying to get them to safety." She started crying again.

"And you did, kiddo. Give us a bump." Finnigan put his fist out, knuckles forward. She burst into a hybrid sob-laugh and reached up to tap her knuckles against his.

She produced a cheap flip phone. "I called my editor at the *Irish Times*. I told them where we were; what was happening. I think that's why the police got involved here."

"We were wondering who bought us the time to catch up."

"Catch up?"

"We were at the base in Kosovo. We got the other sixteen kids out."

Jane started crying into the wad of Kleenex again.

Finnigan grinned at her. "You are one badass reporter, Jane Koury."

C55

Guns N' Roses woke Lazar Aleksić up at shortly after six. *Welcome to the Jungle* ... In truth, he'd slept fitfully throughout the night, anxious for the experience that his partnership with Major Driton Basha would bring him today.

He thought back now to the Epiphany of the Stripper. Lazar called it that, and he thought it rather clever. He remembered the stacked blonde whom he'd brought home from Club Obsidian. He remembered all the things he'd done to her, and ordered her to do. The slut had performed her role admirably. But in truth, a couple dozen whores had performed as well or better since Lazar got his business up and running. The whores had been there when he sold weed. When he'd sold coke and heroin. And when he'd found the network of buyers for the filth. As long as Lazar Aleksić was young, handsome, and rich, he'd have all the whores he needed.

But none of that had given him the experience of the Epiphany of the Stripper. That look in her eyes as she'd sidled up to

Major Basha, all slink and kink. But everything about her had changed as Basha shoved the ice pick into her heart.

The widening of her eyes—all hookers are taught to do that, of course, at the height of passion. But not like this. The sudden intake of breath—they're taught to do that, too. The gasp, the shudder. The well-choreographed but also well-trod path of synthetic emotion. None of it, none of it, held a candle to that moment. The ice pick. The death. The truth of it.

Lazar was hard, anticipating the moment.

Axl Rose screamed from his speakers, and Lazar leapt out of bed. It was Basha—who else ever touched his sound system? He pulled blue jeans up his long legs and over his narrow hips. He crossed the room to his gym bag, unzipped it fully and slowly from one end to the other. He pulled out the new ice pick his posse had shoplifted from the restaurant supply store. It was almost ten inches long, including the black anodized aluminum handle. The spindle itself was more than four inches in length and a quarter inch in diameter. It smelled just a little of linseed oil. It was pristine. It would not stay so for long.

Welcome to the jungle.

Barefoot, bare-chested, Lazar strutted out into the living room of the penthouse suite.

The very first person he saw was a refugee girl, maybe eighteen or twenty. She wore grubby clothes and her hair was a mess. She also carried a smart phone, held up in both hands, horizontal, as if she were taking a picture or a video.

Lazar started to smile, then noticed the lieutenant who sometimes led his security detail was standing by the butterscotch couch, stiffly, almost at attention. His nose was broken, his upper lip split, and yellow half-moons were forming under both eyes.

He heard the iPhone in the refugee girl's hands. She'd snapped a picture of him.

How weird.

"That's a good angle."

Lazar's lusty tunnel vision dissipated. He saw the speaker—a woman, maybe five-ten, dark and slender, wearing all black and with a pistol holster strapped low on her long right thigh. It was a big holster for a big gun, but that thigh seemed to go on for miles. Her T-shirt showed the shadows under her clavicles and outlined small breasts and a long, straight torso.

He spotted another man—wavy hair, several days' beard, also wearing all black, but with a cocky grin.

Two Arabic boys and an Arabic girl, all in filthy, ripped clothes, stared sullenly at him.

The lieutenant still hadn't moved, although blood dripped off his chin.

Lazar's hard-on faltered.

The wavy-haired man lowered the volume on Lazar's sound system. He grinned, all lopsided and overly friendly. He moved with the rolling gait of a sailor.

He nodded to Lazar's right hand. To the ice pick. "What's this?"

The refugee girl snapped another photo of him.

"Who … what the fuck …" Lazar tried to catch up to events, his brain vapor-locked.

"This yours?" the man said, and Lazar realized he was American. "What is that? Is that an ice pick? You got ice in here? You're, what? Making daiquiris?"

Lazar looked around. The bleeding lieutenant, the tall woman with the cowboy holster, the refugee kids, the girl shooting photos. He looked toward the elevator and saw a pair of boots and trousers; someone down and not moving.

"Who the fuck are you?" He winced as his voice broke.

"Us?" the American asked. "Who're you?"

Lazar felt both fear and anger, but subdued by a blend of

power that came from wealth and youth and privilege—the jet fuel that had propelled every encounter in his life. And this guy was asking who *he* was?

"I am Lazar Aleksić! This is my place! What the fuck are you doing here?"

The tall woman turned to the girl with the camera. "Get it?"

She nodded. "Got it."

Lazar thought: *Everyone just smiled.*

But … that couldn't be right.

The bleeding lieutenant hadn't smiled. Nor had the trio of quiet, glaring refugees. The girl with the camera wasn't smiling. And the American had never stopped grinning like a fool.

So when Lazar's brain registered *everyone just smiled*, what it meant was, *the tall woman just smiled.*

The smile of a predator.

The smile of fang and claw.

Welcome to the jungle.

C56

St. Nicholas told Aleksić they wanted Driton Basha.

Lazar gave them Basha. He gave them routes and schedules and the names of buyers. To hell with Basha. Lazar Aleksić could buy a hundred Bashas. And his father would fix this problem easily enough. They want Driton Basha? Lazar would add ribbons, bows, and a gift receipt.

Finnigan asked for access to Lazar's computer. But that was a bridge too far. That was unthinkable. The evidence on his computer would be more than even his father could sweep under a rug. Access to his computer? Now it was Lazar's turn to smile. "Fuck you, bitch! No way."

Finnigan turned to Fiero. "Did he just call me *bitch*?"

"Seems that way." She smiled, turned to Lt. Akil Krasniqi, who was dripping blood on the hardwood floor of Lazar's penthouse. "You," she nudged Krasniqi forward. "In the bedroom."

She turned to Lazar. "Join us, would you?"

She led both men into the bedroom and slid shut the rolling door in their wake.

Jane turned to Finnigan. "What's she doing?"

"Don't worry about it." He made eye contact with the Afghan kid. "English?"

The kid blinked at him.

Jane said, "I think he's Afghan. Poor thing."

"Your media friends are coming?"

"The *Irish Times* reached out to every reporter, correspondent, and freelancer in the region. They're on their way. We can—"

A strangled cry erupted, low and keening, from the bedroom. "What was that?"

"Don't worry about it." Finnigan pointed to the Afghan kid. "Call your buddies and see if we can get someone here who speaks … whatever. Pashto …?"

"Dari," Jane said. "Sure. Good idea." She switched Fiero's phone from camera mode and dialed.

The door to the bedroom slid open. Fiero escorted Lazar Aleksić, who walked stiffly—and a little unevenly, like a drunk trying desperately to look sober. He moved directly to his laptop computer and input codes to wake it up.

He looked unhurt, but as scared as a human can be and still function.

Lieutenant Krasniqi did not emerge.

Fiero nodded to Finnigan. There was … *something*, in her eyes. In the languid movement of her neck and shoulders. Something liquid. And feral.

Jane said, "What happened to—"

Fiero retreated into the bedroom, closed the door behind her. Finnigan said, "Don't worry about it."

The *Irish Times* got the exclusive and a twenty-minute head start. Reuters was the first wire service to pick up the story, which meant every news outlet on earth had it within an hour, and hundreds of them led with it.

It was too good a story not to lead with: the Serbian sex-trafficker, Lazar Aleksić; his connection to a specific unit of the Kosovo Security Force; and of course, his father, Miloš Aleksić, director for the Levant Crisis Group of the United Nations High Commission for Refugees.

Television crews circled the Ragusa Logistics building on Kneza Miloša in Belgrade. Other crews were tipped off to sixteen rescued children being handed over to the US embassy in Sarajevo, Bosnia. Those children told a tale of a massive Viking with an amazing beard, who swept in to rescue them with his band of pirates. When asked, some of the children said he called himself St. Nick. The media chalked that up to the children's post-traumatic stress.

Still other reporters made a beeline north to the Brussels and Paris offices of the UNHCR and its Levant Group. Public information officers issued a couple dozen no-comments, saying UN officials had no knowledge of the wild stories coming out of the former Yugoslavia.

Director Miloš Aleksić was unavailable for comment.

The rule was St. Nicholas Salvage & Wrecking never, ever contacted Judge Hélene Betancourt. The partners didn't have her telephone number or her private email address. They'd never left any electronic trail connecting their illegal and unsavory business with the senior-most jurist of the International Criminal Court.

Thomas Shannon Greyson served as their single point of contact.

Shan, who'd been tasked with getting the partners and the rescued children over the Serbian border, but who hadn't. And who, now, wasn't responding to phone calls, emails, or texts.

Fiero tried yet again as Finnigan helped himself to a bottle of Lazar Aleksić's Champagne. He said, "Still no word?" and poured two flutes.

"The young lieutenant told me something interesting," she whispered. "Aleksić, too. Tell you on our way out."

Fiero stepped to the window and peered down at the pack of reporters on Belgrade's main avenue. She could just barely make out the parliament building from up here. She accepted the glass and sipped.

She turned to Jane. "You'll leave us out of it?"

The British girl had showered—for the first time in over a week—but had no alternative clothes to wear. With her face and hair clean, she looked closer to twenty-five than eighteen. And so far, the adrenaline was doing a fine job of fighting off her fatigue.

"You're part of the story."

"But you owe us," Fiero said. And not in a bargaining tone; just stating a fact.

Jane peered over at the Bakour siblings, who were deep in conversation on the buttery sofa. The Afghan boy sat near them.

"All right," Jane said.

Finnigan and Fiero nodded to each other and finished their Champagne. "We're going to the garage," Fiero said. "Once we're down, direct the car to the lobby. I've … asked the lieutenant to open the doors. Remember, you can only control the elevators from up here, so don't go down to greet everyone."

Jane said, "I won't."

The partners gathered their stuff. Fiero said, "Keep my phone." They had more phones onboard their plane. And she'd wiped it of any incriminating evidence.

Jane stepped into their path before they reached the elevators and threw a hug around Fiero's shoulders, up on her toes, squeezing her tight. Fiero froze, eyes on Finnigan, who rolled his eyes behind Jane's back. Katalin Fiero was *not a hugger* to the same degree that she was *not a fire truck*.

Fiero awkwardly patted the girl on the shoulder and waited to be disengaged.

"God! Thank you!"

"You're welcome."

Fiero disengaged and knelt before the Bakour siblings. She offered her hand to Mohamed, who shook, his face serious and oh so grown-up.

"You did well. Your parents will get here, and they'll be very proud."

"Actually," Jane said, disengaging her hug from Finnigan. "I just spoke to their parents. They made it into Greece. Reuters is chartering them a plane. They'll be here today."

She said it again, in Arabic. The siblings looked stunned.

Finnigan and Fiero moved to the elevator bank and called up one of the cars. As it rose, Jane came to them.

"Our deal is for today. But once I've slept for a couple of weeks, and eaten a lot of food, and slept some more, I am going to find out who you are. And I'm going to tell the world what you did here today."

Fiero studied the girl a moment, then shrugged and turned toward the elevator.

"Publicity is the last thing we want," Finnigan said. "It'd be bad for business."

"But you're heroes!"

"It's your call. But do you really wanna make an enemy of her?"

Jane turned and studied the tall Spaniard by the elevator. She remembered the sudden noises she'd heard in the bedroom, remembered the shock and fear in the eyes of Aleksić.

She turned to Finnigan. "Okay. Good luck."

On the way down to the garage, Fiero said, "Krasniqi, the lieutenant. I asked about Driton Basha. He said the major went to The Hague on behest of the Aleksić family."

"Basha knows Miloš? The old man?"

"When we talked in the bedroom, Lazar gave up his father. The Levant Group director has been perfectly aware of his son's human-trafficking operation."

Finnigan snorted. "Figures."

"There's more. Lazar said his family have come to understand that Judge Betancourt is the true threat. They blame her for our messing about with their mission in France and with the rescue of the refugees. Lazar said the family considers Judge Betancourt to be a mortal enemy of the Slavic people and of Serbians and Kosovars."

The elevator reached the garage level. Finnigan ran a hand through his messy hair. "Well, crap."

Down in the garage, the two corrupt cops noticed the knot of reporters gathering topside. They were more concerned with getting out of the building unnoticed than arresting the guy who'd smashed into their BMW. Besides, a crew of three workers in overalls had entered the garage on board a garbage truck that apparently had access to the garage door code. The crew parked the behemoth well away from the classic cars, and the smash-up of the BMW and Jeep at the bottom of the ramp. The workers climbed out and stood around their truck, leaving a good distance between themselves and the disgruntled cops, who eventually walked up the ramp and snuck past the reporters.

When Finnigan and Fiero got to the garage, they walked over to the three garbage workers and exchanged hugs and handshakes. "Sally," Finnigan said, "Mercer, Gian."

The tall redhead, Sally, rested both forearms over Finnigan's shoulders, as if they were about to slow dance. "I've always had a thing for Scottish guys."

"I'm Irish."

She shrugged. "In the ballpark."

Fiero smiled. "We are done upstairs."

The members of the Black Harts nodded. The crew of thieves had agreed to provide 24-7 surveillance of the Ragusa Logistics building with the understanding that once St. Nicholas was done, they could steal whatever they could get their hands on.

"Reporters are gathering in the penthouse," Finnigan said, as Fiero wandered over to the classic cars. Her plan was simple: steal Lazar Aleksić's Jaguar. Why the hell not?

"Give 'em an hour," he continued. "When they clear out, the place is yours. The shit-heel who owns this building is going to do time for trafficking underage children. And the guy's stinking rich. Anything you take, he can't hawk later to pay for his defense. So, live large."

"That," said Sally, the brassy American, "is most definitely in our wheelhouse." She tousled his wavy hair. "See ya."

Finnigan climbed into the Jag and Fiero revved the engine. The tires squealed as she burst up the ramp and swerved onto Kneza Miloša, accompanied by angry honking. "Here," Finnigan said, rummaging through Lazar's glove box and coming up with a pair of designer sunglasses.

She slipped them on. "Major Basha travels to The Hague, and now Shan isn't answering his phone or email."

"Yeah. And if he's in trouble, the judge is, too."

"Of course." She cut into oncoming traffic to smoke a Nissan, then swerved back into her lane. She caught the signs for the freeway, for the westbound routes to Bosnia and Herzegovina, and to Croatia. And of course, to Lachlan Sumner and their de Havilland. "Why else go after Shan? All he is, is a conduit to Betancourt."

"We gotta get to the Netherlands if we've got any hope of saving them."

She hit the on-ramp doing seventy. "Or avenging them."

C57

Two of the Kosovar soldiers took a break in the spacious kitchen of the flying saucer–shaped house overlooking the North Sea. The boss kept Finnish vodka in the sub-zero freezer, and one of the soldiers—a short, overly muscled bulldog of a man—liked to grab a shot between shifts. The younger, slimmer soldier thought that that was a mistake; he didn't want to be caught lifting booze from the boss. They'd been told to help themselves to his coffee maker or the bottles of still and sparkling water in the fridge. Going for his vodka was pushing their luck, the younger soldier said.

"Pussy," the bulldog replied.

Shortly after they hit the kitchen that morning, Miloš Aleksić strode in with a mobile phone against his ear, looking harried. His salt-and-pepper hair, usually pristine and adhered in place with military precision, stuck up in back and exposed more of his pink scalp than he preferred. The bags under his eyes had turned a deep eggplant, contrasting with the rest of his exposed skin, which had taken on the pallor of undercooked chicken.

"But I *explained* it to you," Miloš pleaded in a tone that suggested he'd made the exact same point a few dozen times. "The media have it *completely* wrong! Couldn't be further from the truth. If I were being *perfectly* honest with you here, I have to say, some of these chaps might be paid according to the *distance* they put between the *facts* on the ground, as it were, and the published version! If you follow."

Miloš walked to the sub-zero, opened it, and retrieved the bottle of Koskenkorva. The soldiers made eye contact. They stayed near the coffee maker.

Marija Aleksić, the lady of the house, entered carrying a vase with a spray of tulips. She poured a little water into the vase and set it on the speckled marble countertop and then did something with her fingertips designed to rearrange the flowers in some manner that escaped the two security men.

"No … yes, see, that's *precisely* the kind of nonsense I mean!" Miloš emphasized into his phone, throwing ice into a tumbler and splashing vodka into it. "I mean, honestly, George! This story is phantasm! It's a work of *fiction*!"

He kept pouring. Marija Aleksić kept batting the tulips the way one might bop soap bubbles with an upturned palm, gingerly, to keep them afloat but intact.

"Preposterous! I mean, *simply* absurd … Yes, I quite agree. Yes … well, take *my* word for … Hmm? Of course! Of course! Thank you … No, thank you!"

He looked at the phone in order to find the END CALL button. He took a significant pull from the glass, thought about it a moment, and added two more fingers from the bottle.

He noticed the soldiers, standing uncomfortably around the coffee machine. "What in God's name are you doing here?"

Marija juggled the blooms in the vase. "They are taking a break, dear. Came in for a cup of coffee. Everyone needs a break.

Workers work best with a bit of relaxation. My father always said so, and he ran a tight ship, I dare say. A *tight* ship."

The soldiers tried smiling. Miloš Aleksić sipped vodka and stared dourly at them. They got the impression that, despite the early hour, this wasn't his first foray into the booze.

"Quite. Well, back at it," he said. He might have been talking about the security men or about his own efforts. His mobile vibrated.

"Ernest? God, yes … Thank you for *all* you … I know. Incredible! *Entirely* unprecedented …"

He stormed out.

Mrs. Aleksić dabbed at the flowers a few more times. She wore a pale-blue twin set with a simple strand of pearls and matching earrings. Her hairdresser had come to the house earlier that morning, and the security guys could smell the cloud of hairspray. As her husband's tirade faded with distance, she turned to the soldiers. Her face lost a little of the blandness she wore like a mask around her husband.

"Mr. Greyson?"

The bulldog shrugged. "Tough guy, madam. Tougher than you'd expect from a poofter like that. But he'll talk. Everyone does. Everyone."

Something changed in her visage; another persona beneath the plump and addled society matron. She said, "We require Mr. Greyson's knowledge of his employer and her security system. You understand this."

"Don't worry. We understand. He'll break."

She listened to her husband extolling yet another old friend over the phone. She tilted her head, studied the tulips a bit.

"See that he does."

They had started with his testicles, though Shan barely remembered that. At the time, the pain had been all he knew. But so much pain had passed since then, it was hard to keep it all straight.

Shan lay on his side, on the floor of a subbasement of the flying saucer house by the sea. He stank of sweat and urine and feces. One eye had swollen shut, and blood oozed from his jagged gum line, where teeth had been removed with pliers. At some level, Shan hated the stench as much as the pain; maybe more. He was an Englishman, a fair-haired son of Eton and Oxford. One does not smell bad. It simply isn't done.

The thought made him smile, and smiling cracked open his split lip.

The stench wasn't all bad. As horrible as the smell of piss and shit, it had masked some of the smell of cooked flesh when the soldiers brought out the acetylene torch.

C58

The ground floor offices of the International Criminal Court were open to the public, and hundreds of lawyers, clerks, civilians, and journalists wandered its halls each day. The judge's chambers were upstairs, and there, the court didn't skimp on security. The teams they hired came directly from the British SAS and the Vatican's Swiss Guard. Judges don't get gunned down in some parts of the world, but they definitely do in others. And to date, no judge of the ICC had been lost to a gunman or a suicide bomber.

The detail assigned to Senior Judge Hélene Betancourt had no intention of breaking that streak.

As Betancourt stepped gingerly into the ground-floor corridor, two men moved into position, as did two men near the entrance of the court, and the monitoring team stationed in an outbuilding, keeping track of each justice. Betancourt had dined with another judge in the so-called Fireplace Room, a ground-floor dining room dedicated to the justices and their guests.

As they chatted, Fiero strode up wearing sky-high heels,

a black suit, and stylishly framed glasses. Her hair was up in a chignon, and she carried a Gucci attaché case. She asked one of the guards in a surprisingly loud voice, "Can you tell me how to get to Saint Nicholas?"

The guard looked perplexed. "To where?"

Betancourt excused herself from her fellow jurist and, with the aid of the cane, came abreast of the hulking guards. "Ask the young woman to come along to my chambers, please."

The nearest guard blinked. He was a thickset man with a shaved skull, a military mustache, and a fine web of scar tissue around his eyes. "Ma'am?"

"We have city maps, don't we?"

Around the corner from Hélene Betancourt's chambers, Fiero pointed to Finnigan, leaning against a water cooler. "May my colleague join us?"

As the guard began to say no, Judge Betancourt said, "Of course." She moved slowly, thanks to a recently broken hip. The guards had to walk at a glacial pace to keep astride her, as did Fiero. The guards looked none too happy about the visitors.

In the antechamber, Betancourt stopped to speak to her security detail, sotto voce. Finnigan and Fiero stayed well back until the jurist nodded toward her office. She ushered them in; the unhappy guards stayed outside.

The space was massive and ornate, with twenty-foot-high windows that looked out on a cool, lush forest and, beyond that, the iron-gray North Sea. The judge favored antiques and dark hardwoods. Her picture frames surrounded original watercolors and pencil sketches rather than photos of herself with famous people.

Fiero slipped off her eyeglasses. "We'd hoped that Shan had

mentioned the name of our organization to you. We couldn't think of another way to get to you."

Betancourt moved slowly around her massive, messy desk. She settled her cane within easy reach and eased herself into her chair. "We had agreed to keep a safe distance between us. Shan always praised the work you do, and I often asked for details, but he insisted on keeping you shrouded."

Finnigan stepped forward. "Michael Patrick Finnigan. This is Katalin Fiero Dahar."

Fiero checked the office windows, standing at an oblique angle—observing, not observed from without. "Shan was supposed to get us out of Kosovo, but he didn't show. We've been unable to raise him since."

"Nor I," the judge said. "The same for his driver, who served as his bodyguard. Two nights ago, Shan received an invitation to meet with Miloš Aleksić to talk about the refugee crisis."

"At night," Finnigan repeated.

The judge lifted one palm off her green desk blotter, rotating at the wrist. Her hand fell horizontal again—the equivalent of a shrug for a person with extreme back pain.

Fiero noted the bulletproof and explosion-proof glass in the window. "Miloš Aleksić."

Finnigan spoke directly to the judge. "You've seen some of the details against the kid, Lazar. He's in this up to his neck. So's his dad."

"I likely won't be able to touch Miloš," she said. "There is very little chance that prosecutors will even bring charges against him. The man has too many friends in too powerful of positions. Oh, he'll likely have to resign, thanks to the scandal. But that's all."

"He'll retire." Fiero addressed the window. "Get a job running a bank, or an international nonprofit."

"Yes, likely."

Finnigan played it through. "So the son is going to prison forever, but the old man's likely okay."

"Mr. Finnigan, do you think that whoever has Shan will trade him for Lazar Aleksić? Is that why he's missing?"

"Nope. Wish it were that simple. But Shan's not the target, ma'am. You are. They grabbed him to get to you."

Fiero turned from the window. "I … *chatted* with Lazar Aleksić in Belgrade. Also to one of the Kosovar lieutenants in charge of the trafficking operation. They told me they blame you. For everything."

Judge Betancourt blinked behind her enormous eyeglasses. "Oh, dear."

"They blame you for the sentencing of the war criminals following the Yugoslavian civil war and the *ethnic cleansing* campaigns in Bosnia and Herzegovina. They blame you for the harsh sentencing of former high government officials. And they blame you for what we've been doing—for destroying their human-trafficking operation. They blame it all on you."

"I see." The jurist nodded ponderously. "And … by *they*, you mean …"

"Miloš Aleksić, ma'am," Finnigan said. "And Major Driton Basha, who's the muscle behind all this. They want payback. They're gonna target you."

"And Shan?"

"Shan's only important as a link to you, ma'am. He's not a prosecutor. He didn't sentence anyone. And he didn't drop the hammer on the trafficking operation out of Kosovo. So if they've got him, we figure it's to get to you."

"My security detail is among the finest in the world."

"Yes," Fiero said. "And Shan knows exactly how they work. He knows protocol and procedure. He knows how to slip people in to see you and how to keep people out."

"Ah." The judge nodded, eyes watery and pale behind her thick lenses. "So, ultimately, you think I'm in danger. And Shan is beyond saving?"

Finnigan said, "I'm sorry. Miloš Aleksić is no idiot. They're not planning on holding Shan for a year or more, to force you to come up with a not-guilty verdict. This isn't a hostage situation. Aleksić needed him to get to you."

She said, "I see. But again, I have security people. I have so many I cannot keep track of their names. If you wish to join my protection detail, I could talk to—"

But she stopped as the partners exchanged glances. She realized that Finnigan looked more than a little uneasy.

The judge said, simply, "Ah."

Fiero said, "We don't want to step between you and the men who are after you. We want to eliminate them before they get the chance to act."

"I cannot sanction violence against—"

"Your Honor," she cut in. "Respectfully, you've never sanctioned anything we do."

Finnigan sat, elbows on his knees, hands clasped, facing the jurist, looking her right in the eye. Waiting.

Fiero leaned back against the wall, arms folded under her breasts, the stiletto heel of one shoe up against the wallpaper. Waiting.

They neither wanted nor needed the judge to sanction what came next.

They just needed her to say she wouldn't interfere.

The room was quiet for a time. The security panes kept out ambient noise. An antique grandfather clock tocked. The sun shone through the window, dappling the well-trod old rugs.

The partners waited.

"Saint Nicholas," the judge said, addressing her green blotter and her gnarled hand with its translucent skin. "He was a Turk. The

Bishop of … Myra, I believe? Fourth Century. Long before he took on the personification of Christmas, he was the patron saint of merchants and brewers; of pawnbrokers and archers; and of thieves."

Finnigan turned in his chair and smiled back at Fiero, who shook her head and smiled, too. Judge Hélene Betancourt was the first person they'd met who connected the name of the company to its origin.

Fiero said, "The patron saint of the necessary. That's right."

The judge gingerly removed her glasses. Without them, she was blind.

Like justice.

She said, "The necessary."

Fiero said, "That's right."

The judge slid her glasses back on. "Do what you must."

C59

Major Driton Basha stood in the den of Miloš Aleksić's North Sea Coast home, a tumbler of scotch in his hand. He wore a raincoat because he always assumed it would be raining in the Netherlands. It wasn't.

The diplomat's huge desktop computer monitor displayed live coverage of the Belgrade crisis, courtesy of Sky News. The images flowed one into another …

- Lazar Aleksić, shirtless, barefoot, and handcuffed, being escorted by police toward a cruiser. His three-hundred-dollar haircut with its red-blond highlights made him look venal, young, and ridiculously wealthy. No crime lord, he—more Justin Bieber than Whitey Bulger.

- The young British journalist who'd apparently been working undercover to infiltrate the trafficking network. She'd appeared on every news show in America and Europe over the past forty-eight hours, the hero of the day and the media's newest sensation.

- The three young, innocent, and put-upon refugees rescued from Ragusa Logistics in Belgrade, with their big eyes and victimized demeanor. His hatred for them flared white-hot. Their older brothers and their fathers were doubtless radicalized Muslims, as they themselves one day would be. They fooled the world at large, but not Basha.

- The sixteen refugees mysteriously delivered to the American embassy—and the American media—in Sarajevo.

- The harsh response from the prime minister of the Republic of Kosovo in Pristina, condemning Basha's unit and naming the major himself. Basha's mug shot—his proud service ID photo—had appeared countless times on Sky News and, he supposed, the other networks.

- The image of KSF regulars taking command of Operating Base Šar, while military police arrested Basha's own people and herded them into a prison truck.

- Still photos and archival video of Miloš Aleksić, director of the Levant Group of the UN High Commission for Refugees. The photo of Miloš looking regal, rich, and untouchable, was accompanied by his written statement, denying any knowledge of the alleged trafficking scandal, and his decision—his *principled* decision—to step down temporarily from the Levant Group. The man in the photo, and in the video footage, contrasted markedly to the unconscious drunk who sprawled, fully dressed, across his bed, on the upper floor of this very house.

The Sky News images began their carousel of shame yet again. Basha blinked, wondering if he were seeing them for the fourth or fifth time. His wrist cramped, and he glanced down to notice the tumbler of scotch and melted ice water in his hand. He didn't remember pouring the drink; he hadn't tasted it. He stepped aside and set it down on a credenza. The glass and the liquor were room temperature.

Marija Aleksić spoke from behind him. "These are trying times, Major."

He spun, surprised. She wore a pale-purple cardigan with a carved ivory silhouette stickpin and a long skirt over sensible shoes. Her hair was perfectly coiffed. Basha stared at her as if she'd sprouted stone wings.

"Trying times?" His voice dripped with incredulity.

She studied Sky News on the desktop monitor for a moment, then turned to him. "Yes."

Basha couldn't help himself—he barked the broken-glass laugh of a man on the edge of a breakdown. "Jesus. *Trying?*"

She watched him a moment. She said, "You are an excellent soldier, Driton."

The segue surprised him. "I … ah, thank you."

"This is a time for strength. For conviction. I'm counting on you."

"I don't see what we—"

"Driton." She didn't raise her voice, didn't show any overt emotion. "General Tito was warned, time and time again, to excise the cancer of Islam from the heart of Yugoslavia. He didn't listen. I rejoiced when Slobodan Milošević rose to power. God knows he tried to rid the Balkans of the Muslims. You, a Kosovar, stood with your Serbian brethren. You were one of his trusted aides. The work you did—in Goražde, in Srebrenica—should have been celebrated by all of our people. As it was, and is, by some of us yet today."

Basha opened his mouth but couldn't think of anything to say.

"The Christian world has learned nothing from the Gulf Wars, the Afghan war, the Arab Spring, the rise of al-Qaeda and ISIS. The Christian world, and Europe specifically, remain mired in a weakling philosophy. We wear the stain of victimhood. Soldiers, such as yourself, are our only bulwark. Our only defense."

Basha blinked. "Thank you. I've … ah, I appreciate your patronage, ma'am. I … may not have been the mentor for Lazar that you'd hoped for, but—"

"Lazar is weak and stupid," Marija Aleksić said, again with no specific emotional tint to her words. She might have been describing an art-exhibit opening. "I've known that since he was a child. Miloš coddled him. Emasculated him with his cars and his flashy clothing. Buying him friends and whores. I had hoped he would come of age—a mother must hope, Driton. But it didn't happen. Now we need to look to the future."

The major glanced toward the loop of news on the monitor, then back to her. "Ma'am?"

Marija looked that way, too. She stood with one foot a bit ahead of the other and angled ever so slightly, with her hands in front of her, one palm up, one palm down, held lightly together. Driton Basha imagined that there were finishing schools that taught society women to stand like that. Just as boot camps teach soldiers to stand at attention.

Basha discovered that he was standing at attention, as he would have in the presence of a superior officer. He didn't remember assuming the position.

"They have played—will play—this story incessantly and forever," Marija said. "Until a new story overtakes it."

"Yes, ma'am."

She turned to him again. "Then we need to create that new story, Driton. That new narrative."

"Ah … ma'am?"

Marija inhaled deeply, as if stirring herself to take on some simple but onerous chore. "You have access to more of these Muslims?"

He thought about it a moment, and remembered driving to the garage on the outskirts of Belgrade, and to the Quonset hut with four Iraqis who were too old for the trafficking operation. "Yes ma'am."

She might have been reading his mind. "Not children. I mean, older Muslims."

Basha colored. "Ma'am, about that. We—"

"Oh, I don't judge you on the … commodity you sold, Driton. The stain of radical Islam brought these ills upon the Muslim people. They got no less than they deserved. But right now, I think we need some of the refugees. Some older refugees. If you follow me."

And, in truth, he started to. "We have some of the bastards stashed away in Italy, just across from the Slovenian border. Four of them. They're probably eighteen to twenty, I'd guess. We'd planned to sell them to a factory owner in Bratislava who needed laborers and wouldn't ask too many questions."

"Get them back, if you can."

"Ma'am." Basha nodded.

"You are going to create a new narrative, Driton. An attack by Europe's Islamist foes on a beloved institution. Thus reminding everyone of who has been truly victimized in this world. And to remind everyone of the face of evil."

"That …" he drifted a moment, then caught the current.

"Yes. Yes, that would work. I see where you're heading with this."

Marija Aleksić turned to the monitor and the news cycle again. "If we strike correctly, and quickly, we can eliminate this silly cow of a judge. The Belgrade case will go before someone who isn't on a fanatical holy crusade. Someone with a reasonable understanding of the threat Europe faces, and must face united. And we shall leave behind a few dead terrorists. With a few of those dreadful suicide vests, perhaps?"

Basha stood tall. "Ma'am."

C60

Finnigan said, "Can you sail a boat?"

Lachlan Sumner sneered. "I'm from New Zealand, mate."

Finnigan took that to mean *yes.*

Bridget Sumner leased them a thirty-foot Pearson with a fiberglass monohull and a cranky old diesel inboard that needed care, feeding, and heavenly intervention. But the stubborn old boat was laid out well enough for short-handed sailing, and Fiero admitted to how she'd crewed the Med on a competitive yacht.

Lachlan and the partners pushed the boat up the North Sea coast, Fiero wearing a bikini top, cutoff jeans, and deck shoes, while Finnigan sat aft with cargo shorts, a baseball cap pulled low, and sunglasses with a cloth loop around his neck. They used an open beer cooler and a magazine to hide a Nikon on a tripod and a 300 mm lens. They sailed north past the Aleksić's UFO-shaped house, then south again. In the afternoon they made the two-way run again, each time switching off how they were dressed and who had the helm and the camera, in case they were observed by the security detail at the house.

Bridget got them a half-timbered cottage near Katwijk aan Zee, in the province of South Holland. There was a good chance that the Aleksić security detail would be checking rental property, so they bought the place outright with well-laundered money provided by Ways & Means in Varenna. The money trail was professionally obscured. He paid for the sailboat, too, adding, "If she were to sink in the North Sea, that wouldn't be the worst outcome in the world."

The partners never asked whose money the banker was laundering. Ignorance is bliss.

Between surveillance runs, Finnigan rumbled around the cottage's kitchen, cooking to relieve stress. He enjoyed cooking more than eating, truth be told. And he was pretty sure that Fiero was the only Spanish woman on earth who couldn't, or wouldn't, boil water.

They sent Lachlan Sumner to Amsterdam to serve as a liaison to Judge Betancourt, not telling him that they had no intention of contacting the judge ever again. But the ruse put Lachlan in a safe place, in the event they were rumbled.

Finnigan and Fiero hadn't even discussed calling in Brodie McTavish and his mercenaries. They were planning on breaking into a home of a high-ranking UN official, all in the heart of the European capital. McTavish would never put his men into such a situation, and the partners would never ask him to.

Finnigan engaged the Black Harts to help with the surveillance. Sally Blue, the statuesque redhead, oversaw the work. Sally always looked like she'd spent the night in 1938, dancing to Glenn Miller. The memorandum of understanding between St. Nicholas and the Harts was the same as always: the troupe of thieves would help with surveillance before the operation, would make itself scarce during the operation, and was free to steal whatever they could get their hands on after the operation. But Sally had never, and would never, risk her people in anything even remotely violent. That wasn't their jam.

"You want to break into that joint?" she said, throwing an arm carelessly but also artfully over Finnigan's shoulder. "That's a sucker bet."

Fiero poured her a glass of Spanish red. "Still …" she said with a shrug, and left it at that.

"Your funeral." Sally hoisted her glass, and the partners did, too. The grifter turned to the schematics of the flying saucer house, which were laid out on the cottage's dining table and weighted down by the wine bottle and plates of cheese and olives. The seaside house looked like a throwback to hip 1970s architecture, but since being purchased by Miloš Aleksić, the building's security had been updated, soup to nuts, by a South African firm that handled the upgrade remodeling of banks and overseas embassies.

"It's the security I'd install if it were my house."

Fiero said, "Haven't you stolen all of your houses?"

"Not all of them. Look at this …" She pointed to the blueprints. "This stone wall surrounding the property? It's rigged with weight sensors. You'd have to go over the wall without touching it. And with three-sixty CC cameras all around the house …" She sipped the crisp, dry red. "Same weight sensors on the roof and the seaside balconies. I thought about suggesting a parachute drop, or parasailing behind that boat of yours. Speaking of which …?"

"Hmm?" Finnigan glanced up. "Oh. You want to steal it when this is done? It's yours."

"You're a doll." She hip-bumped him and turned back to the

schematics. Finnigan could never tell if the Rosalind Russell dialogue was an affectation, or if she naturally spoke like that.

Fiero paced, crossing occasionally to the cottage windows to check their own security. "How would you recommend getting in?"

"I wouldn't."

Fiero turned, wine to her lips.

Sally held the gaze a second, then blushed. "If you had to go in, I'd say go heavy. But you know I'm not actually recommending that, right? Not in a million years. Having said that: if you absolutely needed to get into that house, I'd bring an armored personnel carrier with a cowcatcher, rocket propelled grenades, and guys with Benellis and balls. 'Cause without all that, you ain't getting in. Not no way, not no how."

Finnigan rubbed his neck and lobbed an olive into his mouth. "Our office manager checked the services—cable, groceries, whatever. Nobody delivers anything to the house. The security detail brings in whatever the family needs."

Sally Blue shook her head. "Surprisingly, they've dismissed the usual house guards. They had a contract with Suicide Ride, up till now."

Fiero frowned. "Suicide Ride?"

But Finnigan knew the reference. "Nickname of Sooner, Slye, and Rydell. A huge, multinational private military contractor, headquartered in Texas. These are the guys who roamed Afghanistan and Iraq before the media and Congress wised up. Former SAS, former IDF, former SEALs."

Sally nodded. "That'd be them. Full-bore, balls-out badasses. Fortunately, you won't have to tangle with them. We've watched the Suicide Ride dudes pull out the last couple of days."

Fiero nodded with the hint of a smile. "Military contractors can't afford to get caught breaking laws in the heart of Europe. It's why we haven't called in our own mercenaries."

Finnigan said, "The Aleksićs want another kind of security, now. The kind that doesn't mind full-frontal criminality ..."

"... no matter where it's committed."

Sally Blue smiled as the partners started finishing each other's sentences, unaware of their own cadence.

"Miloš Aleksić is a UN director, or he was until this week," Fiero said. "No matter who's providing house security, they're the least of our worries. We might—*might*—get into a firefight with Aleksić's security detail, and we might even get into the house ..."

"... but any attack would draw local police, Dutch military, and UN security forces," Finnigan finished. "We might fight our way in, but we'd never get out."

The three of them stood, thinking. Sally reached for a tablet computer in her tote bag, unlocked it, and brought up surveillance photos. The first one showed the top of a car and the head and upper torso of Marija Aleksić, looking matronly and prim. She was bracketed by two guys, maybe six-two or -three, with dark hair, dark skin, Ray-Bans, and ear jacks.

"The lady of the house went into Amsterdam yesterday for a meeting of some do-gooder nonprofit she chairs. People for ... I don't know ... the Ethical Treatment of Salad, or whatever. The transit included a convoy of three vehicles, all armored. She had these guys with her. They're with whoever replaced Suicide Ride. We haven't ID'd 'em."

Fiero sipped her wine. "Kosovars."

Sally wrinkled her nose. "You think?"

"Pretty sure."

"Well, we've been watching the joint for three days. That was the first time the lady of the house poked her head outside. No sign of the hubby. And another thing: while Missus Do-Gooder Nonprofit was voting for baby seals,"—she tapped the photo of the two beefy soldiers with one trim fingernail—"more of these

guys flew into town. A bunch more. I had one of my guys dog-
ging them."

The partners exchanged looks.

Sally Blue shook her head. "Five'll get you ten, these boys are
gearing up for the OK Corral."

C61

Fiero found out that her mother would be attending a conference on industrialization and the Visegrád Group—Hungary, Poland, the Czech Republic, and Slovakia—that weekend. The partners used Fiero's former Spanish Intelligence contacts to leak a story that Hélene Betancourt would be making a surprise visit, too. The idea was to draw as much of the Kosovar forces away from the flying saucer house as they could.

Fiero stopped by the de Havilland, moored outside Amsterdam, and switched into what Finnigan called her *grown-up clothes*—the same pumps and severe black suit she'd worn on their visit to the judge. She pinned her hair in a chignon, conscious that doing so exposed her pointed, almost elfin ears—she'd been teased about those ears as a kid, and it still reverberated.

In Prague, she lunched with her mother, Khadija Dahar, who talked a mile a minute about women's health care in China, and the Booker Prize, and the Black Lives Matter movement in the

States. They discussed poets and politicians. Katalin Fiero barely getting a word in edgewise.

Khadija noted that her daughter didn't wear a hijab, her head as uncovered as any modern European woman. But she smiled and said nothing. Khadija's version of Islam was more about the politics of empowerment than tradition. She couldn't very well tell her daughter what to wear.

Khadija had not wanted her daughter raised as a Catholic. Alexandro had not wanted her raised as a Muslim. They never settled on a middle ground, and now they couldn't very well complain about Katalin's absence of faith.

After lunch, they moved to the assembly hall, where Fiero could watch for signs of the opposition. She said, "Judge Hélène Betancourt might be coming."

Khadija Dahar adjusted her hijab, switching her thousand-dollar lambskin clutch to her other hand. "It's worrisome when race and bigotry get entwined in legal battles."

Fiero stiffened. "Meaning ...?"

"Hmm? Oh, I've known Hélène Betancourt for years. She hates the Serbs. *Hates.* It's well established. This entire case ..." Khadija shook her head.

"You don't think the family is involved in human trafficking?"

"Darling, I have known Miloš and Marija Aleksić forever. They've contributed to every humanist, progressive cause I know. Miloš is a fine man. He's on a couple of boards with your father. He has done much good for the refugees over the years. His resignation from the Levant Group was a blow for the cause of refugee rights."

Fiero tried to focus on her mission, even though she'd seen no sign of military-trained lurkers. But she couldn't let it go.

"The son was trafficking children, Mother. He was creating sex slaves from—"

"You don't have to lecture me on feminist issues, darling." Khadija smiled warmly.

"This isn't a *feminist issue*, Mother. He wasn't insulting women. He didn't want them paid less for equal work. He was forcing boys and girls to fuck strangers as slaves!"

Khadija physically stumbled back a step, glancing around the hall to see who had overheard.

"Trafficking is a horror. I know this."

"And the Aleksićs are involved."

Khadija took her daughter's arm. "Don't believe everything the media writes, darling. And remember that Judge Betancourt has made this a cause célèbre. She loathes Serbs; always has. The Aleksić family is of the highest caliber. Patrons of the humanities and the arts. The initial reports of their son's involvement likely are exaggerated. It would be good to keep that in mind."

Fiero saw no way of pushing the topic any further without revealing her role in the entire affair. She stood by her mother, arm in arm, feeling her face burn with rage.

The Kosovar soldiers never showed up.

Later, on the cab ride back to the airport, Khadija took her daughter's arm and squeezed it. "I'm sorry if I snapped."

"Don't be." She squeezed back. "It's fine."

"Actually? I'm pleased to see you get so upset. It would be good for you to be more political, Katalin. Maybe join a political party? Do some volunteer work?"

Her daughter leaned over and kissed her on the cheek.

"I'd love it if my girl became more involved in the good fight," Khadija said.

Her elbow rested against Fiero's hip—right where she normally holstered her gun.

Fiero called Finnigan from her hotel room that night. Trying to lure the Kosovar thugs to Prague hadn't been a bad plan. They remained convinced that Miloš Aleksić and Major Driton Basha would try to kill Judge Betancourt for her role in destroying the life of Lazar Aleksić, and for her role in the war-crime trials of the former Serbian leaders.

But if so, the Kosovars would strike when they were ready and weren't to be drawn out.

C62

From the deck of the thirty-footer, Fiero scanned the nighttime face of the flying saucer house through high-powered binoculars. She watched the two guards on random sweeps.

The Black Harts were watching the house from the land-ward side, just as they were electronically watching the Aleksićs' accounts and holdings.

Finnigan sat on the edge of the deck of the boat behind her, a beer can held between his knees, his knuckles jammed into his thighs, elbows akimbo, staring the thousand-yard stare. "We should get diving gear."

Fiero watched the soldiers on patrol. "Why?"

"See if Aleksić has an underwater tunnel leading to a cave under his house."

She lowered the glasses. "Why would he have that?"

"For his super-secret submarine."

She turned to watch him. He seemed unaware of it, sitting, staring at nothing.

"You think he has a super-secret submarine?"

"No, but it'd be cool."

She turned back and raised the glasses, her energy-sapping frustration turned up a couple levels higher than his. "Don't talk stupid," she snapped. "Stupid makes me crazy."

The *Telegraph* newspaper in England reported that the attorneys representing Lazar Aleksić might drop their client because he couldn't meet their legal fees. Lazar claimed that all of his belongings, stored in the penthouse suite of an unfinished office building in Belgrade, had been stolen shortly after his arrest. Someone had used his own computer to bleed Lazar's trust funds and various bank accounts. Or, so he claimed.

The police weren't buying the story. An international hunt was underway for his stashed fortune.

Finnigan and Fiero sent a fruit basket to Sally Blue.

Sally called in later that day. "Did you read that the investigators are scouring the scum bucket's properties?"

Fiero put her on speakerphone. "Michael's here. Yes, we saw that."

"Well, sugar, my forensic accountants are better than theirs. We found two properties the heat missed. Sending a PDF your way."

The PDF document showed two properties owned by Lazar Aleksić, by way of several dummy accounts. One appeared to be a garage in Vrčin, a suburb of Belgrade, just off the main highway linking Serbia to Kosovo. Google Earth showed it to be a cluster of dilapidated Quonset huts surrounded by a small sea of parking lots and a cyclone fence. A few trucks were strewn about, two with their cabs tilted forward to reveal their engines.

"A trucking company would need a garage," Finnigan said. "But why hide it under dummy accounts?"

"It's between Belgrade and Kosovo," Fiero said. "We passed it when we were chasing those stolen kids and Jane Koury. D'you think they used Vrčin as a sort of staging area when they moved large quantities of victims?"

Finnigan shrugged. "Could be. Makes sense."

They checked out the second address, part of a small, commercial enclave near Trieste, in Italy but within a few kilometers of the Slovenian border. It looked to be warehouse space, or possibly industrial space, well away from any main streets or residential zones.

"No space to park trucks," Fiero observed.

Sally spoke from the iPhone. "And yet owned—through fronts—by a trucking company. The plot thickens."

Finnigan leaned closer to the phone. "Do you have anyone free to check them out?"

"We're stretched thin, boychick. I've got Mercer."

The partners were both going stir crazy. But Finnigan thought back on the moment Fiero had snapped at him on the boat. He said, "Okay, send Mercer to that garage near Belgrade. Fiero can check out the property in Trieste."

That surprised Fiero, but her eyes lit up with the prospect of actually doing something. "You don't mind?"

As a cop and a deputy US Marshal, Finnigan had grown accustomed to long waits on surveillance. Waiting made Fiero even crazier than usual. "Go. Check it out. The Harts and I will keep an eye on things here."

Fiero began packing.

C63

Lachlan Sumner flew Fiero to Venice. She took a couple hours to scan want ads and bought a Honda motorbike and a helmet for cash. Lachlan stayed with the de Havilland as Fiero rode east toward Trieste, finding a room for let over a *taverna*, advertised by a chipped plywood A-board in the parking lot and the single word, *zimmer—room*, better to attract the many German tourists who favor the region. That was ideal for Fiero because, of all of the hoteliers in Europe, the Germans are the least likely to demand a passport. That had been ingrained in her during her early training with Spanish Intelligence.

She paid for the room in cash. In exchange for which she received the key to an ill-kept and airless garret with no TV and no internet connection. Perfect for her needs.

She waited until dark and checked the map she'd made of the area. Tourists can be forgiven for thinking that every square foot of Italy is gorgeous; city planners go to some lengths to isolate the grungier neighborhoods.

Fiero tooled the Honda slowly through the industrial cluster, three blocks wide by three blocks deep, an area that likely had been created in the post–Cold War years in anticipation of brisk trade between Italy and neighboring Yugoslavia. That trade never happened, and the industrial cluster looked lifeless and neglected.

Fiero spotted the small and nondescript factory building, brick and sturdy but unkempt. Streetlights were few. She spotted lights inside the two-story hulk of unreinforced masonry. She saw no signage—Ragusa Logistics or otherwise.

She ditched the bike and the helmet at the far end of the industrial neighborhood. In dark jeans, a leather biker jacket, and boots, she blended well with the shadows. She wended her way back to the building, spotting no other pedestrians; the sector didn't even boast a restaurant or bar to gin up any foot traffic.

What would Michael the Cop do? Fiero asked herself. Michael the Cop would investigate, of course. Usually, Fiero's own inclination was to simply hit people and see what happens next, but for now, she decided to channel Finnigan. She climbed atop a lidded metal garbage can to peer into the lit front window of the building.

She spotted two men. One sat on a folding chair, helping himself to a cup of instant noodles and watching a video on a laptop. The other read a magazine that featured Slavic script on the cover. The remnants of a poker game lay abandoned on a collapsible table. They were drinking coffee, not liquor. They both wore holstered sidearms.

Basha's boys, she thought.

Fiero climbed down and decided that a stable corrugated-metal garbage can that didn't rattle was worth its weight in gold. She lifted it by both handles and carried it around to the side of the building, checked that she was unwatched, and climbed up to peer in another window. She saw a room laid out for assembly-line work. The room had seen no such work in a generation.

Fiero carried the can to the next window, and then the next. She had to climb a fence to get to the back of the building.

She made do and checked three ground-floor windows in back, finding nothing of import.

She climbed another fence to check out the fourth side of the building. That's when she spotted the refugees.

Four of them, maybe twenty years old or a little younger; three men and a woman. The room they were in was squalid, with camp cots and a displaced picnic table, brought in from the backyard likely, liberally speckled with bird shit. Fiero spotted a bathroom with a shower.

She had no doubt that the door to the room was locked from the outside.

Two of the men were asleep. The woman—surprisingly tall and thin—sat on a cot, holding a magazine in both hands, but not reading it; she stared over the top of the pages at the grimy floor. The fourth refugee lay on his back on a cot, one arm under his head, and read a Koran perched on his chest.

Fiero climbed down from the brickwork onto which she'd been clinging. She peered around at the dark street and at the next building over.

She'd found more refugees. So what?

They were clearly older than the children kidnapped by Major Basha's unit. But then again, the British journalist, Jane Koury, had been, too.

Fiero couldn't very well leave them here, in the hands of the

soldiers. And she was in no hurry to head back to the Netherlands, and the endless waiting for an opportunity to get to Miloš
Aleksić and Driton Basha.

Finnigan had been right to send her to Italy. She was losing
her mind, waiting for an opportunity to get to their targets.

Fiero rapped softly on the windowpane with her knuckles.

C64

The partners planned to commit a major crime and they didn't want any link between themselves and Judge Betancourt. But they'd left her with the URL for a chat room with an anonymous communications feature. She could leave them untraceable messages if she were in trouble.

Which she did.

Finnigan sent a text to Sally Blue of the Black Harts letting her know he'd be gone for several hours and asking her to keep watch on the Aleksić house.

The judge provided an address in Rotterdam, only a few miles inland from The Hague. Finnigan checked it out and found it to be a houseboat on the Oude Maas, a bit west of the center of the city. The judge insisted on his going there at noon.

Finnigan rarely carried a gun in Europe but he did that day, untucking a plaid shirt to cover the belt holster of his SIG. He walked around the neighborhood for twenty minutes, seeing nothing that raised his concern, then stepped onto the gangplank of the newish, smallish, and uninspired houseboat, located just south of the urban island known as Krabbegors.

A thickset man with a shaved head answered the door. He wore a starched white shirt that looked naked without a black tie and suit coat, his sleeves upturned exactly one roll over beefy forearms. He had a military mustache and scar tissue around his eyes. Finnigan recognized him as a member of the judge's security detail; they'd met when he and Fiero first made contact with Betancourt. The man was maybe fifty and decidedly unhappy to see Finnigan on his doorstep.

He stepped away from the door and Finnigan entered. The living room had a low ceiling and horizontal windows that were only of use if you stooped or sat on the furniture. The place was soulless, with few personalized tchotchkes around. The furniture was dirt cheap but spotless.

"This was her idea," the security man said in English and pointed to a cordless telephone, which rested faceup in its cradle on a coffee table with the speakerphone light on.

"Finnigan." He offered his hand. The guy paused, then shook.

"Renard. I'm head of her security." He raised his voice and switched to French. "He's here."

The judge's reedy voice sounded from the phone's speaker. "Mr. Finnigan. I assumed you wouldn't want to meet with me in person."

Finnigan sat on the low couch, nearer to the phone, and Renard sat on a chair at a forty-five-degree angle from him, hunched forward, elbows on his knees, and hands gripped together.

"What's up, ma'am?"

"Someone attempted access to the court building."

"How?"

"According to the head of delegate security, unknown persons used a … well, you explain, Mr. Renard."

Renard glowered. The muscles in his jaw and neck never

stopped clenching. "There's a ten-key pad installed in many of the rooms of the court complex. Two days in a row—yesterday and the day before—someone entered the Fireplace Room, the ground floor dining hall, and input an eight-digit code."

Finnigan said, "Who?"

Renard shrugged. "There's not much security on the ground floor. Far too many civilians coming and going."

"A code to do what?"

"Call security," he said. "Activate the police alarm or the fire alarm. Or announce a terrorist incident."

"CC cameras in the dining hall?"

Renard shook his head. "The ground floor has the least security in the complex. It gets better as you move upstairs. And before you ask: Her Honor has not dined in the Fireplace Room since you showed up and warned us about the threat."

Finnigan thought about that for a while. "Whose code was entered?"

"That's the thing. Nobody's. It was an eight-digit code, and all security, maintenance, and administrative personnel are given nine-digit access codes. Here's something else: this happened twice, but the codes weren't identical. They were one digit off from each other."

Finnigan stared at the guy, as if to say, *annnnddd …?*

"I told Her Honor that this wasn't worth bothering anyone with. She felt it important you hear about it."

"Read me the codes."

Renard drew a smart phone and brought up the note function. He read two strings of eight numbers. The last two digits were inverted in the second string.

"What's Shan's code?"

Renard said, "Who?"

"Thomas Shannon Greyson."

"Ah. It's been deactivated."

"Yeah, but what was it?"

Renard seemed to ponder that. "Hold on." He stood and stepped away, into the attached kitchenette, and made a call.

Finnigan turned to the phone resting in the center of the coffee table. "Appreciate you letting us know, ma'am. It does sound weird. I'm not sure that makes it related but—"

Renard said, "Damn it!" He walked back into the living room, and now his face had a pink tinge. "We should have spotted this. Greyson's code. It's the same as the first one, from the day before yesterday, but in reverse order and with the last digit missing."

Finnigan grinned. Someone got Shan's code out of him. He was alive.

Or at least he had been as recently as the day before. Someone had been seeking his security code and he'd given it up, after more than a week's captivity, but scrambled enough to be useless.

But was that all this was? Proof of life and a desperate gamble by a man being beaten, or worse? Finnigan felt his brain whirl, throwing together facts as quickly as he could.

He said, to both the man in the room and the woman on the phone, "What was the name of the dining hall?"

"The Fireplace Room," Renard said. "The fireplace mantle is made from a single redwood tree. It dates back to 1810, when—"

Finnigan said, "Get a hidden CC camera in there, right now. Shan lured one of the guys who's got him into the dining room. Twice. If he's freaking lucky, it'll happen a third time."

"All right, but they can't get to the judge from there. We—"

"Doesn't matter, buddy. Go."

Renard glowered down at him.

Judge Betancourt said, "It seems a sound idea."

He nodded brusquely and walked back into the kitchen, making another call.

Finnigan whisked up the cordless landline phone and moved to the far end of the houseboat, sliding open the glass door and stepping onto the deck. He let the door glide shut behind him. "Ma'am? Renard can't hear us now. Listen: how many rooms on the first floor could Shan have lured these guys to?"

"I'm not sure. A few dozen."

"But he chose the Fireplace Room."

"Indeed. I don't see the importance, though."

He turned back to see Renard in the kitchen, glowering at him through the glass slider. "What are fireplaces famous for? In popular culture?"

"Fireplaces? I'm not …" The jurist's voice faded.

Finnigan grinned. "You got it."

"The means of egress of Saint Nicholas, on the eve of Christmas."

"It's Shan's way of telling us he's alive. And that the bad guys are coming for you. Hang on, I'm getting Renard back on this conversation."

He slid the door open and stepped back in. Renard had returned from the kitchenette. Finnigan said, "Let's say the access code worked, day before yesterday, and somebody set off alarms. Where would you have evac'ed the judges?"

Renard straightened up to his full height. "I've no intention of answering that question."

He thrust the phone toward Renard. "Your Honor? Tell him. Everything. I think I know what the bad guys want. And I think I know what Shan wanted us to figure out. It's time to bring Renard inside the tent. Tell him."

C65

The four refugees were from Mosul, Iraq. Their Arabic was sufficiently different from Fiero's Algerian that they picked their way gingerly through the introductions, like stepping over vines in an overgrown orchard.

Two of them were brothers. The others hadn't met until they'd reached Macedonia. There, soldiers in a civilian truck picked them up and drove them to a Quonset hut in some country— they didn't know which one.

The soldiers had kept their passports and had taken all their money. They could have fled that first building, or this one, but to go where?

The tall, shy woman sat hunched in on herself and barely spoke above a whisper. She kept her hijab close to her face. She identified the civilian truck as belonging to Ragusa Logistics because she read and wrote English, having studied briefly in London before returning home to protect her parents from the rise of ISIS, or Daesh, as she called the group.

The foursome had been taken next by truck to this old factory. Again, they had no idea what country they were in and, despite their fugue of anger, boredom, fright, and sheer exhaustion, their faces lit up when Fiero informed them that they'd made it to Italy.

"We don't know what's next," the eldest boy, twenty, told her. "I speak a little Serbian because my father does business with Serbs. I heard the guards say we would be sent to Slovakia. But that was more than two weeks ago. Now, over the last couple of days, they've changed their story. We're being sent to the Netherlands."

That caught her attention. "Do you know why?"

The foursome shrugged. The eldest boy said, "In Slovakia, we were to work in a sweatshop."

"Have you tried to escape?"

The men glanced at each other. The woman glanced at her shoes.

Fiero pushed them. "What?"

"It's not just that they have our passports and our money," a boy said. "They have guns. And they're soldiers. They know how to use them. Besides—"

Another boy cut in. "A sweatshop in Slovakia, or go back to Daesh? I'll take the sweatshop, thank you please. That's no choice at all."

The others nodded. Except the girl, who might have been nineteen or twenty.

"Not you?"

She shook her head.

"How come?"

She bit her lip, then replied in a whisper. "I have an aunt in Italy. In Rome. Also, nieces and nephews."

Fiero made the *shh* symbol, finger to her lips, and moved to the door connecting their room to the guards. She heard the faint audio of a televised cricket match. She looked back, noting how tall and angular the girl was. She moved back to the cluster of cots, drawing her smart phone. "Do you want to go to your aunt?"

The girl's eyes glittered with tears. She nodded vigorously.

"Do you know her telephone number, or email?"

"Both!"

Fiero quickly tapped out a text message for Finnigan. She glanced at the three boys. "And you want to go north? Even to the Netherlands?"

"If we get to the Netherlands," the eldest said, "my brother and I can get to Brussels. We have family there."

Fiero turned to the girl. "Can you ride a motorbike?"

"Of course not!" She sounded scandalized.

Stupid question. "My name is Katalin. I'm a soldier, too, and my best friend in all the world is a sort of police officer. We are trying to stop these soldiers from kidnapping refugees. Now, I've an idea. It requires everyone to help me fool these soldiers. Are you in?"

All four nodded.

"Okay. Follow my lead."

Before driving back to the rental house on the coast, Finnigan typed up a text message for Fiero. It read:

> Shan's alive. Bravos want to fake a terrorist threat to Courthouse and lure Target out of Courthouse. Got to be an Ambush planned. I brought in Target's security detail. Plan: Let the Ambush happen, w/o Target. When Bravos make move, we hit UFO House. Need you back here Quick. Finnigan.

Just as he was about to hit SEND, a message from Fiero popped up.

MPF: Found 4 refugees being
shipped Netherlands 2night. 3 boys,
1 girl. My guess: Muslim fall guys
for whatever Bravos have planned.
Boys want to go north, girl wants
out. I'm taking her place. After U
get this, giving girl my phone so she
can reach aunt. I'm off comms. Will
find nu phone up north. Should be in
Nthrlnds 2morrow. Don't make move
until U hear from me! Xoxoxo KFD.

Finnigan read it through and groaned. He sent his message, hoping against hope he wasn't too late, thinking, *Xoxoxo, my ass.*

For the first time since this gig started, the partners would be out of touch. And not on the same page.

C66

In the seventeenth century, a Dutch tailor named Pieter de Key moved to The Hague and built a shop and a home for his family of twelve children. The narrow house featured an impressively tall, pointed roof and tightly bunched windows. Each floor was one or two rooms deep, and each featured massive open-beam ceilings. Pieter de Key never imagined that his backyard would, one day, house a portion of the International Criminal Court complex.

In 2010, the Security Directorate of the ICC bought the rights to the old house. They excavated World War II bomb shelters and added tunnels between the court complex and Pieter de Key's tailor shop and home. In the event of a terrorist attack, the justices and senior personnel could be escorted to a subbasement, through tunnels lined with battery-powered lights and forced-air blowers, to the half-timbered house. Once there, simple staff cars could pick them up. Or police cars, or an armored personnel carrier, or a heavy-lift helicopter.

But getting them out of the court complex, in the event of an attack, and into the old house was the first step.

Driton Basha had had access to a wide array of European soldiers during the era of the United Nations' KFOR, or Kosovo Force. Most had been fine and decent soldiers, but a few had been amenable to corruption. Some of them had returned to their home countries after their time in Pristina but had retained their ties to Basha and his unit.

One of those soldiers had sold the major the plans for the emergency evacuation of the International Criminal Court—including the tunnel to the Pieter de Key house—for a mere ten thousand euros. Cheap at twice the price.

If a terrorist alarm went off inside the courthouse building, Basha knew where the judge's bodyguards would take her. His people would be waiting for them. Also, a couple of Muslim immigrants with suicide vests. The judge would be dead, and the Muslims would get the blame.

Basha gathered his strike team inside the flying saucer house of Miloš Aleksić. They had taken over a recreation room carved into the bedrock of the North Sea cliff, moving aside an entertainment center and pool table, to make room for the bivouac. The kitchen, one floor up, had been churning out hot meals for more than a week as the team of nine noncommissioned soldiers and three officers waited for their moment to strike.

Basha gathered everyone at 11:00 a.m. on their second Tuesday in the house. He was accompanied by a captain and a lieutenant—the last officers of his formerly elite squad.

Marija and Miloš Aleksić had made themselves scarce.

"Listen up!" Basha began as the men fell into standing parade rest. Basha nodded to his lieutenant to begin.

The man stepped forward. "At oh eight hundred hours today, I walked into the first-floor dining hall of the court and input a code into the ten-key pad. Within seconds, fire alarms went off."

A soldier raised his hand. Basha nodded to him. "The other times it didn't work, sir. What was different this time?"

The captain said, "Sodium thiopental. Under torture, the prisoner gave us false codes. When we drugged him up, he gave us the real one."

The lieutenant resumed the narrative. "I triggered the fire alarm then sat down and waited to see if I'd get arrested. I guess you know the answer to that. There are no cameras in the Fireplace Room, so the English bastard told us the truth about that, at least. Which means we now control the security override system."

The men grinned.

"At oh seven hundred hours tomorrow, Judge Betancourt is scheduled to arrive at the court. Our surveillance shows she's never, ever late. Captain?"

The senior officer nodded. "The judge's code name for this operation is *Deborah*. At oh seven twenty tomorrow, the lieutenant will again access the security override. He will input the code for a terrorist attack, Level One. Now, everyone? Understand: the code that the lieutenant inputs will show that terrorists are inside the building. And the code is specific to Deborah. She's the target, and she's the one they'll evacuate. Leading the evac will be this man."

They passed around photos of Michel Renard, Betancourt's head of security.

"His code name is *Atlas*," the captain said. "We will be in the evac site, the tailor's house behind the court complex. I'll lead First Team. We'll include the Iraqi shits we're having sent up from Italy. We'll put them in suicide vests and make sure they die on the scene. We'll be able to point to ISIS having planned this entire thing. Second Team will wait outside with the transport. After we make our kills, we will head to the Alpha rendezvous site."

The lieutenant pointed to a map thumbtacked to the wall of the rec room.

"We'll be monitoring all police and military bands. If Rendezvous Alpha is compromised, we'll meet at the Beta or Gamma sites." The lieutenant tapped the wall map twice more.

"Questions?"

Someone raised a hand. "The prisoner …?"

Major Basha stepped forward. "Mr. Greyson is going to attempt to swim to America."

The soldiers laughed.

Access to the North Sea made for a convenient way to dispose of bodies.

C67

For Fiero's plan to work, she was counting on both sexism and racism. And when had either of those ever let her down?

She used grease from the plumbing under the bathroom sink to smudge up her face. She rolled her jeans up to above her calves and borrowed a long, demure skirt form the Iraqi girl—who, by now, had contacted her aunt in Rome and would be on a bus, well on her way to safety. Fiero also borrowed a large and shapeless sweater and the girl's extra hijab.

They had the same height but didn't look particularly alike. Fiero was twelve years older than the girl, but the girl had been painfully shy and tended to hunch, so as not to draw attention. Fiero was counting on the Kosovar soldiers being sexist enough, and bigoted enough, that they hadn't ever looked at the girl all that closely.

When the refugees were paraded at gunpoint into the back of a Ragusa Logistics truck, her guess had proven correct. The guards also seemed to rotate out; these likely weren't the same ones who'd brought the refugees to Italy in the first place.

The truck rolled north over the Alps, through Austria and Germany, then into the Netherlands. In the back, planks had been added above the wheel-well mounds to create two facing benches. Two of the boys sat on the left-hand side of the truck; one rode on the right next to Fiero, but kept a good and proper distance between them. Fiero studied the interior carefully. Tie-down rings studded the interior walls, including the front-facing wall with the narrow, horizontal window separating the cargo bay from the cab.

The drivers stopped occasionally for fast food and tossed the greasy bags and soft drinks into the rear of the truck without comment. Fiero kept her head low each time.

The boys turned to her several times during the trip and asked her what was going to happen to them next.

Fiero's answers had been more or less the same each time.

"If there's trouble, flee. And if there's no trouble—still flee. I'll take care of the rest."

C68

Michel Renard, head of the judge's security detail, used St. Nicholas' voice-over-internet site to call Finnigan, who was making himself pasta with lemon and olive oil in the cottage by the sea.

"A man in a suit walked into the Fireplace Room at oh eight hundred hours and got a cup of coffee," Renard said. "We had hidden cameras placed around the room. When he thought he wouldn't be observed, he keyed in a code on the wall pad."

Finnigan was using the speaker mode on the tablet computer, set up next to the stove. The call had been obscured by a vast lace of intercontinental connections and was untraceable.

"Shan's code?" he asked.

"Almost. No longer in reverse order, but still only eight digits long."

Unbelievable. Whatever they were doing to Shan Greyson, they'd been doing it for more than a week. And he was still feeding them false information.

Renard seemed duly impressed as well. "I wouldn't have thought it possible, but Greyson is really something. I, ah, never thought much of the fellow. I was wrong."

"He's impressed me, too. What happened when the guy keyed in the code?"

"Nothing, as far as the system went. We were watching live on the CC cameras. When I saw him enter the code for a fire alarm, I tripped it manually. He ended up thinking he'd done it. Bastard sat back down and finished his coffee!"

"Wanted to see if you'd arrest him," Finnigan said. "You didn't, and now they think they've got access to your security system."

"We also got fingerprints off the man's coffee cup. He's Kosovar, as you predicted, Mr. Finnigan. And active military. Looks like you were right on all counts."

Finnigan checked his phone, which lay next to the tablet computer. Still no voice mail or texts from Fiero.

"Are you there, Finnigan?"

"Yeah," he said. "My guess is, the guy'll be back. Tomorrow, either when the judge arrives, or the last thing before she leaves. They'll trigger the terrorism alert, expecting you to rush her through the tunnels to that house you told me about."

"And my men will be there to capture them. And you?"

"I'll be around, man. You'll give me the heads-up as soon as the asshole shows up in the Fireplace Room?"

"We will," Renard said. "You've been right so far. We owe you."

"Thanks, man. Good luck."

They both disconnected.

Finnigan checked his voice mail and texts again.

Nada.

He knew what Fiero's Plan A was. He also knew that, so long as Major Basha and Miloš Aleksić remained alive and out of prison, Judge Betancourt's life was on the line.

But Fiero was off-comms. And she didn't know that Shan Greyson was still alive.

Finnigan couldn't picture himself as an assassin. At the end of the day—regardless of the type of paycheck he netted—Finnigan was a cop. Pure and simple.

Killing the bad guys wasn't his style.

But a dramatic rescue?

That was more like it.

C69

Major Basha met with his senior officers, his captain and lieutenant, at 0500 hours in the kitchen of the Aleksić house. The lieutenant made coffee and distributed the cups. "I heard from the men in Italy," he said. "They are en route to the Netherlands with four Muslims. Older ones. In their twenties."

Basha accepted his cup and added milk and sugar. "I saw them in Vrčin, just after they arrived. Three men and a woman, I think. We have suicide vests for them?"

The captain grinned. "Yes, with live explosive. I don't want the CSI people investigating them and finding fakes." Though he spoke his native tongue, he pronounced the letters, *see ess eye*, in English, because he'd seen the TV show.

Basha nodded. "You'll take two of them to the hit. I'll keep two of them here at the house to tie everything together."

He turned his attention to the young lieutenant, who wore a suit and tie with civilian dress shoes. "As soon as the refugees are on the scene, you'll trigger the alarm from the … cafeteria?"

"The Fireplace Room, yes, sir."

Basha turned to the captain. "At which point, the lambs will come to you. Hit them fast. I'll monitor everything from here."

The lieutenant looked at the collection of four Smith & Wesson revolvers laid out on the speckled Formica counter. They'd been loaded and wiped down for fingerprints. The bullets had been wiped, too. They would be left with the dead refugees. "These are fine guns, sir. It seems a shame to leave them with the ragheads."

"The partnership with the Aleksićs has been more than profitable, lieutenant. We'll buy more. And men ...?"

He waited until they both were looking at him.

"The politicians in Pristina have sided with the Muslim scum, as we always knew they would. Most of our men are in the stockade. It goes without saying that we're never going back home. But that doesn't mean the work has to end. Or the profits. There's good money to be had for professional soldiers. And I've never known better."

The junior officers stood a little straighter. The captain said, "Thank you, sir. It's been a good ride, serving with you."

Basha shook their hands. And he offered them a rare grin. "I've saluted my last rear-echelon bastard. I can't trust a military, or a government, that doesn't have my back. So, good luck to you both. When this day is done, we shall make our fortunes when and where we choose."

They thanked him, gathered the Smith & Wessons, and headed out.

The lieutenant drove into The Hague and parked in a public lot a dozen blocks from the International Criminal Court complex. He gathered the empty attaché case he'd bought at a public market in Amsterdam. Forty minutes later, he was through the metal detector at the court complex and walking into the ground-floor Fireplace Room. He ordered a coffee from the waiter, then pretended to check emails on his smart phone.

He sat five meters from the wall-mounted keypad.

In the primary security control room, a guard peered at his black-and-white monitor and reached for his Nextel walkie-talkie phone.

"The same guy from yesterday … Yes, sir … He's sitting at Table Seven. Over."

Two blocks from the court complex, a three-car convoy sat parked. Michel Renard spoke into his matching walkie-talkie, thanked the guard at his monitor station, and switched frequencies.

"It's a go," he alerted the people in the second and third cars. One of those who heard him—in Car Two—was Judge Hélene Betancourt.

"The guards report that the terrorist is back in the Fireplace Room. We have to assume they have the complex under surveillance. This won't work unless our primary is inside. Get the judge into the building and into her chambers. Then wait for my cue."

Finnigan had taken a bus into Amsterdam the day before. He hung around a part of the city that was undergoing a renaissance of sorts, with buildings going up and new streets being paved. He walked the streets, whistling to himself. It was a Sunday, and that part of town, well away from the touristy core, was dead.

He needed a vehicle. A *specific* vehicle.

Twenty-five minutes later, Finnigan snuck into a truck stop and wandered about until he spotted a midsize truck from Ragusa Logistics. He stopped to tie his boot, making sure he was alone, then stood and ran his thumbnail around the edge of the logo.

It was a rubberized, magnetic sheet, exactly like the kind he'd spotted in the garage at the army base in Kosovo.

Finnigan peeled off the logo, rolled it up, and sauntered away.

Later, he'd get around to stealing the vehicle he really needed. And when he did, he'd brand it with the magnetized logo of Lazar Aleksić.

Anyone can steal a car. But to steal it *and* to sign your work with a very lovely fuck-you?

Bitch, please.

C70

Finnigan didn't sleep well. He often didn't before a mission. And never when he and Fiero were out of touch. Well before dawn, he was up and showered and dressed in black jeans and a black sweater and boots. He sent an email to his mom. Just chitchat. His sister Nicole was being promoted to sergeant of the NYPD. His mom beamed: Nicole was well on her way to maintaining the Finnigan tradition.

Yeah, Michael thought, *but which tradition?*

Next, he checked for a text from Fiero. Nothing.

Finnigan popped half a roll of Tums for breakfast and hiked from the cottage to a wooden ravine where he'd left the stolen vehicle, now adorned with the magnetized logo of Ragusa Logistics. He'd picked a good spot to wait; he wouldn't be visible from the flying saucer house. But Finnigan could watch all traffic heading toward, and away from, the house.

Just past 6:00 a.m., a panel truck drove up toward the Aleksić house. It, too, had the Ragusa Logistics banner on the side. Finnigan spotted two men with soldierly haircuts and strong biceps sitting in the cab.

He checked his smart phone.

No word from Fiero.

The panel truck took a corner. In back, Fiero and the three Iraqi boys rocked on their hard wooden benches. There were no windows in the back, other than the one pointing into the cab, and the driver had hung a jacket over a coat hook behind his seat, blocking the view. Fiero had no idea where they were. She just knew they were headed toward The Hague and Judge Betancourt.

She spoke to the boys, but slowly because they had trouble with her Algerian accent.

"These soldiers will meet up with other soldiers. Everyone is going to be armed. It's important you don't do anything stupid. Just do as they say, and we'll get out of this."

She didn't believe that for a minute, but she didn't want the boys taking matters into their own hands.

The eldest Iraqi looked her in the eye and paused. But then nodded. "We're not used to taking orders from women."

"If all goes well, you'll live your lives in the West, meet a nice Muslim girl from the West, and raise daughters in the West," Fiero told him, but with a smile. "Best get used to it."

Twenty minutes later, the panel truck slowed, then stopped. She heard the crunch of small rocks or shells under the tires. She heard the *clank-clank-clank* of a metal gate sliding horizontally on brackets. She pictured the layout of the Aleksićs' house and knew exactly where they were.

She reached instinctively for the left hip pocket of her jeans, under her borrowed skirt. But of course her phone wasn't there. God willing, it was in Rome by now, being used for selfies with a doting aunt.

She had no way to connect to Finnigan.

C71

The driver waited until the gate retracted fully on its motorized brackets, then drove the panel truck into the grounds of the Aleksić family's North Sea home.

One of the solders came out of the house to direct them to the spacious, five-car garage. The driver pulled in, and the soldier lowered the garage door behind them.

The soldiers let the four refugees out of the back. They looked stiff and sore.

The captain glanced at them. They were older than the usual victims—no wonder Lazar Aleksić hadn't been able to sell them to his pedophile clients! But they looked fit enough. The girl was taller than he would have expected. All four looked like able recruits for ISIS or al-Qaeda. Put them in suicide vests and give them the Smith & Wessons, and they'd be believable.

Even the girl. *The ragheads often use female suicide bombers,* the captain thought. *Such lunatics.* He'd grown up with, and adopted, his father's abiding hatred for Muslims. They were virtually a majority in Kosovo. That sat badly with the captain, whose family could be traced back nine generations of patriotic Kosovars.

"Corporal." He nodded to the driver. "Any problems?"

"Operating Base Šar is shut down and most of our guys are in the stockade. I didn't sign up for this to go to prison, Captain."

"Do your goddamn job and keep your mouth shut, and none of us on this mission will be seeing any prisons, Corporal. Now, any problems with the cattle?"

"No, sir," the driver replied. "They just sat there. I've never seen such a useless bunch."

"They won't be useless for long. Two of them come with me. Two stay here with the major."

He turned to the refugees and picked them at random. "The two on my left stay, the two on my right, get them back in the truck. We move out in twenty minutes."

Two of his soldiers brought out four Styrofoam ice chests and set them down in a stack, two wide, two high. The refugees glanced at them, so the captain placed his hand on the lid of the nearest chest. "No touch!" he shouted in English, then again in fractured Arabic.

The refugees either nodded or looked away in fear.

The captain turned to the corporal. "There's sandwiches and coffee and bottled water in the kitchen, through there. Help yourselves. Hit the shitter. I'll go find the major. We're rolling in twenty."

The Kosovars headed out of the garage and into the house. Another soldier walked around to the far side of the panel truck and began digging through a toolbox.

Fiero took two steps to her left, lifted the lid of the nearest ice chest, peered down, closed the lid, and stepped back in line.

The guard reemerged from the toolbox behind the truck.

The youngest Iraqi hissed at her. "He told us not to touch it!"

"It's all right," Fiero whispered. She turned to the eldest boy, the one who spoke Serbian because his father did business in the Balkans. "Did you follow what they were saying?"

The youth had, and translated: the refugees were being split up. And Fiero decided she was in the wrong duo.

A soldier stooped and picked up one of the chests, walking it up the ramp into the panel truck. Fiero turned to the middle Iraqi. "Switch with me."

He said, "Why?"

She wanted to say, *So I don't smack you,* but thought, *What would Finnigan do?* She said, "It is the will of God that you stay with your brother."

"Ah." The kid nodded and stepped next to his older brother.

The Kosovar soldier carried the second Styrofoam chest into the panel truck.

When the driver emerged from the kitchen, he pointed to Fiero and the youngest Iraqi. "You two, back in the truck!"

Fiero replied in Arabic. "Can you tell us where we are going, sir?"

"Shut up that monkey gibberish and get in the truck!"

Convinced that the soldier didn't speak Arabic, Fiero turned to the eldest boy. "Listen, but don't react. There are suicide vests in the white boxes. I'll be back for you, I promise. But if I don't get back in time, do whatever you have to do, but don't let them put these vests on you."

The boy gulped. "By the grace of God, what have we done?"

"You survived. By getting out of Iraq. Do so again. Get out of here as soon as you can. Don't wait for us. And whatever else happens, do not put on the vests!"

"I said, shut up and get in the truck!" the driver bellowed and waved his sidearm.

Fiero and the youngest boy climbed back into the truck, which now featured two ice chests with two fully packed suicide vests.

C72

Major Driton Basha walked down the stone stairs to the wine cellar of the flying saucer house. He kept a guard down here but without the keys to the cellar door. Basha carried those—indeed, he carried Miloš Aleksić's entire key ring for the house and the cars. He unlocked the wine cellar and the stench almost made him gag.

They'd tortured the effete Englishman, Greyson, for a week. They'd tried pain, and that hadn't worked. They'd tried threatening loved ones, but the man had no family. They'd gone through a source in Hungary who'd found a quantity of truth serum on the black market, and that eventually broke him down. Early reports were that the man was a homosexual, but Basha doubted it. He didn't think homosexuals had such guts.

Greyson lay on the rough cement floor. He stank of sweat and shit and piss and burned flesh. All of his fingers were broken, and his face was red and pulpy, one eye closed and oozing pus.

Basha kicked him in the thigh. Greyson moaned.

"It's important to me that you understand what's happening," he said, drawing a handkerchief and holding it over his nose. "Judge Betancourt is a racist fool. She has abused her power to persecute Serbians and Kosovars, and she has helped promote policies that serve Islamic terrorism. She should face a military tribunal for her crimes, and she should be hanged in the city streets. Alas, that's beyond even my reach, Mr. Greyson."

Shan groaned and opened one eye. Blood caked his slit lower lip.

"Thanks to you, she dies today. We drugged you, Greyson. And you gave up your security code. Oh, we know you lied about it at first. More than once. But now we have your code and we'll take the stupid cow's life. And I just wanted you to know this."

"Didn't ..." Shan said. Saying that much made his lower lip bleed again.

Basha leaned forward. "Sorry?"

"Didn't ... code ... Fireplace Room ..."

Basha laughed and nudged him with the toe of his boot again. "Oh, yes. So sorry to be the bearer of bad news, but we did use your code in the Fireplace Room. It does work. And in ..." Basha made a show of pushing back his sleeve and checking his watch, "... a little over an hour, we will use your code to kill the race-traitor bitch. I'd like you to stay alive until that's done. I'll check with you later. For now, please, ah ..." he glanced around, "... enjoy the wine selection."

Basha turned and exited, locking the door behind him.

On the freezing cold floor, Shan risked splitting his lip even further by forming a ghostly, wan smile.

Fiero, the young Iraqi, and two Kosovar soldiers dressed in civilian clothes rode in the back of the panel truck. Two ice chests sat side by side in the middle of the floor, surrounded by everyone's knees. Both guards sat on the right-hand planks that rested above the wheel-well mounds. Fiero and the refugee sat on the left side. Fiero leaned back against one of the many tie-down rings.

She glanced toward the envelope-shaped window leading to the cab. The driver's coat still hung there—Fiero couldn't see where they were going, but the driver and the soldier riding shotgun couldn't see into the back, either.

Two minutes outside the grounds of the flying saucer house, Fiero adjusted her hijab, freeing her shoulders. She leaned forward. "Permitted?" she said in English, and reached for the nearest cooler.

"No!" one of the guards spat. "Don't touch."

Fiero let thirty seconds pass. She leaned forward again and reached for the cooler. "Permitted?"

"I said no, goddamn it!"

The nearer soldier made a fist and swung horizontally to backhand the insolent woman.

Fiero leaned back, dodging the blow from the seated man, which threw him off-balance.

As his fist windmilled past her face, she made a spear of two knuckles and lunged forward, driving them into his windpipe.

Fiero rose out of her seat, rocked by the strength of her legs, and drove the point of her elbow into the second guard's nose. His head snapped back into one of the iron tie-down rings.

She followed with her left elbow into the ear of the first guy, then used the rebound to drive her left fist into the second man's neck, just under his ear.

Fiero fell back into her seat.

The whole attack took a shade under two seconds.

The first guy's eyes rolled up into his head and he flopped over to his right and slid to the floor by the ice chests. The second guy's eyes rolled up and he followed his friend to the floor.

The Iraqi youth gaped.

Fiero unwound the hijab. "Ever jump from a moving truck before?"

"I … how … what? No!"

Fiero smiled. "Want to try?"

As soon as Fiero spotted the suicide vests, she understood what the soldiers planned: Kill the judge and leave behind fall guys. Muslim fall guys. Europeans would be quick to blame Islamist extremists for the attack.

She stepped to the back of the panel truck and gingerly opened the door enough to see where they were: on one of the local access roads between the flying saucer house and the urban center of The Hague. She remembered that the route featured right-angle intersections with stop signs, not the usual roundabouts. They'd reach the A44 within a few minutes, where their speed would pick up considerably.

She beckoned the youth to the rear of the cargo hold. "We're going to reach a series of stop signs. At the first one, hop out."

"And then?"

Fiero said, "Hide in the ditch at the side of the road until the truck is out of sight."

The truck braked. The kid looked perilously close to a heart attack, but he swung his legs over the tailgate and hopped to the pavement.

Fiero didn't follow. The truck started moving again, and the kid watched with pathetic eyes as she accelerated away.

The thing about suicide vests is: suicide is not their primary mission. Wearing one *is* suicide. But that's a by-product. They should be called homicide vests.

That's because, if they are configured correctly, the vests direct the energy of their explosion outward. Away from the wearer. With a well-packed vest, an estimated 80 percent of the energy is directed outward.

It's the other 20 percent that kills the wearer.

Fiero glanced at the tie-down rings all along the inside walls of the panel truck.

Removing the hijab, she knelt and lifted off a Styrofoam lid. She gingerly pulled one of the vests out of its ice chest, studying it. It appeared to be well made. She opened one pouch, smelled the explosive, and used her thumbnail to make a crescent moon indentation in the material—to make sure it was what she assumed it was, and not some newer, high-tech explosive with which she had no experience. The rig featured shoulder straps and a canvas belt to be secured around the waist of the martyr, like a hiker's backpack, but designed to be worn in the front, over one's chest.

She moved forward and attached one half of the belt to one of the tie-down rings, to the left of the cab window. She attached the other half of the belt to a ring on the right side of the window.

The vest hung against the forward wall of the cargo space, splayed like an animal pelt.

She searched the two dead guards and took both of their side-arms and also a mobile phone. Then she moved to the back of the truck and waited for the next stop sign.

As soon as it came, she bunched up the long skirt and deftly hopped out the back. She planted her boots shoulder width apart, aimed a stolen Glock back toward the interior of the truck, left hand bracing her right wrist, and waited.

The driver pulled through the intersection.

Fiero let it get ten meters—about far enough that they'd spot her in the rearview mirror—and fired.

Her slug sailed through the cargo space and slammed into the vest.

The driver braked hard, the tires squealing.

She fired a second shot.

A third.

The third bullet did the trick. The vest exploded.

The blast kicked her like a mule, and she stumbled back but stayed upright. She'd hung the vest with the inside of it facing her. It was that 20 percent of energy that staggered her.

The rest of the energy shredded the front wall of the cargo space, ripping through the cab, peeling off the roof like the lid of a can of dog food, pulping the torsos of the two soldiers, shattering the windshield and ripping the bonnet off its hinges, throwing it forward like a giant's discus and exposing the engine.

Fiero unsnapped the skirt and let it fall to the tarmac, rolling down the legs of her jeans past her calves.

She heard an engine and turned. Behind her, a subcompact car slowly edged forward, the driver doubtless thinking there'd been some sort of collision ahead of him.

Fiero waved to the driver and removed the oversize sweater, letting it fall to the pavement in a heap. She tapped Finnigan's number into the stolen mobile.

The car was a cheaply made, top-heavy Fiat Panda. The driver wore a plaid jacket and a pencil mustache, and he rolled down his window to ask if she was all right.

The phone connection clicked. Finnigan said, "Hello?"

"It's me. Hold on." She showed one of the stolen guns to the Panda driver. "Get out of your car please, sir."

The driver said, "What's going on? I don't—"

"Now, sir." She tapped the gun barrel against the door fame. The man scrambled to climb out of the subcompact.

Finnigan bellowed over the line. "Where the hell are you?"

Smoke unfurled from the ruined panel truck. The Panda driver hurried away from his car, eyes flicking from the wreckage to the madwoman with the gun. Fiero climbed into his car, throwing it into gear, and performed a quick K-turn to head back.

She put the stolen mobile phone on *speaker* and set it on her lap. "Michael? We were just at the Aleksić house! Three refugees and me. In a panel truck."

"I'm parked just outside the grounds," Finnigan said. "I saw your truck enter and leave."

Fiero drove the clunky, underpowered Panda, glancing in the rearview mirror to see the roiling column of smoke rising from the remains of the panel truck. She shouted over the noise from the open window. "One refugee was with me! Two in the house! Michael, they have suicide vests!"

"Shit!"

She stomped on the gas. Stomping on the gas in a Panda doesn't have any particular impact on the speed of the car, she discovered.

Finnigan said, "So they kill the judge, leave dead Muslims on the scene in suicide vests. Change the narrative from *Judge halts trafficking of Muslim refugees* to *Islamists assassinate judge.*"

"We have to get into that house."

He said, "Got it covered. You coming?"

"Fast as I can."

The Panda all but hyperventilated.

"Hey," he said. "Glad you're alive. How'd you get out of the freaking truck?"

"Let this be the lesson of the day," Fiero said. "Never put a bitch like me in a truck full of explosives."

When she was within a kilometer of the stone wall surrounding the seaside home, Finnigan stepped out of a small cluster of cypress trees and flagged her down. He ran ahead, down an unpaved access lane, until she spotted the most unlikely of vehicles—a massive cement-mixer truck, its enormous cauldron slowly rotating.

Fiero pulled in next to it. The cement mixer dwarfed the Panda.

Finnigan eyed the subcompact and grinned. "Wow. You stole this?"

"Shut up. It was the first car on the scene."

"No, no. I like it. Really. Outstanding gas mileage. And, you know … cupholders."

She threw her arms around him. "Fuck you, Michael."

He squeezed her. "You, too."

They pulled apart. "Soldiers have been leaving the house in small groups for the last hour. Not in caravan, but separately, so they don't draw attention. The hit's going down." He stepped onto the running board of the cement truck and threw open the driver's door.

Fiero circled the big engine—the grille was as tall as she. She climbed in on the shotgun side. "The judge is safe?"

"Yeah."

She noted his beloved Halligan bar resting against the gearshift.

"The Kosovars will wait until the Iraqi refugees and the suicide vests arrive before attacking her office. And, since the refugees aren't coming …"

"You bought us a little time," Finnigan finished her thought. "Most of the bad guys are clustered at the court complex. It's now or never."

Fiero was about to check the magazines in the guns she'd

stolen when she glanced behind the driver's seat and saw her gym bag, filled with her own guns. "You shouldn't have!"

"What do you give the girl who kills everything?"

She began her prefight check of the familiar guns.

"Hey, Shan's alive."

Her eyes popped wide. "Oh my God! You're sure?"

"He was as of yesterday. This just became a rescue mission."

Fiero drew her SIG Sauer P226 pistols out of the bag, checked their magazines. She said, "Among other things, yes."

The cement truck left the access lane and Finnigan turned it toward the Aleksić estate.

"Panda. Good choice."

She grinned and flashed him two raised fingers, knuckles first.

C73

Driton Basha had set up his command post in the Aleksićs' kitchen. Why not? It was spacious and well lit, and the butcher-block island was large enough to lay out a city map and the police- and military-band radios they'd brought. Plus: coffee. Always important.

He and a sergeant were able to monitor all first-responders in The Hague, as well as military bands. They also had purchased access on the black market to normally encrypted radio frequencies favored by the security unit in the International Criminal Court.

Basha's chess pieces were aligned:

His lieutenant in the Fireplace Room would start the ball rolling.

His captain would lead the assault forces.

Two of the refugees, with their vests and guns, should be arriving at any minute.

The Fireplace Room. Sobbing, half-mad with pain, Shan Greyson had told them this was the least-secure spot in the court complex, with no cameras. He'd insisted upon it.

Something about that nagged at Basha. Something about the Fireplace Room. If only—

He heard a roaring boom from outside and, for a second, wondered if the extra suicide vests had exploded in the garage. Alarms began blaring.

Basha shouted, "Where's the breach?"

The soldier looked at the panel of blinking red lights. "Um ... everywhere!"

Basha grabbed his firearm and raced out of the kitchen, down the short hall and into the living room.

A wall exploded. Timber and glass and insulation flew horizontally, as if a tornado had touched down.

The grille of a Kenworth truck appeared through the dust, right before Basha's eyes. *Inside the house!*

The maelstrom of material reached him, and he ducked, arms over his head, crouching low. Bits of wood smacked him in the shoulders and across his back.

He tasted blood, and it clicked.

Fireplace.

St. Nicholas.

Major Driton Basha had led his troops into a trap. Not one set by those damned bounty hunters. No, this trap had been set by the hopeless and helpless, broken and bleeding Englishman tied up in the cellar.

The state-of-the-art alarm system was designed to identify any specific type of intrusion—one alarm if anyone climbed over the stone wall, another if motion sensors aimed at the lawn were tripped, another if the front door lock was jimmied.

Slam a cement truck through the gate, gouge up the lawn with its oversize tires, and drive the front into the house like a cannonball, and the state-of-the-art alarm system became as useful as a yapping Chihuahua.

The east side of the flying saucer house began to collapse in on itself, the massive cement truck having destroyed one of the load-bearing walls. Part of the second floor and the curved stairway fell against the front left fender of the Kenworth. Water sprayed from cracked pipes.

Fiero rolled out of the passenger side and saw a big guy with a shaved skull and a gym rat's physique struggling through the smashed furniture to get to her. He looked like he weighed three hundred pounds of pure muscle and meanness. He dragged an H&K MP5 submachine gun in his wake. Fiero spotted the guy's ballistic vest, so she shot him in the hip.

The biggest, brawniest badass on the planet can't advance on you with a shattered pelvis. The guy collapsed to his knees, firing the MP5 downward, the bullets smashing into the hardwood floor.

Fiero stepped closer and shot him through the top of his skull, driving the bullet straight down through his brain and spine and throat, and into his chest cavity. He was dead before Fiero's shell bounced off the floor.

To escape the truck, Finnigan had to shoulder open his door; the frame had bent upon impact with the house. He saw a man with close-cropped hair and a bull's neck rise from a crouch, turn, and sprint toward the almost-ruined stairs. He recognized the guy from the reconnaissance photos Bridget Sumner had provided before the assault in Kosovo: Major Driton Basha.

Finnigan ducked back into the cab as part of the ceiling fell—right where he'd been standing. He grabbed the long-handled Halligan bar, climbed out again and looked around at the devastation.

The house wasn't going to stay standing long.

He circled the front of the truck. He and Fiero spotted each other.

Finnigan pointed. "Basha! Heading upstairs!"

A wooden beam crashed down from the ceiling, and part of the outer wall of the house began to sag.

Two missions then: get Basha; get Shan Greyson.

Finnigan did the math.

Rescue and retribution.

Cop and spook.

He knew what separating from Fiero meant at this moment. He knew how she'd react.

"I got Shan! You get Basha!"

She blinked in surprise. "You're—"

"Go!"

Fiero nodded, understanding the full depth and breadth of Finnigan's decision.

She headed for the stairs.

It's a cliché to hold a prisoner in the basement or subbasement. But in his time as a cop and a US Marshal, Finnigan had found it almost always worked out that way. Nobody holds a prisoner in a room with a lovely view.

The door to the basement was locked, the door fairly modern and the lock substantial. Finnigan shoved the arched, adze-like fork of the Halligan between the door and the doorframe, gripped the other end of the bar, and yanked. The wooden door cracked, wood splintering. The deadbolt had been jarred halfway out of the wall. He stepped back and kicked the door, right under the knob, and it bounced open.

He affixed the Halligan bar to a loop on his belt. He drew his handgun and took the stairs slowly. The postmodern house groaned and, even down in the bedrock basement, Finnigan could hear and feel the destruction upstairs. He found a rec room and the remnants of a military bivouac, with boxes of supplies, including ammunition, and that gym–locker room funk of too many men cooped up for too long.

No sign of a hostage.

He winced as timbers fell to the floor above his head. Time was running short.

Finnigan figured a guy like Director Miloš Aleksić would have a fancy wine cellar in his fancy UFO house. He went looking for it.

He found it, along with a soldier. Finnigan turned a corner, and the guy was almost nose to nose with him. The soldier drew his sidearm and Finnigan grabbed his wrist, pinning it down.

Gunfights are a difficult proposition when opponents are close enough to grapple. The soldier struggled to aim his gun, but Finnigan stepped in tight and used his gun as a club, swiping it across the guy's cheek and slicing skin to the bone.

The soldier had had the wherewithal to wear a bulletproof vest. Finnigan thought, *Good for you, pal,* and kneed him in the balls.

The soldier dropped like an anvil.

Finnigan threw the soldier's gun the length of the rec room. He stepped over the guy, toward a wooden door rounded at the top and slotted into a stone doorway. This lock was even older and heavier than the one in the kitchen, and it wasn't a modern, hollow-core wooden door. The Halligan could get it open, but not quickly.

He drew his gun and aimed it like they taught him: forty-five degrees up, forty-five degrees in. He fired, and the bullet smashed both the door's lock and the faceplate of the doorframe. From that angle, the bullet lodged in the wall, rather than traveling through the door to hit who-knows-what beyond.

He turned his back to the door and kicked it open with his heel, spinning in, gun raised.

Shan Greyson moaned and squinted into the light that poured into the wine cellar.

Finnigan made the sign of the cross, almost bursting into tears of joy. He ignored the stench, knelt and drew a knife from his hip pocket, cutting the tape off Shan's ankles and wrists. The tape came away with bloody strips of necrotic skin. Shan's face was swollen, sweaty, and red; one eye was swollen shut, and teeth were missing. Finnigan wouldn't have recognized him if he hadn't been searching for him.

"M-Michael ..."

Finnigan helped him to his feet, but his body was like a bag full of broken glass. Finnigan lifted him up and threw one of Shan's arms over his shoulder. Shan's ankles and feet were broken.

"God ... didn't ..."

"I know. I got you."

In the corridor, the soldier struggled to rise. Finnigan picked up the Halligan, swung it overhand, cracked it against the man's hand. Fine bones crackled. The man shrieked.

"Get up!" Finnigan shouted, hoping he spoke English. "House is coming down. Get out!"

In his arm, Shan gasped. "Hel ... Hélène ..."

"She's safe, man. You did it. We got her."

C74

Alarms shrilled. With a tortured crack, part of the second floor began to collapse.

Driton Basha made it to the master suite, with its 120-degree, curved floor-to-ceiling windows facing the North Sea. The suite was spacious, with low ceilings and recessed lights. The bed itself was huge, more or less square, as wide as it was long, with a thick ruffled comforter in Easter-egg colors.

Basha shouldered his way into the room and spotted Miloš Aleksić lying facedown on the bed, wearing pinstriped trousers and one sock, no shoes, and an undershirt. Three bottles of whiskey, mostly empty, lay or stood on the side table. An alarm clock was visible through a standing bottle, its number bloated and deformed by the curve of the glass, blinking *12:00.*

The siren shut up and the lights shut off as the power failed in the building.

Marija Aleksić sat on the edge of the bed in a long skirt and twin set, with her matching pearl necklace and earrings. She held a Colt .45 revolver, which looked comically oversized in her dainty hands. She just stared at Basha standing in the doorway, water dripping off his clothes.

Miloš Aleksić snored.

"Muslims?" she asked in a casual, street voice.

Basha wished. "Mercenaries. Bounty hunters. We—"

The left-most pane of glass in the window shattered as its frame warped. Lightning-bolt cracks spread across the ceiling, and Basha felt the floorboards reverberate under his boots.

"We have to hurry, ma'am. Miloš—"

"—is not the man I'd hoped he would be." Marija turned at the waist, placed the revolver against the back of her husband's head, and pulled the trigger.

The boom was ungodly loud, and the blast spread the man's skull and brains and spinal fluid in a florid fan across the mint-green accent wall beyond the bed. His body twitched once, as if an electric current passed through it, then settled again into the divot he'd occupied in the bedspread.

"Jesus!"

Marija turned back to the major. She rubbed her wrist, sore from the recoil. "Goodness, that's loud."

Basha gaped. Blood glistened on her ivory silhouette broach, and dripped off her forearm.

"I couldn't be a soldier, Driton. My family would never have permitted it. I am not a politician. I did not study law. I have served our people as well as I could, in the only way I knew how."

"We have to leave! Now! We—"

"I supported Milošević. I stood in awe as this great man explained to the world the moral imperative of ethnic cleansing."

Basha's mind whirled. *The psychotic bitch is giving a speech?*

"I thought perhaps his administration would rid us of the Muslim threat for—"

Fiero swept into the room. Her eyes locked on the armed woman sitting by the headless cadaver on the bed.

Basha reacted quickly, throwing back an elbow, catching her square in the chest. Her clavicle cracked. She gasped and stumbled back, her gun falling to the floor.

Basha turned and grabbed her by the throat, raising his own gun.

Fiero smashed her knuckles into the inside of his elbow and his hand spasmed open, the gun spiraling away.

Basha dragged her over his hip and used a judo throw, sending her crashing into the carpet.

Fiero hit the ground and scissor-kicked, taking Basha's ankles out from under him. He landed on his ass.

Fiero rolled over, her left knee pinning down his gun hand, threw her right knee over his chest, and punched him in the throat.

Basha used his superior mass and strong legs to buck her off. She did a somersault, coming out of it into a standing crouch.

Basha rose, too, holding a gun.

But the blow to his windpipe had taken the fight out of him.

Fiero pivoted and kicked, her boot higher than her own head. Her heel shattered Basha's nose and sent bits of cartilage and bone ricocheting into his brain.

The dead man stood a moment, but only because his autonomic nervous system hadn't gotten the message yet.

That's all that saved Fiero.

Marija Aleksić raised the long-barreled Colt in both hands and aimed at her. Fiero spotted it and ducked as Basha's body swayed unsteadily on its feet. She put the dead major between herself and the big revolver.

Marija fired, the sound deafening. The bullet smashed into Basha's back, dug through his chest, exited under his pectoral, and ripped a gouge out of Fiero's right arm.

Basha's corpse folded into her and they both tumbled.

Fiero struggled to free herself from the dead weight, her own torso and arms now covered in his blood and hers. She felt something hard under his left thigh and reached for it.

Basha's Glock.

Marija tried to aim at her. But firing the big Colt twice had cost her dearly. She could barely lift it, and the recoil had sent pain reverberating through her hands and wrists and elbows. She struggled to aim.

Fiero, up on one elbow, legs trapped under the corpse, drew Basha's auto left-handed and aimed first.

Marija paused, then let the cumbersome gun come to rest in her lap.

The house shuddered.

Fiero kept the pistol steady as she fought to get her legs out from beneath Basha. Pushing with her right arm brought searing pain that jolted up through her shoulder.

Marija studied her. Fiero freed her legs.

"Driton told me about a bounty hunter who rescued the Muslim scum. St. Nicholas. He said a woman was among them. A Muslim woman. Is that you?"

Fiero rose to her feet. Water-soaked hair hung before her face, and blood oozed down her right arm, dripping off her knuckles.

She surprised herself. "Yes. I'm a Muslim woman." And thought, ridiculously, *If my mother could see me now!*

That was shock setting in, she realized.

The house groaned. A guillotine of plate glass, hanging from the upper frame of the shattered window, broke free and fell to the floor. Shattered shards bloomed in every direction.

Marija didn't appear to hear it. "Will the major's men succeed in killing the judge?"

"They won't. She's safe."

Marija's shoulders slumped. "How fitting, that a Muslim like you would destroy everything."

"You're the one behind all this? Behind your son?"

Marija said, "I'm a patriot. I wouldn't expect you to understand."

Fiero fought the pulsing pain. She held the Glock in her left hand and snapped her head to the side, hair swinging away from her eyes. "You're Lazar's mother. He's your only son?"

"He is."

"I imprisoned him. For life. He'll die there."

A dark cloud occluded Marija's eyes. A bottomless well of hate rose, contorting her face. She looked to her right, at the corpse of her husband. She looked back at the major's body, crumbled artlessly, like garbage tossed to the ash heap.

She looked Fiero in the eye.

"A foolish name. St. Nicholas!"

"The patron saint of the necessary."

"The necessary?"

Fiero said, "Yes," and shot Marija Aleksić in the forehead.

C75

Finnigan got Shan to the five-car garage and selected a brand-new Lexus coupe with diplomatic plates. He got the Englishman lying down in the back seat before he noticed two Iraqi boys, standing and shivering on the far side of the car, their eyes like saucers.

"Go!" Finnigan bellowed and waved his gun.

The kids tore out of there and sped across the spacious lawn, leaping over the tire tracks gouged into the pristine grass. Finnigan watched and spotted the soldier he'd kicked in the balls, just now painfully climbing over the ruined stone fence.

Finnigan ran back toward the house.

As he did, Fiero appeared in a second-floor window. She swung one long leg out onto the roof, then twisted and followed with her torso and shoulders, her head, and her brace leg. She turned and Finnigan saw water and blood dripping off her clothes.

He peered up at her.

She made the cutthroat gesture, her hand to her neck, and he understood what that meant. She began using a rose bush's lattice to climb down.

Finnigan ran into the ruined house. He climbed up onto the running board of the cement truck and activated the slowly revolving cauldron. With a bass groan, it began to rotate along its long axis.

Their resident thief, Sally Blue, had said the various alarms at the house would make sneaking onto the property difficult. That's why Finnigan decided to use a truck and to ram his way in, setting off every alarm all at once to slow down the defenders' response through shock-and-awe. But he specifically selected a cement truck with a full load of cement to bollix the crime scene. In the event that he, Fiero, and Shan got away today, he didn't want local police knocking on their door in the next few days. Nothing screws up a crime scene like a ton of wet cement. He quickly wiped down the cab for fingerprints. He got out and hit the lever to begin dumping wet cement into the spacious living room.

He caught up to Fiero in the garage. "You're bleeding?"

She'd grabbed a clean shop rag from the tall tool kit and was using her teeth to tie it around her upper arm. "Shan?"

He led her to the Lexus and showed her their friend, passed out in the back seat and ruining the creamy upholstery. Finnigan climbed in behind the wheel and Fiero took shotgun, but sitting backward, reaching over the headrest to brush stray blond hair away from Shan's good eye.

"Katalin," the Englishman murmured. He dredged up the macabre ghost of a smile.

"You can't die. We haven't been paid."

"Might've … misplaced checkbook …"

She leaned over the seatback and felt her eyes turn hot. She blinked back tears. "Shhh. We have you."

Finnigan pulled away and raced down the curved path for

the gate. He noticed the part of the wall he'd smashed through; the impact had knocked over the gate. They spotted the two Iraqi brothers, sprinting into the cluster of trees that Finnigan had used earlier to hide the cement truck.

The partners and Shan Greyson were a good three kilometers from the collapsing flying saucer house when they passed the first of seven police cars, racing the opposite direction.

Kosovar Team One, under the command of Basha's senior officer, waited for the refugees with their suicide vests to arrive. When they failed to show—and the truck didn't reply to radio calls—the captain decided they could wait no longer. He sent the order to his lieutenant in the Fireplace Room.

The lieutenant rose from his table and tapped the false code into the ten-key pad on the wall, announcing a terrorist assault on the building. He waited to hear the alarm and frowned as the silence reigned. Three seconds later, guards with machine guns stormed in from the kitchen door. The lieutenant was on his knees, hands laced behind his head, in under ten seconds.

Team One stormed the historic house of the tailor, Pieter de Key, expecting to find Judge Hélene Betancourt emerging from an escape tunnel. Instead, they faced a fully armed and armored counter-terrorism unit with gas masks and bulletproof shields. A few shots were fired, but most of the Kosovars followed their captain's lead and dropped their weapons without incident.

The Public Affairs Officer of the International Criminal Court held a press conference, in which she tied the attempted attack on Judge Betancourt with the rescue of the refugee children in Belgrade and Sarajevo. A very young reporter recently hired by the *Times* of London, Jane Koury, covered the press conference and got her first byline on Page 1, above the fold.

Hélene Betancourt pulled strings at a private hospital outside Amsterdam, on whose board of directors she sat. Shan Greyson was taken there, and a team of top-flight trauma surgeons worked on him for six hours before announcing that he was out of the woods. They saved his eye but couldn't be sure if he'd ever walk again. However, he would live.

The doctors also treated an unnamed woman—tall, dark of hair and skin—with a gunshot wound to her right arm and a cracked sternum. The woman left in the company of a wavy-haired American who seemed to complain a lot.

Judge Betancourt handled all of the medical bills. Someone apparently forgot to alert the police that one person had been tortured and another shot.

The appropriate paperwork went missing.

C76

A week passed.

In Kyrenia, Cyprus, Lachlan Sumner relaxed by taking apart the Pratt & Whitney engines of their beloved de Havilland DHC-6-300 Twin Otter. He stripped them down and tuned everything himself.

Bridget Sumner updated the partners on the *business* of their business, including expenses accrued in Italy, France, Slovenia, Serbia, and the Netherlands. She announced that a check had been cut by one of the elegant, historic, and deeply corrupt f banks and deposited in their own elegant, historic, and deeply corrupt Cypriot bank. No forensic accountant on the planet would ever find a link between the transaction and the Honorable Hélene Betancourt.

Finnigan asked Bridget to use some of the proceeds to lease a spacious house perched high on a cliff in beautiful Bellapais, just outside Kyrenia, for the remainder of the summer and fall. As soon as his doctors gave the okay, Shan Greyson would be convalescing in the Mediterranean sun.

Fiero took two days off and visited her parents in Madrid. She made up a story about hurting her arm in a car accident. Her parents wanted to know about her work as an analyst for the European Union, and they wanted details about her relationship with Michael Patrick Finnigan.

Khadija Dahar wanted to know if it was true romance.

"It's true," her daughter said. "It's not romance."

Alexandro Fiero bemoaned the stories coming out of the Netherlands and Serbia regarding the admirable Aleksić family, including the tragic homicides of Marija and Miloš Aleksić. Surely the macabre stories of their son's crimes were being hyped by the international media!

"Surely," his daughter muttered.

Finnigan, for his part, flew commercial to Newark and met with several contacts in the US Justice Department, who confirmed the news that an assistant district attorney in New York was putting together a case—a new case, a big case—against former NYPD captain Patrick Finnigan. The sources wouldn't, or couldn't, go on the record. But the case was described as "open and shut" and "a career-maker."

He visited his mom in Queens. He ate unbelievably good pastrami, as well as world-class bagels. He ordered a box of Dunkin' Donuts and had them FedExed to Ways & Means in Varenna, Italy.

He took a subway into Manhattan and ate a sandwich across the street from a Starbucks and an NYPD precinct building. It took forty minutes before he spotted Sgt. Nicole Finnigan and two other female cops, stepping out for coffee.

Nicole looked good. She looked strong and happy.

Finnigan finished his sandwich and headed back.

Finnigan had time to visit his father on Long Island. He even drove close enough to see the house. He never climbed out of the car.

Police continued to investigate the deaths of Marija and Miloš Aleksić. The first day of the investigation was hampered by the hazards of the flying saucer house—investigators determined that it was too dangerous to enter due to the structural damage caused by the cement truck. To add to the complications, the truck had dumped its load of wet cement, which inundated the ground floor and essentially tombed-off the basement and wine cellar of the great house. Engineers pored over the house for a day and a half before the first-responders were allowed to enter.

When they finally gained entrance, police found three bodies in the master suite. Marija and Miloš Aleksić lay on their bed, crosswise to each other, arms and legs spread, and looked like nothing so much as a human hashtag. A third body lay on the floor near the bed. They linked a gun in the hands of Marija Aleksić to the bullet that had taken off her husband's head. That gun also was linked to the chest wound of an as-yet unidentified male. That corpse held an Austrian-made pistol which, tests showed, had shot Marija Aleksić between the eyes.

The obvious conclusion was a love triangle gone horribly awry.

That theory would be blown to hell in a month when a fourth body—that of a Kosovar soldier carrying a machine gun, a bullet wound through the top of his skull—would be jackhammered out of the cement in the living room, and when investigators found the remains of a military bivouac in the house's basement, complete with firearms, ammunition, and blueprints of the International Criminal Court complex.

The partners didn't properly reconnect until eight days after leaving The Hague aboard the de Havilland. They met in the Turkish restaurant below their office and above the winding and scenic boardwalk that surrounded the tiny, picturesque marina. Finnigan got there first and ordered bread and hummus and olives, plus a red wine from a vineyard co-owned by Alexandro Fiero.

His partner arrived on the new motorbike she'd just purchased—she'd gotten a taste for them in Italy. And besides, the leather went well with her goth/bad-girl fashion sense.

"Riding a motorcycle with a bullet wound to your arm and a cracked sternum," Finnigan said. "That seems reasonable."

"Fashion over function," she murmured, unzipping her painted-on leather jacket and flopping down on the red leather bench next to him. She noticed the label on the wine bottle and smiled. "I love this wine. Thank you."

They waited until the appetizers arrived, and Finnigan filled their glasses. "So, here's some good news. Lazar Aleksić got stabbed in jail."

Fiero touched her glass to his. "Lovely."

"Better news: he didn't die. Which means he's free to heal up, go back, and get stabbed again."

They ate in silence. The coast of Turkey hovered blue-green across the sparkling water. Unbidden, the proprietor brought them a platter of copra and baked sea bream. He didn't offer the dish often, but knew it to be a favorite of his upstairs neighbors.

They dug in.

After a while, Fiero spoke without looking up from her plate. "D'you remember what you told me when we started this company, three years ago?"

Finnigan spooned a little more of the citrus sauce onto his fish. He ripped off a quarter moon of the aromatic flatbread.

"I told you we'd be great catching bad guys. Me a cop, you a spy. We'd get the assholes nobody else could touch."

"Yes. And d'you remember your one absolute condition?"

"We'd break rules. We'd break laws. But we wouldn't be assassins."

They ate in silence.

"Do we need to talk about—"

Finnigan said, "Nope."

"Are you sure?"

He sopped up juices with the bread. "I knew what would happen when I went after Shan and sent you upstairs after Basha. I'm as guilty as—"

"Guilty? Michael, that family was corrupt. Their family creed was based on a psychotic level of bigotry and hatred. They were going to kill Hélene Betancourt. They turned their house over to a death squad. Marija Aleksić had murdered her own husband. She told me she was fully aware that her son was trafficking immigrant children. They condoned the torture and maiming of Shan."

"Look, I said ..." Finnigan paused, regathering his thoughts. "You're not wrong. Okay? You did the necessary thing. The thing I couldn't do. And I was there the whole way: eyes wide open."

"But there's more than that," she said, and took his hand in hers. "All I could see was vengeance. I went into that house to kill Basha and the Aleksićs. That's *all*. You went in to save Shan."

Finnigan sat back. He paused, then squeezed her fingers in his fist.

"Your way saved Shan," she said. "Your way also resulted in the arrest and trial of Lazar Aleksić."

"And your way saved Judge Betancourt," he said. "Your play was the only one left on the board. Given their money, their power, their position, they'd have gotten away with it and tried again. And again. They were gorilla-shit crazy. There was no other way. I get that. I didn't, but I do now."

They sat for a while. They stared out at the Eastern Mediterranean, watched the gently bobbing sails of the boats heading into and out of the marina.

After a while, Finnigan sighed. "I wanted to grow up to be a policeman, like my old man. Turns out, my old man is a hood, forever on the take. You wanted to grow up to protect the world and to be a force for peace, like your parents. Turns out, your gifts lie in being just as ruthless as your enemy."

Fiero squinted into the westering sun. She used a knuckle to dab at her eyes. "Sounds about right."

Finnigan drained the last dregs of the Spanish red into both glasses and held his up.

She matched the gesture.

"St. Nicholas isn't the patron saint of the desired," he said. "He's the patron saint of the necessary."

They toasted.